PRAISE FOR *THE NINJA LIBRARIANS: THE ACCIDENTAL KEYHAND*

★ "So madcap that it's hard to turn the pages fast enough to keep up. Well worth a spot on library shelves…but it won't stay there long."

—*Kirkus*, Starred Review

"The melding of fantasy, adventure, and history is enlightening… Readers who miss the collegial, magical setting of Hogwarts will enjoy exploring Petrarch's Library."

—*School Library Journal*

"Delightfully funny from the first page, this middle-grade time-travel adventure is surprisingly full of fun and action. Downey's hilarious debut is perfect for any library-loving reader and those who never considered librarians to be cool."

—*Booklist*

"The delightful premise will be an obvious hit with librarians and their fans… The multiple allusions to history's unsung heroes of intellectual freedom will likely send a few readers to the 900s."

—*Bulletin of the Center for Children's Books*

"Fun-filled, fast paced, and alive with details to appeal to all of the senses, including a sense of adventure."

—*Richmond Times Dispatch*

"A rollicking adventure with a smart heroine, heaps of mystery, and the whole of history to explore. It's like finding Lara Croft running your local library!"

—Lissa Evans, author of *Horten's Miraculous Mechanisms*

The NINJA LIBRARIANS

Sword in the Stacks

Jen Swann Downey

sourcebooks
jabberwocky

Published by Sourcebooks Jabberwocky, an imprint of Sourcebooks, Inc.
P.O. Box 4410, Naperville, Illinois 60567-4410
(630) 961-3900
Fax: (630) 961-2168
www.sourcebooks.com

Library of Congress Cataloging-in-Publication data is on file with the publisher.

Source of Production: Worzalla, Stevens Point, Wisconsin, USA
Date of Production: April 2016
Run Number: 5006449

Printed and bound in the United States of America.
WOZ 10 9 8 7 6 5 4 3 2 1

For John and Jackson and every other valiant spirit

CHAPTER 1

LYBRARIANS WITH A Y

TWELVE-YEAR-OLD DORRIE BARNES WAS on pins and needles.

And thumbtacks.

The thumbtacks were plastic—and scattered the length and breadth of Great-Aunt Alice's shabby ballroom where the Barnes family did most of its living and dining and everything-else-ing. The reason that Dorrie, coffee can in hand, was crawling among the thumbtacks—and occasionally upon them, feeling slightly mocked by their cheerful colors—was that she had a four-year-old sister. A sister who had thought it made perfect sense to create a thumbtack garden beside the sofa and even more sense to run over it with a vacuum. The results had been spectacular.

Only a minute before, the tacks had been zinging through

the air, ricocheting with hard pings off windows and Great-Aunt Alice's piano, embedding themselves in lampshades and couch cushions, and sending four members of the Barnes family streaking for cover. The fifth member—the perpetrator of the event—had simply squealed in delight. The sixth member—Great-Aunt Alice—had not been home at the time. Even if she hadn't been halfway around the world, it's quite likely she would still have escaped the need to streak for cover since, preferring order to chaos, she visited the Barnes on their side of her decrepit mansion as rarely as possible.

The reason Dorrie was on pins and needles was because a week ago, she'd been abruptly sent home from Petrarch's Library, the headquarters of the Lybrariad, a society of warrior lybrarians who took very unkindly to people who set fire to books or tossed writers into rat-infested dungeons. Hypatia, the director of Petrarch's Library, had given Dorrie only the haziest idea of if or when she'd be invited to return.

Since the lybrarians who occupied Petrarch's Library were just as likely to spend a Monday morning rappelling down a cliff with swords clamped between their teeth as shelving books…

And since Dorrie had longed to chase down villains with a real sword ever since she could hold a fake one…

And since, while staying in Petrarch's Library, Dorrie had unexpectedly served as the Unofficial Temporary Apprentice to Hercule-Savinien de Cyrano de Bergerac—possessor of the finest sword skills and grandest nose of the seventeenth century—and wanted to serve as Savi's Extremely Official Until-the-End-of-Time Apprentice more than she wanted her heart to keep beating…

Dorrie was finding the uncertainty excruciating.

Much worse than the pain caused by the thumbtack that had just driven itself into her knee.

"This is why we can't have nice things," said Dorrie's father, breaking into her thoughts. "Like appliances."

Dorrie glanced over at the corner of the ballroom-declared-kitchen to see him lifting several tacks out of a pot of clam chowder with a slotted spoon.

"Or electricity," said Marcus, Dorrie's fourteen-year-old brother, chasing a blue one around the top of his snare drum.

"Well, who left the vacuum out?" Dorrie's mother asked as she coaxed several more tacks out from between the crevices of her keyboard.

"Well, what sane person would ever think she'd use it as a deadly weapon?" Dorrie asked, neatly side-stepping her mother's question.

"I'm not *she*! I'm *Miranda*!" bellowed Miranda from the high stool in front of the sink, to which she'd been banished.

"*She* is a menace," said Marcus, sucking on a punctured finger.

Miranda, her red curls in their usual state of defiant chaos, began to fill the sink with water. "*I* am an artist."

Dorrie went back to gathering and let Petrarch's Library take shape clear and bright in her mind's eye. She saw it first as a bird would, rising to its towering heights on its sea-encircled island, where it touched hundreds of points in time but belonged to none of them. Dorrie beat her imaginary wings so that they bore her through a window and through a good number of the library's jumbled chambers and corridors. In the walls of some stood the black, stone archways that connected Petrarch's Library to smaller, time-anchored libraries in ancient India and the Aztec Empire and medieval West Africa. The lybrarians called the libraries that lay on the other side of archways Spoke Libraries.

Even if Petrarch's Library hadn't connected to hundreds of centuries, Dorrie would have found it astounding. Dozens of floors tall, immensely wide, and peppered with courtyards and gardens, it was made up of squashed-together Ghost Libraries— libraries that had been destroyed in their own times and places but lived on as part of Petrarch's Library. Dorrie had found that they had melded in the most odd and surprising ways, creating an interlocked labyrinth of staircases, chambers, and passages. The shelves, racks, and trunks in the Ghost Libraries still groaned with their collections of stories, speeches, and histories that people had scribbled onto parchment, paper, and papyrus—or pressed into tablets of mud and wax or painted on billowing lengths of silk.

From the moment she'd left Petrarch's Library, Dorrie had

felt driven to return, but as the days had slipped by in Passaic, New Jersey, with no word from the lybrarians, her mood had slid from alert hope to creeping doubt to outright despair that she'd ever hear from them again—especially now that the Foundation, the Lybrariad's old enemy thought to be defeated, had returned from the future more powerful than ever.

She'd begun to wonder if she really had spent two months in Petrarch's Library with Marcus while time virtually stopped in Passaic. That very morning, she'd yanked open her top dresser drawer, flinging underwear left and right in search of the balled-up argyle sock she'd hidden. Relief had filled her when a good shake had sent the silver keyhand's armband tumbling out of the sock and onto her bed.

Feeling only a little stupid to be whispering to a sock, Dorrie had repeated the words Hypatia had spoken when she'd given the armbands to Dorrie and Marcus as a token of her trust in them.

"We would have offered to take you on as full apprentices…"

Dorrie idly shook the can of tacks and frowned. *Would have.* The words had been spoken and the armbands given when Dorrie, Marcus, and the lybrarians thought they might never possibly see each other again. But now that Dorrie's own Passaic Public Library was to stay connected to Petrarch's Library as its official twenty-first-century wing and Dorrie and Marcus *could* serve as apprentices, the question was…would the lybrarians still want them?

A firm knock nearly made her drop the can of tacks. Dorrie glanced at the back door and felt the hairs on the back of her neck rise. Three silhouettes could be made out through the door's curtained window. With her heart beating wildly, she scrambled to her feet and ran to the door, Marcus on her heels. Together, they wrenched it open.

"Mistress Wu!" Dorrie shouted in great relief, recognizing the broad-shouldered figure of Hypatia's assistant.

Mistress Wu had exchanged the long kimono she wore in Petrarch's Library for a lilac pantsuit, a white blouse, and a patterned scarf tied in a billowy bow around her neck.

"Phillip!" Dorrie cried, throwing her arms around the soft middle of the first lybrarian she had ever met. Phillip wore a jaunty fedora, out from under which two clouds of red, frizzy hair insisted on their freedom. "You're here! And…"

Dorrie's eyes traveled upward to take in the figure that loomed behind Phillip and Mistress Wu like a mountain in the background of a vacation photo. Bald as a melon and thick with muscle, he wore a cardigan knit with a pattern of cats.

"This is Menelik," said Phillip, following Dorrie's gaze. "He's been watching over your family's home, just in case the Foundation has other operatives in Passaic."

Menelik gave a small nod, the flowered shoulder bag he carried shifting slightly.

"So sorry we've kept you waiting," said Mistress Wu, both hands curled around the handle of a briefcase. "So many meetings. So much going on."

"Did you get Petrarch's Star back?" Dorrie couldn't help but blurt out. Petrarch's Star was a thick stone star covered in runes. A stone whose existence the Lybrariad had only just learned about. A stone capable of blowing holes into the past—and into Petrarch's Library itself. A stone, Dorrie now knew, the Foundation wanted to get its hands on very badly.

"Not yet," said Phillip. "But we have a large number of lybrarians hunting for Mr. Gormly."

Hot anger toward Mr. Gormly shot through Dorrie. He'd betrayed the Lybrariad and disappeared with Petrarch's Star.

"Excuse me," came Dorrie's mother's voice. "But do we know you?"

Dorrie whirled round to see her parents standing in the doorway. She glanced back at Phillip and Mistress Wu. "These are our parents."

Phillip held out his hand. "Philippus Aureolus Theophrastus Bombastus von Hohenheim." He wiggled his fingers slightly, but neither of Dorrie's parents took his hand. "Or Paracelsus if you'd like." His fuzzy eyebrows danced a little. "Or plain old Phillip is fine."

Still, Dorrie's parents hesitated.

"I'm Wu Yongtai," tried Mistress Wu. "Phillip and I, and

the rest of the staff, think a good deal of Dorrie and Marcus and—"

"Our parents that we haven't explained anything to yet," Dorrie clarified in a rush.

"Oh," Mistress Wu said, taken aback. "I see." She collected herself. "Well, we've come to discuss with you the possibility of offering Dorrie and Marcus apprenticeships."

Dorrie and Marcus let out twin whoops, and Marcus offered Dorrie a high five. The relief and excitement bounding through Dorrie made her miss his hand, but she didn't care.

"What sort of apprenticeships?" asked Dorrie's mother, sounding bewildered.

"With them!" said Marcus, jerking his thumb toward the visitors.

"They're lybrarians with a *y*," announced Dorrie over the sound of Miranda sloshing water on the floor inside the house.

"With a…?" Dorrie's father began, a sharp note in his voice. "Where did you meet these people?"

"In a dark alley," said Marcus. "They leaned out of a van and offered us candy."

"He's kidding, he's kidding!" cried Dorrie.

"Oh, dear," said Mistress Wu, her eyes fixed on something inside the house. "While I as yet have only the most rudimentary understanding of electricity and appliances, I do wonder if the little girl should be doing that."

8

Everyone turned to see Miranda preparing to drop the plugged-in family toaster into the overbrimming sink.

"Miranda! No!" cried Dorrie's mother.

Before Dorrie could even think of moving, Menelik's hand twitched, and the toaster, as if it had suddenly developed a will, flew out of Miranda's hands, its cord ripping from the wall as it fell with a harmless crash onto the counter. A boomerang clattered to the floor.

Dorrie's father charged inside and swept Miranda up off her perch and into a suffocating embrace.

"Thank you," said Dorrie's mother breathlessly, staring at Menelik with her hand on her heart.

"Yes, thank you, Menelik," said Mistress Wu, nodding at him. She blinked at Dorrie's mother. "Perhaps we could come in now and discuss matters?"

"Of course, of course," said Dorrie's mother, looking highly flustered but making way.

Mistress Wu bustled inside. "Such an interesting walk over from the Passaic Public Library. Hitching posts that take coins. Ingen—" She broke off, taking in the highly disorganized state of the Barnes' book collection with the sad horror usually reserved for a grisly traffic accident. Hastily, Dorrie picked up a dictionary lying open on the floor, its spine tortured into an arc. She shoved it onto a shelf.

"Please sit down," said Dorrie's mother, gesturing to the

kitchen table as Dorrie's father, still looking suspicious, placed a jar of pickles on it as if not yet completely convinced the visitors deserved them.

Soon, all were seated around the table except for Menelik, who had lowered himself into the scarred leather chair by the woodstove and pulled a ball of yarn and two wooden needles from his bag, and Miranda, who had planted herself near Menelik's knee to stare fixedly at his now-flying hands.

Mistress Wu blinked at Dorrie's mother and father in turn. "How are you at believing the impossible?"

"What kind of impossible?" Dorrie's mother asked slowly.

Dorrie could hold herself back no longer. "Impossible like, last week, Marcus and I fell through a hole in the floor of a secret room behind the janitor's closet in the Passaic Public Library into a much, much bigger library underneath it with thousands of rooms. It's called Petrarch's Library, and it's the headquarters for a secret society of lybrarians with swords who rescue people who get into trouble because of stuff they write, and now we want to be their apprentices and help them fight people who want to steal writing from the world."

"Surprise!" shouted Marcus, throwing his hands up in the air.

Chapter 2
Whim's Gift

DORRIE'S PARENTS STARED FROM Dorrie to Marcus to Mistress Wu to Phillip.

"Okay…what's the joke?" demanded Dorrie's father.

"If I may," said Mistress Wu.

For the next hour, she described how Petrarch's Library had first sprung into existence around the shocked fourteenth-century poet Francesco Petrarch.

"He was tending a cooking fire on a mountainside meadow at the time, having spent the day traveling. Night had fallen, and after a sound like the crack of a whip, five walls began to heave their way upward out of the earth around him, spreading and stretching toward one another until he stood at the center of a vast towering pentagon, with only the star-studded sky above for a roof. He saw that one wall was stone, one wood, one iron, one brick, and one paper.

Dorrie listened raptly because she'd never heard the story of the Library's beginning.

"In each wall appeared a black archway, pricked as full of searing starlight as the sky above. In a short time on the other side of four of the archways, four rooms coalesced out of the dark. One was full of books, one of mud tablets, one of papyrus scrolls, and one of wooden blocks. In time, Petrarch would learn that each was a library that lay in a different wheren."

"A wheren is a particular place and time," said Phillip. "Eleventh century Rome or fourteenth-century Kathmandu.

"It means 'where' and 'when' all in one word," added Marcus.

"But what about the fifth archway?" asked Dorrie impatiently.

"The fifth archway showed Petrarch sky, a bit of land, and beyond it, a sea," said Mistress Wu. "Passing through it, he found himself no longer in a mountain meadow, but standing on a rocky island beside a five-sided tower, the sea stretching in all directions."

Mistress Wu explained how Petrarch's Library had grown steadily larger over the four hundred years it had existed.

"How could it not?" she asked, taking out a handkerchief and looking as devastated as only Mistress Wu could look.

"Every time someone destroys a library out in the wherens or lets one fall to wrack and ruin, its ghost squeezes into Petrarch's Library where it can." She dabbed at her eyes and then perked resolutely up. "But it's no graveyard." She explained how new archways materialized every so often, secretly connecting Petrarch's Library to lively, perfectly functional Spoke Libraries in new centuries.

When Mistress Wu seemed to have finished, Phillip reached for a pickle. "During the first hundred years the Lybrarid and Petrarch's Library existed, a good portion of Europe and North Africa and the Near East was still under the control of the Foundation."

"The what?" asked Dorrie's father.

"The Foundation," repeated Mistress Wu.

"Bad, bad people!" said Dorrie.

"Total control freaks," added Marcus.

"I'm sorry," said Dorrie's mother, as though she'd heard just one incredible thing too many. "But I've studied a good bit of history, and I've never heard that Europe, North Africa, and the Near East were ever under the control of something called the 'Foundation.'"

"You wouldn't have," said Mistress Wu. "Because the Lybrariad has spent the last four hundred years—Petrarch's Library time—changing history out in the wherens as we've fought the Foundation. The Foundation is now only a shadow of a footnote of a legend." She made her voice gentle. "The history you currently know isn't the history that always was."

Dorrie's mother stared at Mistress Wu, looking flushed. "I...I...feel a bit dizzy."

"And half like you might have to throw up?" said Dorrie eagerly. "That's how I felt when I first heard how it all worked!"

"An entirely natural reaction," said Mistress Wu. "Very disorienting. Do you need to lie down? Do you want a cold compress? Menelik knows some wonderful Persian lullabies."

"Oh, she's fine," Marcus answered for his mother. "Mom loves amusement park rides."

"All right," said Dorrie's father, a scoff in his voice. "What was this Foundation all about then?"

"Back in Petrarch's day," said Phillip, reaching for another pickle, "the Foundation kept tight control over the people in its territory. Part of how they did it was to keep written language all to themselves."

"No one but Foundation members could learn to read and write," said Mistress Wu. "The skills were closely guarded secrets forbidden to most people, and the penalties for teaching or learning were..." She glanced at Miranda, who was now curled up asleep between Menelik's feet. "Severe. Over time, the Lybrariad succeeded in chiseling away at the Foundation's control of reading and writing, and our work shifted to rescue missions."

"Rescue missions?" said Dorrie's mother faintly.

"Oh yes," said Mistress Wu. "Once more people could write, you wouldn't believe how often they would be locked up in cold, damp places or chased around with flaming torches and portable guillotines. Even with the Foundation vanquished. All because of an unpopular thought scribbled here or an opinion printed there. We lybrarians don't go for silencing people with threats and abuse, and we swore to protect writers from such tormenters."

"It takes many lybrarians to conduct the rescue missions," said Phillip. "The Lybrariad regularly trains librarians with an *i* into lybrarians with a *y*. If you permit Dorrie and Marcus to train as apprentices, they'll learn research and reference skills, along with how to gain entry to a locked room, set a broken bone, ride anything with four legs, practice all seventeen uses for a flaming arrow—"

Dorrie's father pushed his chair back, and Dorrie had the terrible sense that he was about to flee back to his workshop in the yard. "I truly wish warrior lybrarians did gallop around the world shooting flaming arrows, but I can't listen to any more of this elaborate fantasy."

Mistress Wu glanced at the untidy teetering piles of books spread across the ballroom. "Would you be more convinced of our claims if we did a speed cataloging and shelving of your book collection?"

"Or Dorrie could stand up against a wall and Menelik could outline her in throwing daggers," suggested Phillip.

"*No!*" cried Dorrie's mother and father together. "That... that won't be necessary."

"He does have truly phenomenal hand-eye coordination," Mistress Wu said with more than a hint of pride.

Dorrie's father stood. "We'd have to be mad to believe you."

"But it's all true," cried Dorrie. "Marcus and I spent months in Petrarch's Library!"

"Now just stop it," said Dorrie's mother, her voice shaking. "I think I'd know if my children disappeared for a day, let alone months."

"But we did," said Marcus. "You just didn't realize that we were gone because time just about stopped in Passaic while we were in Petrarch's Library."

Dorrie's mother stood as well. Her expression gave the clear message that as far as she was concerned, the meeting was over.

Inspiration seized Dorrie. "Call Great-Aunt Alice! She knows all about it. You'd have to believe her. She doesn't know *how* to make something up!"

"Plus, she's old," added Marcus. "And old equals credible."

"I don't know what exactly is going on here," said Dorrie's father, "but I'm not going to bother Great-Aunt Alice while she's on her first vacation in a decade to ask her if she's visited any magical libraries lately."

"She's not actually on vacation," said Phillip delicately. "She's being credible at the International Librarians'

Conference. She's recruiting librarians with an *i* interested in training as lybrarians with a *y*."

Dorrie's parents gaped at Phillip.

"She asked me to give you this," said Mistress Wu, pulling from her briefcase one of the sky-blue envelopes that Great-Aunt Alice favored. She handed it to Dorrie's father. "It explains everything."

With clumsy fingers, Dorrie's father tore it open and unfolded the matching piece of stationery within. Heads together, Dorrie's parents scanned the lines of writing, and then slowly looked up.

For a moment, all that could be heard was the clicking of Menelik's knitting needles. Dorrie was sure her parents were deeply pondering the fact that Great-Aunt Alice had never made up anything in her life and looked severely down upon anyone who did.

"Either she's lost her marbles—" said Dorrie's father at last.

"You know she hasn't!" said Dorrie.

"Or…" his voice trailed off.

"They're telling the truth," said Dorrie's mother, looking wonderstruck.

Mistress Wu beamed. "Now that we're all agreed that Petrarch's Library exists, I'm afraid I must warn you that your family may be in some danger from the Lybrariad's enemies."

Dorrie's father dropped back into his chair, his eyeglasses

sliding down his nose on impact. "Danger? What kind of danger?"

Mistress Wu adjusted her scarf. "A week ago, right in your backyard, a loathsome man named Mr. Aldous Biggs viciously attacked Dorrie and Marcus and your aunt Alice."

"What?" exclaimed both of Dorrie's parents.

At the mention of Mr. Biggs's name, Dorrie had felt a twinge of fear, remembering his pitiless eyes. The little bottle he'd left behind felt cold in her jeans pocket.

"He also threatened the life of Kash, one of our lybrarians," said Mistress Wu.

"She means Elder," said Dorrie. Elder was an old friend of the family. Old like Great-Aunt Alice old. "Kash is Elder's real name."

"Elder is a lybrarian with a *y*?" asked Dorrie's father, as though trying to mentally fit a lawnmower into a matchbox. "But…but…we've played *golf* together!"

"Kash always was fond of the game," said Mistress Wu wistfully. "The scamp broke more than a few windows out on the Commons when he was younger." She frowned slightly. "Which was, of course, just a few weeks ago, Petrarch's Library time." She gave herself a little shake. "Well, the important thing is that thanks to Dorrie and Marcus, he's been reunited with the Lybrariad, even if he is eighty-two now."

Dorrie's mother sank back into her chair.

"His bullet wound is healing nicely," said Phillip, picking with fascination at the pickle jar's plastic label.

"Elder's been shot?" cried Dorrie's father, his eyes blazing.

"And can you believe he still insisted on going to the International Librarians' Conference with Alice," said Mistress Wu, her voice trembling with admiration.

"Which brings us back to the danger," said Phillip. "The Lybrariad is concerned that Mr. Biggs may have cronies in the area, which is why Menelik has been watching your house this last week."

As Dorrie's parents gaped at Menelik, he nodded serenely and shot a needle through a loop of yarn.

"But what would they want with us," said Dorrie's mother.

Phillip and Mistress Wu exchanged glances.

"Mr. Biggs came to Great-Aunt Alice looking for a powerful stone called Petrarch's Star," said Phillip. He seemed to be choosing his words carefully. "It seems the Foundation has risen from its terrible ashes, and Mr. Biggs serves it."

"I thought you'd...you'd...vanquished the Foundation," said Dorrie's father.

"We had," said Phillip. "In the past. Kash discovered that the Foundation has been operating with great strength in future centuries. Ones with which Petrarch's Library doesn't yet connect."

Like the Lybrariad, it possesses a headquarters that lies

outside time," said Mistress Wu. "The Foundation calls it 'the Stronghold.' Until recently, it only connected to centuries *after* the twenty-first."

"But now they're connecting to earlier times," said Dorrie. "Like ours!"

Mistress Wu nodded. "And ancient Athens and Egypt."

Dorrie's father's eyes nearly crossed.

Phillip leaned forward. "From what Kash could glean while a prisoner in the Stronghold, the Foundation operates in the future in the same cruel way it operated in the past. Unfortunately, it has definite plans to re-conquer all the earlier centuries."

Dorrie's blood ran cold.

Her father staggered toward one of the kitchen cupboards. "I need a cup of chamomile tea."

"Why is the Foundation coming back now?" Dorrie's mother asked.

Phillip and Mistress Wu shared another long look. "Because they only lately learned how to use Petrarch's Star to break into the past."

"We have to get the Star back!" cried Dorrie, jumping up, possessed by the urge to search the streets of Passaic for Mr. Gormly that very minute.

"Indeed," said Phillip. "But there's more to the story, and its possibly good news. Kash found out the Foundation needs more than just Petrarch's Star to succeed in its plans."

"What else," whispered Dorrie, sitting back down.

"Something called 'Whim's Gift,'" said Phillip. "Petrarch's Star has to be put inside Whim's Gift to force it to do the Foundation's bidding."

"How is that good news?" asked Marcus as Dorrie's father set a tray of jiggling teacups on the table.

Phillip happily reached for one. "Because whatever version of Whim's Gift that the Foundation used to break into Athens and Egypt is no longer available to them. Broken or lost, Kash supposes.

"Is it some kind of box or machine?" asked Dorrie.

"We don't know," said Phillip. "But the Foundation is now desperately trying to make a replacement. It buys us some time."

"So what happens if the Foundation takes over the past?" asked Marcus.

Mistress Wu's eyes snapped with anger as the kettle began to shriek. "It would seek to enslave people again, no doubt. Taking back written language would likely be one of their first moves. The Lybrariad will be doing everything in our power to stop them."

Dorrie's father began to pour hot water into the cups, spilling a great deal of it on the table.

"In the meantime," said Mistress Wu, looking at Dorrie's father with some concern, "we'd like Menelik to stay with you. Great-Aunt Alice has offered her room."

"All right," said Dorrie's mother. "If you really think it's necessary."

"Good," said Mistress Wu briskly. She sprang the catches on her briefcase and removed a sheaf of papers. "Now, I wonder if we can discuss the matter of the apprenticeships."

Dorrie heart skipped a beat.

Dorrie's father chugged what was left of his chamomile tea.

"I want to make it clear," said Mistress Wu, "that Lybrariad's offer has nothing whatsoever to do with the fact that Dorrie and Marcus inadvertently managed to become keyhands."

"Keyhands?" said Dorrie's mother, lost again.

"Not just anybody can go skiffing through the archways," said Phillip. "It takes a particular lybrarian known as a keyhand to do that job. Three for every century. If you're not a keyhand, you'll bounce right off an archway, like a bird against a plate of glass. We plainer sorts of lybrarians count on the keyhands to get us in and out of the wherens."

"And Dorrie and Marcus are keyhands?" asked Dorrie's father.

"Only technically," said Mistress Wu and Phillip together.

Dorrie tried not to be hurt by the distinct relief in their voices.

"As a rule, keyhands are chosen from among the most experienced and able of our lybrarians," said Mistress Wu. "Dorrie and Marcus came by their abilities, well—"

"It happened accidentally," said Dorrie. "Because we fell

into Petrarch's Library a few seconds after it connected with the Passaic Public Library."

"But they are in very good company," said Phillip. "The third keyhand for twenty-first century Passaic is a fine upstanding mongoose."

Dorrie's father rubbed his temples.

"Say it loud; say it proud," said Marcus, holding up a raised fist.

Dorrie rolled her eyes. "His name is Moe. He escaped from this kid at the Pen and Sword Festival we went to last week. Marcus and I tried to catch him. He ran into the Passaic Public Library and then into the secret room behind the janitor's closet, and then we all fell into Petrarch's Library."

"Big splash," said Marcus.

"They landed in our Roman bath," explained Phillip.

"Dorrie got an extra seriously weird power that not even the real keyhands have," said Marcus.

Dorrie's face went red as her parents' eyebrows went airborne.

"Don't worry," said Marcus soothingly. "It's nothing too freaky. Normal keyhands only have the power to get through one archway each, but Dorrie can get through any of them."

"But why?" asked her mother.

Slowly, Dorrie pulled a small walnut-shaped silver vial from her pocket and laid it on the table, where it rocked for a moment on its rounded side. Though made of silver metal like her armband, the bottle dully refused to reflect the light from the windows. "I think this had something to do with it."

"What is it?" asked her father, poking it experimentally.

"It belongs to Mr. Biggs," said Dorrie. "I drank something out of it, and it made this happen." She held up her thumbnail, which had been black as pitch ever since the day she'd fallen into Petrarch's Library—black like all of Mr. Biggs's nails.

"Why, on Demeter's great, green, globulous earth," asked Dorrie's mother, who seemed to be attempting to employ calming yogic breathing, "were you drinking out of a stranger's…flask?"

"I didn't know I was," said Dorrie, impatient to get back to the subject of the apprenticeships. "Miranda emptied it into my orange juice when I wasn't looking."

"She pickpocketed Mr. Biggs when he was here," added Marcus.

Menelik looked with interest over his knitting at Miranda's slumbering form.

"Of course she did," said Dorrie's father. He turned to Mistress Wu. "Well, what exactly did our daughter ingest?"

"The Foundation's operatives call it, 'Traveler's Tea,'" said Phillip. "They must drink it to travel in and out of the Stronghold.

"So can we train?" Dorrie cried, unable to bear the suspense any longer.

"May we," corrected Phillip, Mistress Wu, Menelik, and her parents in unison, startling one another.

"Sure. That," said Marcus.

Dorrie's gaze darted from her father's to her mother's face, her breath held, hoping that the interest they shared with the lybrarians in good grammar might have tipped the balance in a good way.

Dorrie's mother spoke first. "It...it...does sound like a marvelous—"

"Insanely marvelous," broke in Dorrie's father.

"—opportunity," finished Dorrie's mother. "But it would be a very big change for all of us. I mean...uh...just the time-travel element..."

"A very big change," repeated Dorrie's father.

"You always tell us that change is good!" Dorrie cried.

"Well, yes," Dorrie's mother replied, reddening a little, "but I meant trying a new kind of vegetable or taking a pottery class or something."

"You're only twelve and fourteen," said Dorrie's father, "and it just all sounds so...dangerous."

"Oh, it is," said Phillip. "Terribly, fantastically dangerous. Especially since particularly difficult times may lie ahead for the Lybrariad."

Dorrie's mother visibly gulped.

"On the bright side,' said Phillip. "In four hundred years,

the Lybrariad has only lost one apprentice, and that was entirely her fault because she insisted on doing foolish things with tungsten."

Mistress Wu pushed the sheaf of papers across the tablet to Dorrie's parents. "Here are some written materials about the apprenticeship program—do burn them when you're done reading." She folded her hands. "Now. We organize the year into quarters in Petrarch's Library. The summer quarter begins on the first of July, in three days' time. It would be sensible for Dorrie and Marcus to arrive a few days in advance, to prepare."

"We'll get to stay with the other apprentices in the attics," said Dorrie and realized immediately that she'd taken a wrong turn.

"Stay?" said her mother, newly alarmed, her teacup clattering against her saucer.

"Oh," said Mistress Wu, looking with sudden great pity at Dorrie's mother and father. "I'm sorry we didn't make that fact clear. As apprentices, Dorrie and Marcus will indeed need to stay with us in Petrarch's Library. There are practicums, you see, and—"

"For how long?" demanded Dorrie's mother.

"Well, a quarter runs three months and—"

"Three months!" cried Dorrie's father. He rounded on Marcus. "What about your friends here? What about that band you were going to start with that boy with that hoop in his eyebrow?"

"You can't stand that kid!" said Marcus.

Her father swung back around to face Dorrie, looking shocked. "And what about the Passaic Academy of Swordplay and Stage Combat? I thought you loved being part of that."

"I did," said Dorrie, feeling her heart squeezing painfully on its own mixed feelings. "But that was all pretend. And this is real. I have the chance to really learn how to use a sword and do something that counts with it."

"What about your sister—and us?" asked Dorrie's mother, her voice choked. "I can't not see my children for three months!"

"Yes, I imagine that would be simply wretched," said Mistress Wu, her eyes looking filmy.

"Couldn't they come home for a visit or two?" asked Dorrie's mother.

"In future quarters, yes, that will be possible," said Mistress Wu, blotting her eyes. "But this quarter, given the situation…"

Dorrie looked anxiously from her mother to her father, even as they were exchanging the same kind of look with each other. "Please," she whispered.

Finally, Dorrie's mother squeezed her husband's hand and then turned back. "You can give this a try for one of these… quarters, and then we'll see."

"A try," Dorrie's father repeated firmly.

"And getting maimed or killed will simply not be tolerated," added Dorrie's mother, tears in the corners of her eyes. "That happens once, and we're done."

"Well, of course we'd be done," Marcus said. "We'd be dead."

Dorrie kicked him hard under the kitchen table as an abounding joy nearly lifted her out of her chair.

Chapter 3

An Inconspicuous Entry

TWO DAYS LATER, DORRIE and Marcus were walking quickly along Grand Avenue toward the Passaic Public on their way to begin their apprenticeships. Mistress Wu and Phillip had outlined the plan for Dorrie and Marcus's return to Petrarch's Library at the conclusion of their visit with the Barnes.

"Lybrarians-in-training Mr. Louis P. Kornberger and Ms. Amanda Ness will help get you into the staff room, of course," Mistress Wu had said.

"They've been accepted?" Dorrie had cried joyfully. She'd worried the Lybrariad wouldn't invite her favorite local librarians into the training program. Especially Mr. Kornberger, who, though Dorrie loved him, lacked perhaps the more obvious lybrarian warrior qualities.

"What if Scuggans gives us trouble?" Marcus had asked.

Mistress Wu had sifted through her papers. "Ah, yes. Mr. Richard P. Scuggans, director of the Passaic Public Library." She had looked up. "According to Amanda, he's taken a couple weeks off to recover from"—she had consulted her papers—"a personally traumatic recent event."

Dorrie had snorted. "He *can't* mean Mr. Gormly stealing his clothes." The last time she had seen Mr. Scuggans, he'd been pelting past the Passaic Public Library's magazine rack wearing nothing but a "Where Will a Book Take You Today" poster.

"That was way more traumatic for us," Marcus had said.

Mistress Wu's brows had risen as her eyes scanned the page further. "It seems Mr. Scuggans has officially banned you both from the library. For releasing a rodent onto the premises. Just as well he won't be there when you arrive. The Lybrariad would appreciate an inconspicuous reentry, please."

Now Dorrie glanced behind them again as she'd done regularly since they'd left the house.

"Can't you use a mirror or listen for footsteps or something?" asked Marcus, hiking his backpack up higher on his shoulder. The neck of his ukulele stuck out of the top. "You're appalling my inner stealth master. And if my outer stealth master was here, you'd be appalling him too."

Dorrie laughed out loud at the thought of Master Casanova,

the Lybrariad's white-wigged stealth and deception master, walking beside them down the potholed street.

"And if Mr. Biggs does have friends looking for us," continued Marcus, "you are totally skywriting our position."

"I'm not worried about friends of Mr. Biggs," said Dorrie, facing front again. "I'm worried Mom and Dad are going to catch up to us and tell us we can't go after all."

Marcus took a sharp right around a corner, departing from their usual route.

"Hey," said Dorrie, stopping. "Where are you going?"

"Well, no sense taking the obvious route then."

Grinning, Dorrie ran after him.

After some devious twisting and turning of Marcus's design, the library came into view. Dorrie felt a bit of the lump in her throat returning from the night before when Miranda had insisted the whole family squeeze onto the couch to watch *Willy Wonka and the Chocolate Factory*. She'd refused to skip the "Cheer Up, Charlie" song and had wailed through it inconsolably until Menelik had promised to knit a coat for her invisible dog.

Thoughts of Ebba, her best friend among the apprentices, and Savi waiting for her somewhere in the tangle of Petrarch's Library chased away the lump. Despite the boarded-up window on the second floor and the paint peeling off its door frames, Dorrie felt the Passaic Public Library looked beautiful and dignified, its red bricks glowing with late-afternoon light.

She and Marcus hurried up the steps. Joining a horde of preschoolers being coaxed along by a weary-looking woman, they pushed through the swinging glass door. A few steps in, Dorrie heard a voice that made her freeze.

"I've already explained the situation to you, Mrs. Jackson," said Mr. Scuggans from behind the circulation desk. He was readjusting his toupee with the aid of a pocket mirror. "You cannot check a book out without a library card, and I cannot possibly issue you a library card without seven forms of identification, including a birth certificate."

"But you know, all my possessions were lost when my apartment building burned down last week," said an elderly bent woman. She held out a newspaper. "You can read about it yourself."

Behind Dorrie, one of the preschooler's lunchboxes clattered to the floor. Dorrie seized Marcus's arm and yanked him behind a bookcase.

"*No noise*," said Mr. Scuggans, sounding enraged. "*At all.*"

Dorrie cautiously peeked through a gap in the books and saw Mr. Scuggans glaring at the preschoolers, one eye twitching convulsively.

"Please," the old woman said. "I've been taking out books here for fifty-three years."

"I'm sorry," said Mr. Scuggans, going back to his pocket mirror and sounding nothing of the sort. "No exceptions."

In the week since Dorrie had seen him, his real hair had developed a gray undercoat, giving his groundhog-colored toupee the look of a mismatched teapot lid.

Marcus elbowed her. "What's he doing here?"

Mr. Scuggans promptly gave them an answer. "Now if you'll excuse me, I am expecting the Mayor of Passaic and representatives of the local media any minute now." He breathed on his watch and rubbed it on his shirtfront. "It may interest you to know I am receiving a special commendation for courage in the line of duty. Were you aware a dangerous criminal came through the library recently?"

"Yeah, and Mr. Scuggans ran around in circles screaming, 'Help! Police!'" whispered Marcus. "How is that courageous?"

Dorrie looked across the tables and bookshelves to the spot where the staff room door beckoned. It was tantalizingly close, but getting to it from where they were would put them directly in Mr. Scuggans's line of sight.

"And where are Mr. Kornberger and Amanda?" Marcus asked.

"Let's sneak back out and go around to the back door," said Dorrie. "We can come up the basement stairs and get to the staff room without him seeing us."

Marcus nodded, and they crept back out the way they'd come in.

Around back, Marcus yanked on the gray metal door, but it was locked tight. "Now what?"

Dorrie stepped back. A window a ways down the wall and not too far above their heads was half-open.

A minute later, Dorrie was crouched against the brick wall, and Marcus used her as a human ladder. "Why exactly did I volunteer to be on the bottom?" she panted as his sneaker nearly took off her ear.

"Pride," said Marcus. "It's so easy to use against you."

The window screeched as Marcus forced it farther up.

"Which room is it?" panted Dorrie.

"Bathroom."

Marcus's weight disappeared from her back. A moment later, she heard the sound of something metallic hitting something hard with great force and a great gushing. Marcus appeared in the window utterly soaked. "I may have broken a small piece of plumbing."

Behind Dorrie came the sound of cars rolling into the graveled parking lot.

Dorrie whirled. A long, black car with little fluttery flags affixed to the hood was pulling in.

"I think," Marcus said conversationally, "that the Mayor's here."

She tossed her pack to Marcus. "Give me your hand!"

He threw the pack behind him and had just reached down when the back door was flung open and Mr. Scuggans appeared. He and Dorrie stared at each other for a horrified silent instant.

"You!" cried Mr. Scuggans, his eyes wild, his voice saturated with loathing.

"Jump!" yelled Marcus.

Dorrie leaped as well and high as she ever had, just managing to grab hold of his hand, her toes scrabbling at the bricks.

"Help!" cried Mr. Scuggans, waving his arms at the people getting out of the cars. "Illegal ingress! Illegal egress! Trespass! Stop them!"

Behind her, Dorrie heard the sound of running feet. Marcus gave a mighty heave, and Dorrie managed to get her chest over the sill, but she felt Mr. Scuggans's hands clamp around her ankle. He gave a yank, and she nearly fell, clawing at the sill. A brick came away in her hands and plummeted out of sight. Dorrie heard a thud accompanied by a shriek, and suddenly, her foot was free.

She tumbled through the window and onto the floor.

"That hoodlum threw a brick at me!" shouted Mr. Scuggans from outside.

"What'd you throw a brick at him for?" asked Marcus, dragging her to her feet.

"I didn't," Dorrie protested, not thinking it was the right time to go into details.

Slipping and splashing through the great puddle of water that now covered the floor, they streaked for the door and nearly collided with Amanda and Mr. Kornberger on the other side.

35

"By the bard's beard!" said Mr. Kornberger, his curly hair wild. "Where have you been?"

"Where were you?" Dorrie hissed.

Amanda hurried them toward the staff room door, her hundred braids swinging. "When Mr. Scuggans showed up, he sent us to clean up the staff room for his interview. Mr. Kornberger slipped out to try to intercept you, but..."

Thundering steps on the stairway from the basement announced that Mr. Scuggans and the others were on their way up.

"Just tell him we got away through the front door!" said Dorrie.

Amanda hurriedly pushed Dorrie and Marcus into the staff room. "We'll stall them as long as we can!"

Dorrie and Marcus sprinted for the janitor's closet, slipped in, and closed the door behind them.

"I'm not sure that was entirely inconspicuous," said Marcus, locking it.

"Francesco's going to kill us," Dorrie said, panting as she dug in her pocket for the little length of flat metal Phillip had given her to pry up the worn plank that hid the mechanism that opened the door. Crouching, she levered one end upward. The plank rose silently on a well-oiled hinge, revealing a small wheel in the cavity below. Left or right, Dorrie thought to herself, suddenly unsure.

"Button, button, who's got the button?" said Marcus.

"*Willy Wonka* quotes not helpful," hissed Dorrie, taking hold of the wheel.

"Well, c'mon, already!"

Dorrie chose left and gave the wheel a twist. The back wall of the closet swung away from them on one side, golden light burnishing the rags and paint cans.

CHAPTER 4

AMONG FRIENDS, MOSTLY

ONCE INSIDE THE SECRET five-sided room Great-Aunt Alice's father had made when he'd built the Passaic Public Library and in which the entrance to Petrarch's Library lay, Dorrie slammed the door behind them.

"Hold!" rang out a pleasant, if tense, voice.

Dorrie spun around. In some ways, the room was just as it had been when she'd passed through last. The gas lamp still hissed softly from its ceiling fixture. The bookshelves still held their fantastic collection of books and things it was hard not to want to pick up. The gaping hole that connected the Passaic Public Library to Petrarch's Library still glowed blue-white around its jagged edge in the center of the room.

On the other hand, a row of computers now sat on the heavy wooden table with its carved dragon legs. Dorrie instantly resented their modern glow. But there was no time to dwell on the change. Behind the computers stood five vibrantly alert lybrarians, all with their eyes on Dorrie and Marcus. Dorrie knew they were lybrarians because one held a throwing dagger, two held slingshots, and another a thick staff. They had all made attempts at twenty-first-century dressing. It hadn't gone perfectly well. A grandmotherly-looking woman was wearing a tube top over a suit jacket.

"Weapons away," said the fifth lybrarian in the same pleasant voice Dorrie had heard before. She was plump with a soft puff of a bun and friendly, if watchful, brown eyes.

The other four lybrarians secreted their weapons, seated themselves, and immediately began tapping at their keyboards with great focus.

"I'm Rachel Davis," said the fifth as she slipped a pair of headphones down to rest around her neck. "Acting keyhand for twenty-first-century Passaic." She gestured to the typing lybrarians. "We've been assigned the mission of finding Mr. Gormly and Petrarch's Star. The Passaic apprentices, I presume?"

"Indeed," said a deep voice off to one side, sounding distinctly unenthusiastic.

Dorrie jerked her head around to see a tall man with an eye patch and graying dark hair standing close to one of the bookcases. One of his hands rested on the pommel of a long sword. He held a fat stack of folders in the crook of his other arm.

"M-master Francesco..." Dorrie stammered. Her stomach quivered unpleasantly as it always did in the presence of the director of security for Petrarch's Library. His craggy face looked as fierce and as thunderous as ever, and his thin, waxed mustache was still jet-black. She shot Marcus a quick look, wishing her clothes weren't soaked and that she wasn't panting.

"Well," said Lybrarian Davis. "A pleasure to meet you."

Dorrie wasn't at all sure Francesco shared her feeling. During Dorrie's time in Petrarch's Library, Master Francesco had looked upon her with the utmost suspicion, expressing more than once his belief that if she wasn't out to harm Petrarch's Library, she wasn't there out of a love for the Lybrariad's mission either. Only his daughter, Millie, had seemed to think less of Dorrie.

He seemed about to speak when, from one of the back corners of the room, angry chittering sounded. In a large cage, Moe the mongoose began to hurl his long, glossy brown body from side to side. He paused for a moment to bare his teeth.

"There's the keyhand we all know and love," crowed Marcus.

Francesco looked pained.

Even though Dorrie knew she pretty much owed her life to Moe, she still had a hard time seeing the charms in him that Ebba did. She glanced at the hole in the floor, remembering how Mr. Gormly had hurled Moe into the Roman bath far below after Moe attacked him.

"An apprentice named Ebba has been in here five times

already today," said Lybrarian Davis, returning to her computer. "Her most updated message is that the apprentices are waiting for you in the attics and that you should come quickly because Sven will be reading out celebratory refreshments."

"Oh! Thank you!" said Dorrie, feeling a surge of intense pleasure.

She and Marcus tore for the jagged hole. Sven was the acknowledged champion of conjuring sweet, delicious things out of books.

"Just a minute," said Francesco, his voice commanding.

Dorrie and Marcus skidded to a stop, and Dorrie turned slowly to face Francesco.

"Welcome back," he said, his tone neutral, revealing nothing. "Before you reenter Petrarch's Library, I want to make sure we are perfectly clear on a point. You, Dorothea Barnes, are not—at any time or for any reason or under any circumstances—to employ your ability to navigate the archways of Petrarch's Library."

Dorrie flushed. "I wasn't planning on it."

"See that you don't change your plans or you will find that your apprenticeship has ended."

Dorrie nodded, the thought chilling her.

There was a burst of sound from Lybrarian Davis's headphones. Hurriedly, she slipped them back on. "Davis here. Go ahead." She froze for a moment and then reached for a pad. As she scribbled down a string of numbers and letters, a fierce glow that verged on triumph appeared in her eyes. "The end," she said crisply and tore the earphones back off. The other lybrarians had stopped typing and were looking at her expectantly.

"Lybrarian Petrov found the spot where Mr. Gormly has been staying," Lybrarian Davis said, her voice rich with satisfaction. "In an abandoned warehouse by the river."

Dorrie's breath caught. A cheer went up from the lybrarians.

"Is he there?" Francesco demanded.

"Not at the moment," she said, "but Petrov has reason to believe he'll be back and that Petrarch's Star is still in his possession."

Rich relief flooded Dorrie.

"Get three more mission lybrarians over to that address," Francesco commanded a lybrarian wearing a cowboy hat set with a great number of rhinestones. He turned to Dorrie and Marcus and pointed at the hole in the floor. "And you. *Go!*"

As he hurriedly began to talk with the other lybrarians, Dorrie, with Marcus on her heels, sprang for the rough wooden steps the lybrarians had built to reach the jagged hole from the lip of the Roman bath below. Had they not been keyhands, the hole would have behaved as if it were simply a transparent piece of the floor: solid and unyielding. But for Dorrie and Marcus, the invisible barrier became penetrable. Descending through it, Dorrie felt the familiar warmth engulf her—almost pleasant compared to the searing heat she'd felt her first time through.

When her head dropped beneath the level of the barrier, she paused, thrilling to the sound of the bath's gently slapping water, giddy with happiness. She was back in the wild jumble of Petrarch's Library—and Mr. Gormly had been found!

On fire to tell the other apprentices what they'd heard, Dorrie and Marcus pelted through the set of swinging doors that led into the Gymnasium, bumping into the weapons training mistress, who was carrying an armload of javelins, and nearly knocking her off her feet.

"More care, please!" cried out Mistress Mai with more surprise than anger. "I'd prefer to be taken out in the line of duty than by a door!"

"Sorry!" Dorrie called out. She sprinted across the room, hoping to see Savi dueling another lybrarian, his rapier flashing, but he wasn't there.

After exiting through another door, they careened up and down stairwells and through familiar library rooms and corridors—some grand, some shabby. Dorrie slowed to a panting halt when they reached one of the black stone archways.

Above it, white letters twisted to spell out "Athens, 399 BCE" between two images of a crossed pen and sword. To its left, an ancient water clock slowly trickled out the minutes. To its right, a calendar carved into the wall showed the current date in the wheren on the other side of the archway. Dorrie knew the archway well having once fallen through it accidentally and then snuck through on purpose during the last quarter. She jumped back when the sweaty-armed housekeeper she, Marcus, and Ebba had met while in Athens pushed a mop into view.

"I can never get used to the fact that people on the other side of the archways can't see us," Dorrie said.

"She's probably still cleaning up after that riot we caused," said Marcus.

"We?" said Dorrie indignantly as she watched the woman attack the pigeonholes full of scrolls with a dust rag. "That was all you."

Last quarter, Dorrie, Marcus, and Ebba had slipped through the archway to look for a scroll they'd lost in the little, tiled Spoke Library on the other side, only to be mistaken for hired servants and sent to pass out wine and grapes at a party. There'd been musicians, and Marcus, unable to resist, had taught the drummer, Timotheus, a few choice seventies rock rhythms. There had been a violent reaction from the partygoers. Chairs and wine bowls had flown.

"Who knew they were so set in their musical ways?" said Marcus.

Dorrie stared at the housekeeper's retreating back. They also hadn't known they'd run into Mr. Biggs there.

When they at last reached the whitewashed wooden door

that led to the Apprentice Attics, Dorrie heard voices arguing on the other side. Not stopping to listen to the words, she threw the door open to the room the apprentices called "the den."

Inside, the apprentices were sitting and lying and perching in remarkably creative ways on the worn furniture around the rough, brick fireplace, their attention focused on an older apprentice named Amo that Dorrie didn't know very well.

"You're back!" shouted Ebba, leaping off the arm of one of the sturdier battered armchairs.

She and Dorrie flung themselves at each other and hugged fiercely, laughing, the yellow cloth band that held Ebba's dreads back falling over her eyes. Around them, general whooping and hollering ensued. Dorrie and Marcus were treated to a wide variety of welcoming gestures, including a punch on the arm each from Sven, who wasn't a big fan of speech; a hot baked potato each from Mathilde ("I just read them out!"); and a fervent "*Finally!*" from Kenzo, who, too young to be an apprentice, still spent as much time in the den as possible.

Saul, who was older than Marcus, waved from where he sat perched on a table next to Fatima, another apprentice Dorrie didn't know very well yet. A blue smudge of ink lay across a cheek, and two short plaits of dark, gravity-phobic hair shot out from the sides of her head. She was plinking a stringed instrument that lay in her lap.

Izel, Millie's best friend, experimented with a couple

forbearing looks, as if she thought Dorrie and Marcus were getting far too much attention. Dorrie was mildly relieved to notice that Millie, for once, wasn't beside her or anywhere in the den for that matter.

"I was afraid your parents wouldn't let you come!" said Ebba.

Dorrie grinned. "They almost didn't."

Many hands pulled Dorrie and Marcus toward the fire. With deep pleasure, Dorrie let herself be tossed onto the balding horsehair couch, a good many of the apprentices piling on after her.

"Can Sven read out the marshmallows now?" begged Kenzo, trying to reach a floppy magazine that had been jammed behind a stack of battered books on the mantelpiece.

"I've got so much to tell you!" said Ebba.

"Me too!" said Dorrie. She was about to blurt out what she'd heard from Lybrarian Davis when Amo spoke.

"Excuse me." Dorrie saw he was standing beside an easel. He pushed his spectacles up the steep grade of his nose. "Welcome back and all that, but we were in the middle of talking about this quarter's attics cleanup."

Audible groans rose from the apprentices.

"This is important," shouted Amo. "Do you want to fail the inspection?"

"If we fail, none of us gets to take practicums this quarter," explained Ebba to Dorrie and Marcus.

"No group of apprentices has failed in ages," said Mathilde.

"Yes, but this place has never been more disgusting!"

Dorrie glanced around. The floorboard cracks held stale popcorn. A loaf of moldy French bread stuck out from beneath a chair. Random belongings, crumpled paper, and abandoned half-filled mugs covered the tabletops. In short, it looked just the way it always did.

Mathilde yawned. "So what? It's always disgusting the day before the inspection."

"And then we clean it up," said Saul. "And Mistress Wu passes us."

"Last quarter, she almost didn't," said Amo. "If Izel hadn't fake-cried, we'd have failed."

Izel batted her eyes and did a little curtsy. Some of the apprentices snickered.

"Here," said Fatima, jumping off the table and going over to the fireplace, where Kenzo was now practically trying to climb the chimney to get at a magazine. She plucked it down and tossed it to Sven. On its cover, a woman in a bun painted a vase below the words *Saturday Evening Post*.

"I can't afford to be barred from practicums this quarter," said Amo, looking like he might really cry himself. "I've got my lybrarian field trial after this quarter, and if don't improve my spear-throwing, I'm going to fail my personal weapon skills demonstration."

"All right, all right," said Mathilde. "Don't get your dashiki in a double Windsor. We'll clean it all up tomorrow like we always do."

"That's not good enough!" said Amo. "Which is why I'm proposing we start cleaning up tonight."

A mutinous roar rose up from the apprentices. Sven stopped leafing through the magazine.

"How could you even *suggest* such an outrageous break with tradition?" blazed Mathilde, her voice filled with mock indignation.

"We have all day tomorrow," said Fatima. "The inspection isn't until 2:00 p.m."

Amo snatched up a piece of thin paper from the easel. Dorrie saw that the words at the top spelled out "Summer Quarter Practicums." She longed to look at it more closely.

"I can't take any chance," said Amo, jabbing at the paper with his finger. "I *need* to take Spears, Axes, and Cats: Throwing Objects with Precision and Flair!"

Mathilde snatched the paper from him and did her own jabbing. "Well, I have every fervent intention of taking Acquiring Written Artifacts by Women Who Nobody Has Bothered to Publish—taught by the one and only Rachel Davis, mission lybrarian and suffragist extraordinaire—and you don't see me jumping around in a panic."

Hearing Lybrarian Davis's name, Dorrie again remembered the news she had to share.

"Let's just vote," said Sven in his quiet, stolid way.

"Something most women out in the wherens never get to do," said Mathilde sniffily. "But fine." She raised her hand high in the air. "All in favor of ruining one of our last nights of ease and sloth, say 'aye.'"

Nobody spoke.

Amo glared at her. "All in favor of *not* waiting to the last minute to clean up and yet guaranteeing we'll all get to take our practicums, say 'aye.'"

Again, nobody spoke.

Marcus looked from Mathilde to Amo. "I'm pretty much confused, but I don't think we're doing any window washing tonight."

"I. Made. You. Pie charts," said Amo stiffly, and raking them all with a highly disappointed gaze, he tore the papers from the easel and stalked into his bedroom, closing the door loudly behind him.

The ceaselessly burning wood in the fire made a popping sound.

"Sheesh," said Mathilde. "Save me from acting like that when I'm a senior apprentice."

Dorrie could wait no longer. She struggled forward out of the pile of apprentices and perched on the edge of the sofa. "We saw Lybrarian Davis out in Passaic."

"You did?" said Mathilde, looking rapturous and dropping

to her knees. "What was she like? How long is she staying in Petrarch's Library? Did she talk about her practicum?"

Marcus tilted his head back thoughtfully. "Confidently insouciant. No idea. And did not mention it."

Mathilde looked disappointed.

"But listen!" Dorrie said. "While we were talking to her, she got a message. The Lybrariad has found Mr. Gormly's hideout!"

Chapter 5
Marshmallow Talk

T HERE WERE GASPS AND cries of excitement from all over the room.

"They're going to stake Mr. Gormly's hideout out," said Marcus. "Which, let me just say, is very hard to say."

"And they think he still has Petrarch's Star," added Dorrie. Everyone began to talk at once.

"The lybrarians could be surrounding Mr. Gormly this very minute!" said Ebba, her eyes shining. "Maybe they already have the star back!"

"That would be a relief!" said Fatima.

Dorrie threw herself back on the cushions. "Especially if the Foundation has already rebuilt that Whim's Gift thing."

The apprentices looked at her blankly.

"You haven't heard?" Marcus asked.

Mathilde poked at Sven with the toe of her pointed shoe. "The marshmallows, Sven. This conversation most definitely requires marshmallows."

While Sven leafed through the magazine, Dorrie and Marcus took turns explaining how the Foundation needed Whim's Gift to make Petrarch's Star work. Dorrie broke off midsentence as Sven bent over an advertisement showing snow-white marshmallows spilling out of a cardboard box. She knew it took great imagination and focus to read objects out of books and that not everyone in Petrarch's Library could do it. Those who could were usually able to read out only one sort of thing. Ebba could read out animals—though since last quarter, when she'd read out Roger, an aurochs the size of a moving van, she'd been forbidden to exercise her skill without express permission.

Lightly, Sven dropped his fingers onto a clump of words below the picture:

ANGELUS MARSHMALLOWS ARE FLUFFY, DELIGHTFUL, DELICIOUS—A MASTERPIECE OF THE CONFECTIONER'S ART.

"So what does Petrarch's Star look like anyway?" asked Fatima.

Dorrie looked up with a start, realizing that among the apprentices, only she and Marcus had ever set eyes on it. And they only for a brief moment.

"Well," said Dorrie as Sven began to slowly draw his fingers together as if trying to catch hold of a tiny dropped bead. "It's made of gray stone, and it's thick. Like a…like a…biscuit or something. And it's got marks carved into it."

"I heard Hypatia talking to Master Callamachus about it at breakfast yesterday," said Saul. "She said Kash made a rubbing of the marks, and they're the same ones that Petrarch used in that journal you got from your great-aunt Alice."

Dorrie whipped around to face him, feeling stupid that she hadn't realized this herself. "I guess they were," she said.

"That might explain Hypatia's message," said Ebba, picking a piece of papyrus off a table. "A messenger left it for you a few hours ago."

Taking it, Dorrie scanned the words. "She wants to borrow the journal." Hurriedly, she reached for her pack and pulled out the little book with its bumpy spine and cracked leather cover. All the apprentices gathered around and stared at the title's worn gilt lettering.

"Still not moving," said Marcus.

During the last quarter, one of the strangest and most glorious things about Petrarch's Library that Dorrie had discovered was the fact that she could pull just about any book or mud tablet off any shelf in the library, and no matter what language it had been written in, the symbols would twist and reshape themselves into English words. For Ebba, they would reshape themselves into Songhai. For Kenzo, Japanese. But the words in the little red book remained stubbornly inscrutable.

Dorrie flipped it open. There were a few surprised murmurings from apprentices who'd never seen the journal. The shape of a star had been carefully cut out of just about all the pages. Only a few in the front and the back had been left intact. Faded words filled the pages, written with the strange collection of symbols known as Petrarch's alphabet.

"Hypatia said the marks on Petrarch's Star don't shift either," said Saul, staring at the star-shaped cavity.

"But why don't they?" asked Kenzo.

"Probably because the words aren't written in a real language," said Saul.

"Don't say that in front of the Archivist!" warned Mathilde. "He'll start gibbering all wild-eyed about how it's most certainly a language."

Dorrie and Marcus's eyes met. While they'd never actually spoken to the lybrarian known as the Archivist, they'd met him on their first day in Petrarch's Library, when he'd arisen drunk and disheveled from behind a table, nearly scaring them to death. It was his job to document the changes in history that occurred every time the Lybrariad ran a mission.

"Well, if it's not a language, what else would it be?" asked Dorrie.

"A code," said Izel, her eyes glittering with the pleasure of a spilled secret. "That's what Lybrarian Della Porta thinks. The lybrarians have brought him in to try to break it."

Dorrie got distracted at that moment by the fact that between Sven's fingers, the corner of a cardboard box had appeared. She watched in awe.

"Read it! Read it! Read it!" the other apprentices began to chant.

Sven's face reddened, and the box slipped backward.

"Quit that," said Mathilde. "You sound demented, and you know how Sven hates attention."

A dead silence took hold, and staring eyes replaced the encouraging cries.

"Well, that's not much better," muttered Sven, but nevertheless, he succeeded in again coaxing the corner of the box out, and then as the page of the magazine flexed and widened, the whole box emerged from between two lines of words.

This time he grinned, red faced, as the cheering resumed.

Soon, great gobby marshmallows were hanging over the fire, impaled on a variety of weapons and a few sharp sticks gathered for the purpose, and the apprentices were swooning at the taste.

"I bet Mr. Biggs wishes he was enjoying one of these about now," said Mathilde as she jammed a fifth marshmallow onto the tine of a grappling hook hung from one of Sven's fishing poles.

For the first time, it occurred to Dorrie that as a prisoner of the Lybrariad, Mr. Biggs could be somewhere very nearby. The thought made her look around nervously. "Where exactly *is* Mr. Biggs?"

Marcus stuffed another marshmallow in his mouth. "He better not be sleeping in my room."

Everybody laughed.

"Don't worry," said Ebba, grabbing Dorrie's hand and pulling her over to the tall windows embedded in the far wall of the den. "He's far, far away!"

From the window, Dorrie could see down one side of the steep mountain of Petrarch's Library. Because the Ghost Libraries that made up the mountain had all arrived with their own weathers and times of day, a patchwork quilt of snow, mist, and rain; dusk, dawn, and blazing midday sun hovered just above their rooftops. Higher up, spread over it all, was a clear moonlit night that had set the surrounding sea to glinting.

Ebba pointed at a dot in the waves far from the shore. "He's out there. On Crackskull Island."

"And what about Mr. Lamb?" asked Dorrie grimly. Mr. Lamb worked for Mr. Biggs. He'd twisted Marcus's arm almost to the point of breaking it, and Dorrie hated him.

Ebba pointed at a distant dot of stillness in the waves. "There. On Crackskull Island."

By squinting, Dorrie could finally make it out.

"And that nasty other man with the stringy hair?"

Ebba moved her arm slightly to the left. "The lybrarians put him on Bloody End Island."

Dorrie stared at Ebba. "The lybrarians aren't... I mean, they wouldn't..."

"What? Kill them?" said Fatima.

"Sounds good to me," said Marcus.

Although Dorrie knew he was kidding, his words chilled her. As frightened of them as she was, she didn't want the two men to die.

"No one's killing anyone," said Saul. "The islands are just called that because they're hard to get on or off without major injury or death. Weird crosscurrents and lots of pointy rocks."

"Plus, sharks are attracted to the islands for some reason— and electric eels and highly poisonous jellyfish—and the beaches around the islands are covered with toxic sea urchins," said Ebba. "The lybrarians rowed Mr. Biggs and Mr. Lamb out there the day after you left."

"Phillip wanted to just catapult them there," said Mathilde, "and good luck to them on the landing, but he didn't get his way."

"I hope those islands are perfectly infested with chiggers," Dorrie said through gritted teeth.

"Oh, they are," said Ebba cheerfully.

"Given his taste in pets..." said Mathilde, when they'd all settled back down by the fire. "He probably enjoys chiggers."

"Whatever happened to Darling?" Dorrie asked, reminded of Mr. Biggs's pet monitor lizard. The last time Dorrie had seen the animal, Ebba had been cradling it in her arms and worrying about whether the belt secured around the lizard's frothing, thrashing jaws was too tight.

Out of the corner of her eye, Dorrie could see Mathilde waving her arms frantically as if to redirect an oncoming bus.

"Oh," said Ebba, a gulpy catch in her throat. "Francesco said she was a menace and that I couldn't keep her."

"Ebba was trying to convince him to let her keep that monster in here!" said Izel indignantly, primly holding her slowly toasting marshmallow a good two feet away from the flames.

"She's not a monster," said Ebba, her own indignation aroused.

"If you overlook her bacteria-ridden deadly bite," said Marcus.

"Marcus!" said Dorrie.

Several tears spilled out over Ebba's bottom eyelids.

Mathilde swung her newly loaded grappling hook back over the fire. "He didn't say the deadly bite was a *bad* thing."

"The lybrarians are just going to release her out in some remote wheren," said Ebba. "Where she doesn't know anybody. When she's been a pet all her life."

"They're putting her back in her natural habitat," said Izel. Ebba choked back a small sob.

"Izel!" said Mathilde, turning to fix her with a meaningful stare. The marshmallow on her grappling hook began to smoke ominously.

"What?" said Izel. "At least they're not going to just lop the thing's head off."

Mathilde's marshmallow burst into flames. She jerked the grappling hook out of the fire, using more force than strictly necessary. The marshmallow sailed over the couch. Fatima shrieked as it narrowly missed her head. For a moment, there was silence, and then everyone burst into laughter, including Ebba.

Dorrie hugged her knees happily. "I'm so happy to be here. I really wasn't sure the Lybrariad was going to want us to come back."

"Of course they'd want you back!" cried Ebba. "If it hadn't been for you and Marcus, Mr. Biggs would have killed Kash and done who knows what other terrible things, and we wouldn't have captured him."

At that moment, Saul trod barefoot on the marshmallow that Mathilde had flung, which resulted in loud recriminations and the throwing of pillows. For the next ten minutes, the apprentices chased one another loudly from one end to the other, around and over the furniture. Amo's easel was upended.

When the tumult died down, Dorrie finally had her first chance to look over the list that Mathilde and Amo had been snatching back and forth. Old-fashioned-looking writing across the top spelled out:

Summer Quarter Practicums

OFFERED TO APPRENTICES, LYBRARIANS-IN-TRAINING,

AND ANY ACTIVE LIBRARIAN WISHING TO

DEVELOP USEFUL KNOWLEDGE AND SKILLS

Dorrie scanned hungrily down the page, her heart pounding with excitement. Under the library administration section was a practicum called:

A Lot of Written Material in One Place: How to Organize Absolutely Everything. Taught by Mistress Minchu Wu, assistant to the director of Petrarch's Library

Another practicum listed under patron services was titled:

Flattering Your Way to the Perfectly Bloodless Prison Break. Taught by Giacomo Casanova, staff lybrarian, department of mission planning

Looking at a section called "Surviving Your Lybrarian's Day," Dorrie immediately wanted to take every practicum listed, which included:

First and Last Aid: When Nobody Else Is Coming

Finding Food Where There Doesn't Appear to Be Any

Damp Dungeons, Desolate Moors, and Dreary Parties:
How to Survive Inimical Environments with Style

She was just looking over

Swords, Daggers, and Coffee Can Tops: A General Survey
of Sharp Edges and Their Uses. Taught by Amita Khan,
Spoke Lybrarian, Karakarum, Mongol Empire

when Izel suddenly spoke to her. "I can't believe you were even worried that the lybrarians wouldn't let you come back."

Her head still full of practicum visions, Dorrie looked over to where Izel sat adding stitches to a piece of cloth stretched over an embroidery hoop.

"I mean, the lybrarians need you. They had to take you back." Izel gave Dorrie a sidelong look. "How else can they travel back and forth to your century? I mean, you are the keyhand."

"They don't need Dorrie and Marcus to get into the twenty-first century," said Ebba stoutly. "They have Moe."

"Well, yes," said Izel. "But they can't depend on one mongoose for access. And anyway, Dorrie has her special power, remember? She can travel through *any* archway. That has to be useful to the Lybrariad."

Dorrie's face burned as most of the apprentices looked at her.

"It's nothing to be ashamed of," said Izel, giving a little laugh that made Dorrie's skin crawl.

"Who said we were ashamed?" Dorrie asked.

"Yeah," said Marcus, crossing his feet on one of the ottomans. "I'm perfectly happy to be used. It's obvious the Lybrariad just wants me for my ukulele."

There was scattered snickering.

"I'm just saying, you two were shoo-ins," Izel said in an overconciliatory voice that somehow nettled Dorrie.

"Hypatia would never have invited them to be apprentices if she didn't think they belonged here," said Mathilde. "Period."

Izel pulled up a long stretch of thread, her darting fish eyes swimming back to Dorrie. "Is your thumbnail still black?"

Dorrie held it up boldly, trying not to show her ambivalent feelings about the mark that had made so many apprentices and lybrarians suspicious of her during the previous quarter. "Same old, same old."

The den door opened. Dorrie was grateful for the

interruption until she saw it was Millie. She had stopped short, her bulging satchel hanging heavy on her shoulder, her eyes barely visible beneath her dark bangs. For the briefest of moments, Dorrie and Millie gazed at each other.

Dorrie lifted her hand in greeting, but Millie only turned and began finding a place to hang her sword belt on one of the overburdened hooks beside the door. Not sure what else to do with her awkwardly aloft fingers, Dorrie ran them through her hair.

"Where have you been?" asked Izel, a note of abandoned complaint in her voice.

"Main reference room." Millie strode to her bedroom, let herself in, and closed the door firmly behind her.

"I don't think she missed us," said Marcus.

"She's been helping Master Callamachus."

Dorrie remembered that he was the director of the research department.

"The research lybrarians are so overworked right now, and Millie is really worried," said Izel, who seemed to be savoring the opportunity to share her friend's distress.

"Everyone's been worried," said Fatima. She yawned hugely, stood, and stretched. "I'd better go to bed. I've got about five hundred pounds of news to gather from the Spoke Lybrarians tomorrow."

Although still preoccupied with Izel's words, Dorrie was dimly aware of a wave of sympathetic murmuring.

65

"What for?" asked Marcus.

Fatima stepped over Saul's long legs. "Because I'm apprenticed to Master Benjamin Franklin, keeper of the Lybrariad's printing presses and editor in chief of *Gouty Ben's Weekly Digest*."

Dorrie had been hardly listening, but she looked up at the mention of the familiar name.

"Benjamin Franklin is a lybrarian?" cried Marcus.

"And a ruthless newshound," Fatima called back over her shoulder.

One by one, the apprentices said good night. Dorrie shouldered her pack and followed Ebba into their little slope-ceilinged bedroom. It was exactly as Dorrie had left it, with its two narrow beds covered with patchwork quilts taking up much of the room, and one little, round window set near the floor on the wall opposite the door. Even the old-fashioned green dress she'd worn all last quarter still hung from a nail on the wall.

"You know you *can* have that washed," said Ebba, jerking her chin at the dress as she got into her nightgown. "Or you can turn it in to the circulation desk and get something entirely new. Like…jodhpurs if you want."

Dorrie laughed weakly. A soft, sighing tornado of disturbing thoughts set off by Izel's words began to spin around her head.

"Izel's wrong," came Ebba's firm voice out of the darkness a few minutes later, after they'd snuggled beneath their quilts.

"I know," Dorrie lied, trying to keep her voice light and not trusting herself to say more.

"Hypatia would never have invited you to become apprentices if she didn't think you were worthy of the training. That's just not like her!"

Dorrie faked a yawn, the tornado still whirling but more slowly now. "I know." She pulled the quilt up farther. She thought of Hercule-Savinien de Cyrano de Bergerac. Savi. He believed in her. He'd accepted her as his apprentice. When the quarter began, she would work so hard that no one in Petrarch's Library would even think for one instant that she didn't deserve to be an apprentice or a lybrarian when the time came.

She was enjoying a pleasant imagined scene—in which she and Savi discovered Whim's Gift hidden in a wall behind an oil painting in seventeenth-century France—when her gaze fell on her moonlit thumbnail. Sitting upright in a rush, she angled her hand to find the best of the moon's light and peered more closely at the nail. It almost seemed as though a thin, pale crescent had formed at its base. She felt her pulse quicken and reached over to shake Ebba awake but then hesitated.

Izel's words danced again in her ears. What if the lybrarians did only want her for her power? And what if the power wasn't going to be hers forever? What if the power was something that could disappear along with the blackness of her thumbnail? She thought of Mr. Biggs's vial where it lay at the bottom of her backpack under her bed. Packing in Passaic, she'd thrown it in at the last minute. For the first time, she wondered if there was any Traveler's Tea left in it.

"I *am* a true apprentice," she said in a fervent, hoarse whisper, staring at the moon in the distance. She was here to train and become a real lybrarian, just like Savi had done before her, and she was going to fight the Lybrariad's battles at Savi's side, no matter the color of her thumbnail.

Chapter 6
Not My Best Angle

WHEN DORRIE WOKE, EBBA was already dressed and the den was alive with sound. Dorrie's thoughts immediately zoomed to Petrarch's Star. "You think they caught Mr. Gormly?"

Ebba grinned at her as she threw the quilt back on her bed. "Let's go find out."

As Dorrie was tucking Petrarch's journal into her apprentice satchel, Marcus flung the door open, nearly knocking Ebba to the ground. He had his apprentice's satchel slung across his chest. Out of it stuck the neck of Fatima's balaban. "Two questions: Did you bring styling mousse? And can I borrow it?"

"Why would I pack—" Dorrie stared at him. "Did you *part* your hair?"

Marcus gave it a pat. "Egeria could be goddess-lurking anywhere."

Ebba and Dorrie exchanged looks. Egeria was a sixteen-year old lybrarian, the youngest member of the Lybrariad. She knew everything there was to know about plants, taught food foraging practicums, and, unbeknownst to her, had become the object of Marcus's unbridled and determined affection during the last quarter.

Out in the den, a good number of the apprentices were digging through the room's mess for misplaced cloaks, the practice weapons they were supposed to make a habit of carrying around, and favorite pairs of roller skates. Loud cries of "Have you seen my scabbard?" "You're sitting on my satchel!" and "Where is my wax tablet?" filled the air.

Dorrie tugged on Mathilde's sleeve. "Any news?"

"Nope," said Mathilde, unearthing a battered-looking admiral's hat from beneath a pile of pillows. "But then no one's made it out of here yet."

A morose, eardrum-shaking bellow rose from somewhere beneath the window.

Marcus backed against the wall. "Is that..."

"Roger," the apprentices said together.

"Don't worry," said Mathilde, jerking her head toward the windows. "He's four floors down in the yard."

"That's way too close," said Marcus.

Dorrie understood his feelings. Roger, who had great affection for Ebba, had a talent for destructive rampaging when in search of her.

"I wonder if he needs more water," said Ebba, concerned.

Izel wrinkled her nose. "What he needs is a bath! I can't believe the lybrarians are letting that smelly old cow live here."

"While I was visiting my parents, he kept breaking out of the pen the riding master made for him," explained Ebba.

Dorrie knew that Ebba's parents, along with a lot of other people who'd been rescued by the Lybrariad, lived in Haven, the little village on the other side of the island.

"He just about gave Master Al-Rahmi a heart attack one night," said Izel. "Stuck his head through the window of the book repair and preservation department workshop."

"A closed window," added Mathilde.

"He got a *terrible* gash over one eye," said Ebba.

"Roger, not Master Al-Rahmi—in case you're wondering," said Mathilde.

At that moment, Amo stalked out of his bedroom, paused to give the gaggle of apprentices a look of deepest reproach, and let himself out of the attics without a word.

"Sheesh," said Mathilde, jamming on her hat. "You'd think inspection was an hour from now." In a noisy, jostling scrum, the apprentices followed Amo. Ten minutes later, Dorrie burst with them onto the green expanse of the Commons. The large rectangle of gardens and grassy areas and small groves of trees lay in the uppermost reaches of Petrarch's Library, surrounded on all four sides by Ghost Libraries standing shoulder to shoulder. With great pleasure, Dorrie breathed in the familiar mixed scents of garden blossoms, grass, and sea air.

Their feet loud on the crushed-shell path, the apprentices started toward the west end of the Commons, where the ancient Library of Celsus stood, grand and pillared. Tallest of the buildings fronting the Commons, it served as the lybrarians' meeting hall and post office. Behind the great statue of Athena, Hypatia had her office.

Marcus stopped short in front of a little, brick Ghost Library that was being battered endlessly by golf-ball sized chunks of hail. "Get my mail for me."

He loped off across the Commons toward one of the gardens Egeria tended. With no idea what he was up to, Dorrie and Ebba joined the lybrarians hurrying up and down the Celsus's broad steps and passed through the middle pair of towering bronze doors.

Dorrie made a beeline for the wall across from the mailboxes on which hung portraits of all the staff lybrarians and keyhands. Beneath Savi's, the brass plaque read "Out."

Disappointed, Dorrie joined Ebba at the mailboxes. Dorrie's was empty. Hurriedly, she slipped Petrarch's journal into Hypatia's box.

Marcus was waiting for them at the bottom of the steps. He held a small bouquet of flowers that looked like their stalks had been chewed off by an angry badger. "For Egeria," he said by way of an explanation. "It's a classic gesture."

Dorrie shot him a look. "But aren't they from her own garden?"

Without answering, Marcus took off in the direction of the Sharpened Quill, the tavern that stood on the opposite end of the Commons and in which the lybrarians and apprentices ate most of their meals.

At the Sharpened Quill, the casement windows were thrown open wide beneath the building's homely yellow-brown thatched roof. Stepping around the usual scattering of bicycles and carts at the entrance, Dorrie pulled open the heavy wooden door.

Inside, the tables were already crowded with lybrarians. A pleasant din of conversation accompanied the clinking of silverware and the clonk of tankards of mead and water.

"Bacon," murmured Marcus, setting off at once for the serving tables.

Dorrie grabbed Ebba's hand and followed, taking advantage of Marcus's wake. Everywhere she glanced, Dorrie was pleased to see many of the lybrarians she'd come to know. She watched Ursula, the director of the human repair and preservation department, pull a chair up to a table, her dark corkscrew curls already escaping from her morning bun. She must have said something amusing because Phillip, already seated, threw his head back and laughed. He noticed Dorrie, tapped Ursula's arm, and they both waved.

Grinning, Dorrie waved back, filled with hope that their light spirits meant the Lybrariad had indeed found Petrarch's Star.

After she and Ebba had served themselves, they headed for the apprentices' long trestle table and sat down. It was already quite full, and most of the apprentices were poring over practicum lists.

Marcus squeezed in beside them, looking disgusted. His flowers had sustained serious damage. "Never get between Master Al-Rahmi and a platter of crullers."

When Sven put his list aside, Dorrie pulled it toward her and brushed toast crumbs off it. "Is Principles of Lybrarianship any good?"

"I don't know," said Ebba, reaching for a pitcher of water. "Who's teaching it?"

"Hypatia."

"Oh, well, then it can't be bad."

"I know, but it sounds kind of...quiet."

Ebba shrugged. "Word gets around about boring practicums, and I've never heard anyone complain about that one. Hey, Mathilde!" she shouted up the table. "Didn't you once take Principles of Lybrarianship?"

Mathilde had no list and was busy making failed snatches for Saul's. "Saul and I both did. Maybe two years ago."

"Was it more than sitting and talking and taking notes?" asked Dorrie.

Mathilde and Saul stifled laughter.

"Trust me," said Mathilde. "You won't be bored."

Dorrie scanned the room for the director of Petrarch's Library and saw her at last in a corner, wearing a sky-blue chiton, her scarred face looking tired but serene enough, her graying curls loose. To one side of her sat the Archivist. His hair a wild thicket, he was chewing slowly and darting uneasy looks at a man sitting on her other side who was talking and cutting up a sausage with great gusto.

"That's Lybrarian Della Porta," said Izel, having followed Dorrie's gaze. "He's teaching Codes, Invisible Inks, and Smoke Signals: Keeping Communication Maddeningly Secret. I've already decided to take it."

Dorrie looked away. Not because she was squeamish about watching people eat sausage but because she still felt uncomfortable whenever she caught sight of the Archivist. Not just because of how he'd scared her and Marcus that first night, appearing in an avalanche of the oranges he'd read out, but because when she and Marcus had fled, terrified, they had accidentally ripped a page out of an important book in Petrarch's Library's main reference room. The book was from a set known as the *History of Histories*, a record of all the missions the lybrarians had ever completed.

The Archivist had been blamed for the missing page, and because she'd been worried that the Lybrariad would kick her out of Petrarch's Library, Dorrie had taken her time admitting the truth. She hunched down a little, feeling ashamed. She had never really apologized to the Archivist for that.

Yawning, Fatima appeared at the table with a plate of eggs and sausage, her arms loaded with newspapers. She dropped down hard on the bench. "I'm supposed to deliver these to Francesco's office, but if I don't eat something first, I'll never be able to make it up all those tower stairs."

Dorrie understood, having once had to climb the long, cold, circular stone staircase herself.

Fatima flopped the newspapers on the table. "They're from your wheren, actually."

"Hey, my parents get this," said Dorrie, picking up a copy of the *Passaic County Ledger*. Her mother checked it for yard sale advertisements, and her father said he read it mostly to smell the ink and feel nostalgic.

Marcus tossed a practicum list to one side. "Done and done." He pulled Fatima's balaban out of his satchel.

"Which ones are you taking?" asked Fatima, reaching for a the salt.

Marcus gave the balaban a strum. "Cloaks, Hoods, Tunics, and Wimples: How to Dress for Mission Success, taught by Master Obaji, staff lybrarian and director of haberdashery

76

services." He strummed again. "'Don't Let a Fashion No-No Nix Your Rescue Fix.'"

"And…" said Dorrie, turning a page of the *Passaic County Ledger*.

"Everyday Stealth and Deception," her brother said, coaxing a pretty little melody out of the instrument. "I have *got* to get one of these."

"Is Fatima ever going to get a chance to play that again?" asked Mathilde, pouring syrup on her pancakes.

"We are the music makers," said Marcus. "And we are the dreamers of—"

Marcus's words and playing came to a sudden dissonant end. Dorrie looked up to see Egeria standing beside the apprentices' table, her long, auburn hair hanging over her shoulder in its usual braid.

The balaban leaped from between Marcus's hands like a wet watermelon seed and noisily bounced on the wooden floor. His face scarlet, Marcus dove for it.

"Sorry to startle you," said Egeria, the small gap between her front teeth showing as she smiled. "Just wanted to say 'welcome back.'"

"Hi," said Dorrie, looking with some concern at Marcus, who had dropped the balaban again.

"That sounded lovely," said Egeria.

"You're welcome," croaked Marcus, finally gaining control of the instrument.

She waved and continued on to the serving table.

"I mean, thank you," Marcus said far too late.

"Hey," said Mathilde. "Anyone want to go swimming after breakfast? Last day of interim and all?"

"Does no one remember that we have the entire attics to get clean by two o'clock?" cried Amo.

At that moment, the usual twirling of monocles and eyeglasses signaled the beginning of announcements.

Ebba brushed crumbs off her hands. "If the lybrarians have Petrarch's Star back, this is when we'll hear about it."

Mistress Wu stood, and the room quieted.

Dorrie listened intently, her fingers crossed.

"Well, here we are just a few short days before the start of the summer quarter. Apprentices, please note that all practicum and apprenticeship request forms must be in my mailbox by eight o'clock this evening.

"As many of you already know, our regularly scheduled Lybrarians Council will be held tomorrow evening." She took out one of her handkerchiefs. "Mr. Biggs, the Foundation operative who attacked our own Kash with such viciousness, will be in attendance for part of that meeting. Lybrarians-in-training and apprentices are welcome to attend, but please sit in the rear of the room, and do not in any way impede the proceedings."

A chill danced down Dorrie's back at the thought of seeing

Mr. Biggs again, but she could hear excited murmurs from many of the other apprentices.

"And while we're on the subject of viciousness," continued Mistress Wu, "I'm afraid I must report that the monitor lizard kept as a pet by Mr. Biggs escaped before it could be transported to New Guinea and is likely somewhere in the library."

There were many gasps of the unhappy sort in the room. But beside her, Dorrie felt Ebba suck in her breath with relieved joy.

"Because this is such a dangerous creature, if you encounter it, you must either give it wide berth or…" Mistress Wu glanced at the apprentices' table, her handkerchief hand twitching, and Dorrie had a bad feeling about what was coming next.

"You must aim to kill."

Ebba gasped again but this time in horror. Dorrie squeezed her hand.

"That's all for now," Mistress Wu said hurriedly. "Enjoy your preparations for the summer quarter."

Dorrie stared from Mathilde to Marcus as the volume in the room rose again. "I guess they didn't get the Star back."

"Or if they did," said Mathilde, "they're not telling us lowly apprentices."

"I'd better get these to Master Francesco," sighed Fatima, gathering up her bundle of newspapers.

Disappointed, Dorrie began to fold up the *Passaic County*

Ledger, only to freeze halfway through the operation. She stared at the newspaper's back page bug-eyed. It held an enormous photo of Dorrie scrambling through the window of the Passaic Public Library the day before.

"What is *that* all about?" cried Izel in a near-shriek. "'Juvenile Delinquents Plague Passaic Public Library. Mayor's Office Plans Investigation.'"

The apprentices crowded around the open newspaper. Dorrie groaned inwardly.

"On July first," read Marcus, "a juvenile delinquent broke into the Passaic Public Library and threw a brick at library director Richard P. Scuggans before eluding capture." He punched Dorrie on the shoulder. "Wow, you sound dangerous!"

"For the last time, I didn't throw a brick at Mr. Scuggans!"

"What happened then?" clamored the apprentices.

As quickly and with as little detail as possible, she told them the story.

"Just what our newest Spoke Library needs," said Millie, stuffing the book she'd been reading in her satchel. "Publicity."

"You think I'm happy about it?" Dorrie thrust the paper at Fatima. "You'd better go ahead and give it to Master Francesco."

Marcus pursed his lips together like Veruca Salt's mother. "Someone is going to be very unpopular around here."

Dorrie hadn't needed Marcus to tell her that.

As Fatima hurried away, Mistress Wu materialized beside the table.

"Well, I'm sure you already have the attics shipshape for inspection," she said in a determined sort of way.

Caught off guard, Dorrie and the other apprentices gave one another sidelong glances.

"Hardly a thing left to do really," said Amo, a desperately fake smile pasted on his face.

"Excellent," said Mistress Wu. "I only stopped by to say that I must attend an important meeting this afternoon during the usual inspection time, but not to worry, Mistress Lovelace said she wouldn't mind doing the inspection for me."

A horrified silence took hold of the table as, after patting Mathilde's shoulder, she trundled off.

"Mistress Lovelace," Ebba whispered with something like terror in her voice at the thought of the meticulous director of the circulation department. Staring at her practicum list on which she'd drawn a great big heart around Lybrarian Davis's practicum, Mathilde began to hyperventilate.

"So much time and so little to do," said Marcus cheerfully. "Wait a minute. Strike that. Reverse it."

"We're doooooooomed," said Amo.

Chapter 7
BROOMS, BEDS, AND BANGS

PEOPLE!" SHOUTED MATHILDE AS the apprentices swarmed back into the attics. "Our hour of darkness is upon us."

"Oh, *now* you see the problem," said Amo.

Dorrie felt a surge of panic as she looked around at the chaos.

Mathilde leaped onto a chair and shoved her admiral's hat backward on her brow. "Listen up, you lazy dogs! We have five hours to transform this filthy, verminous nest into something Mistress Lovelace will interpret as clean! We need drop cloths. We need whitewash. We need colossal amounts of soap!" An unpleasant thought seemed to seize hold of her, and she grabbed two of the three corners of her hat. "We may need inspirational quotes!"

The apprentices spread out over the den like a plague of

locusts, stripping it of sweaters, baked potato skins, books, swords, apple cores, broken quills, crumpled paper, pewter cups, accordions, and roller skates.

Looking only a little smug, Amo handed Mathilde his pie chart, and she began shouting out assignments.

Izel objected to hers. "Floor scrubbing won't work for me. I'm very prone to splinters."

Mathilde's eyes nearly crossed. "I'm about to be prone to violence."

"Okay, okay!" said Izel, picking up a bucket.

For two long hours, the apprentices swept and mopped and shoved furniture from one end of the den to the other. They cleaned the fireplace, polished the doorknobs, and splashed vinegar water on the windows.

"You," Mathilde said, pointing at Millie, who'd just come down from hunting cobwebs in the rafters. "Get us two more buckets of clean water."

"You," she said, pointing at Dorrie, Marcus, and Ebba after Millie had left the den, buckets banging with ill humor. "Strip the beds and pull the mattresses into the den."

"Why are we doing this?" asked Dorrie as they wrestled with the first mattress.

"Have to empty out the old straw," huffed Ebba, "and stuff in fresh."

It didn't take long for Marcus to decide his role was to call out instructions to Dorrie and Ebba while they did the sweaty maneuvering.

"Just help us!" snapped Dorrie as she and Ebba dragged Millie's mattress off its wooden frame.

Instead, Marcus pounced on a frog-green book that lay balanced on the crisscrossed ropes. "Teen-girl diary treasure!" He opened its cover, making a creaking sound.

As a keeper of a diary back in Passaic, Dorrie felt a flare of compassion. "You can't read that."

"Even if it is Millie's," added Ebba.

He paid no attention and began to read out loud, keeping Dorrie and Ebba at bay as they tried to snatch the book from his hands. "'The history of Frey Tomas de Torquemada is not so much the history of a man as that of an abstract genius presiding over a gigantic and cruel engine of its own perfecting.'"

"Put it back!" Dorrie yelled as their struggle toppled a stool.

Marcus only held the book higher. "'Through the records that survive, we may observe its cold, smooth action and trace in this the awful intelligence of its architect.'"

Even as she lunged for the book again, Dorrie felt uncertainty. The words Marcus had read didn't sound exactly like thirteen-year-old diary writing.

"Relax," said Marcus, letting Dorrie have the book. "It's not even a diary."

Dorrie looked down at the cover. "*Torquemada and the Spanish Inquisition: A History*," she read aloud.

"Cheery subject," said Ebba.

"What are you doing?" rang out Millie's voice from the doorway. She strode to Dorrie, snatched the book out of her hands, and hugged it to her chest. "Get out!"

Dorrie hesitated, feeling both ashamed and unfairly accused. Before she could work out what to say, Millie seized the stool as if to throw it, sending Dorrie, Marcus, and Ebba scurrying from the room.

"What was that all about?" said Marcus.

"I don't know, but thanks for making things worse between me and Millie!" said Dorrie, irritated.

When they were done with the mattresses, Mathilde sent Ebba to fetch more water and, to Dorrie's dismay, thrust a paintbrush in Dorrie's hands and told her to go help Millie whitewash a wall.

Dragging her feet, Dorrie joined Millie where she had spread out a drop cloth close to a section of the wall. Millie glanced at her, startled, and then her eyes narrowed.

Dorrie took a deep breath. "I wasn't messing with your stuff. Marcus was fooling around. I was trying to get him to put the book down. That's all."

Millie slapped at the wall with her own paint-laden brush. "Don't think just because you stole keyhand powers, I'm going to suck up to you like everyone else."

Dorrie stared at her, feeling slapped herself. During her week in Passaic, she had let herself hope that even if she and Millie weren't destined to be the best of friends, they wouldn't have to be enemies. The hope fizzled.

"I didn't 'steal' keyhand powers." Dorrie said in a low voice.

"Acting like you're really one of us," muttered Millie, her lips barely moving.

"I'm not acting anything," Dorrie flung back, nauseated by the words. She thrust her brush into the whitewash bucket and attacked the wall grimly, battling an urge to fling some at Millie. Dorrie could feel Millie's determination to cover more wall faster and more thickly and with better results. Her teeth clenched, Dorrie increased her own painting speed.

In other parts of the attics, copious amounts of water were being spilled, sweat flowed freely, and the apprentices were managing to find ever more creative methods of getting in one another's way.

"We're running out of time!" cried Mathilde, helping push the last of the mattresses out the den window. They landed with a thud on the others four stories below. "Kenzo, run down to the circulation department. When Mistress Lovelace leaves, run back here and tell us. Saul, you and Marcus go down to the yard and start emptying the old straw out of the mattresses."

Dorrie watched Saul peer out the window. "Not while Roger's eating one of them."

"He won't hurt you," said Ebba. "Marcus isn't worried."

"Not in the least," said Marcus as he calmly swept a patch of floor.

"See!" said Ebba triumphantly.

Marcus poked the broom under a chair. "Because I'm not going down there either."

The vein crossing Mathilde's forehead began to throb noticeably.

Ebba grabbed Dorrie's hand and towed her toward the den door. "We'll do it."

Dorrie forced herself not to drag her feet.

Down in the yard, Dorrie and Ebba emptied and restuffed the mattresses with furious energy. Roger helped by sending fresh jolts of energy into Dorrie's weary arms every time he snorted or breathed down her neck when she least expected it. Mathilde helped by sticking her head out of the window every five minutes, asking if they could go faster and describing in great detail her plan to have them walk a very short plank into a crocodile-infested bucket of dirty mop water if they didn't.

At one point, through a haze of straw dust, Dorrie saw Sven clamber out on the windowsill high above. With no hesitation or fear, he reached up to release a great coil of rope that was hanging from a pulley set above the window.

Ebba jammed in another handful of clean straw and

snorted. "He's willing to do that, and yet he won't spend a little time with Roger."

Dorrie watched Sven send one end of the rope snaking down to the ground. He looped the other end over the pulley and disappeared back into the attics with it. "So that's how we're getting the mattresses back up."

"Two at a time," said Ebba.

"Hurry!" Mathilde shouted down.

"She is *way* worse than Amo," muttered Ebba as she and Dorrie buttoned up the last mattress.

In a few minutes, they had the first pair of mattresses trussed up.

"Ready?" cried Mathilde from the window, her eager hands on the rope.

Kenzo suddenly appeared beside her, panting. "Mistress Lovelace is on her way!"

"Nooooooo," cried Mathilde, beginning to haul furiously on the rope.

Ebba turned to Dorrie, looking dismal. "No way can we get all these up there before Lovelace gets here."

"People!" cried Marcus, pushing Kenzo aside and pointing at Roger now busy eating the wooden frame off a window. "We've got to work smarter, not harder."

A grin split Ebba's face. "Roger could pull half the mattresses up at once."

Or a third of them anyway. Fifteen minutes later, Dorrie sat atop the last stack of eight trussed-together mattresses. She snaked the end of the rope into one last granny knot. The other end had been thrown down for the third time to Ebba, who had tied it again to Roger's great leather collar. Led by Ebba across the yard away from the windows, he had lifted the first two stacks up as though they were made of cobwebs.

Finished with the knot, Dorrie was about to climb down when Roger snorted loudly and bolted forward at a gallop, sending her rocketing upward, holding on to the rope for dear life. She screamed.

"No, Roger!" Dorrie heard Ebba call. "Come back!"

Dorrie forced herself to look up. Seated upon the mattresses, her arms and legs wrapped around the rope, she was hurtling toward the enormous whirring pulley. She was going to smash into it. Instead, the mattresses jerked to a sudden dead halt. Dorrie gulped for air, listening to the rope supporting her gently creaking. She was dangling three-quarters of the way up to the attic windows.

Marcus was leaning out of one of them, his hand on his heart. "Gah! Don't scare me like that!"

Dorrie was about to bellow back indignantly, but a glance down at the ground made all the important working bits of her throat seize up.

"I think something stung him!" called Ebba. There was a

sound of great effort in her voice. Dorrie guessed she was using all her strength to hold Roger still.

Mathilde pushed back her admiral's hat. "Dorrie, this is no time to be fooling around."

"I'm not fooling around!" Dorrie shrieked as the mattresses dropped several feet.

"Please stop making loud noises," pleaded Ebba. "I can't hold him still."

Dorrie, now at the level of a lower window, peered through it into an unfamiliar room. She had the mad idea to kick the glass in and try to scramble to safety that way. She was about to swing her foot when a movement caught her eye. On the other side of the window, Egeria stood with her arms around a young, dark-haired man. His clothes were dusty, and his boots coated in mud as though he'd traveled a long way. As Dorrie watched, he and Egeria kissed.

The mattresses dropped another few feet. Dorrie couldn't help but shriek again. Egeria broke off the kiss and looked at Dorrie wide-eyed. Another drop put Egeria out of sight. The mattresses spun madly.

"I'll have you down in a minute, Dorrie," called Ebba.

Above her, Dorrie heard Kenzo's panting voice again. "Lovelace is five rooms away!"

Dorrie licked her lips and stared down at the ground for a moment and then back up to the attics' window, sweat pouring off her palms. "Make me go higher!" she forced herself to shout.

"Are you sure, Dorrie?" Ebba asked.

Dorrie nodded vigorously. She wanted this wild ride to be over, but more than that, she wanted to save the apprentices' practicums. She heard Ebba encouraging Roger forward. The rope creaked ominously, and then Dorrie felt herself rising.

Above her, Egeria and the young man Dorrie had seen her kiss appeared in the attics' window, shouldering Mathilde and Marcus aside.

"It's the Bang!" Dorrie heard Izel say breathlessly.

Though he was only a little older than Marcus, the young man's arms were thick with muscles. His teeth were refrigerator white.

"I've got you," he said, grabbing Dorrie around the waist as she came level with the attics' window.

Dorrie felt mammoth gratitude, mixed with resentment for Marcus's sake.

With great difficulty, she persuaded her fingers to release their hold on the rope. Bang dragged her over the windowsill and lowered her onto the floor.

To anxious questions of "Are you okay?" Dorrie nodded, getting awkwardly to her feet. "Get the mattresses in! Keep going!"

As Sven struggled with the knot that bound the mattresses together, Marcus offered Bang a high five. "Thanks a lot. She's the only sister named Dorrie I've got."

Bang looked curiously at Marcus's hand and then put an arm around Egeria. He chuckled, his white teeth showing. "Anyone the love of my life cares about, I care about."

Marcus stared at Bang, his high five still hanging.

"We'd better go before Mistress Lovelace gets here," said Bang, grabbing Egeria's hand. "Wouldn't want her to think you apprentices had hired in help."

Giggling a little, Bang and Egeria made for the attics' door, which suddenly burst open.

Kenzo skidded in. "She's coming up the stairs."

Dorrie flew with the other apprentices to return the mattresses to the beds.

There was no time to think about Marcus's feelings.

CHAPTER 8
DON'T EAT THE BAKLAVA!

I T WASN'T UNTIL MISTRESS Lovelace had finished running her white-gloved finger over the last bit of baseboard and declared the attics "clean enough" that Dorrie remembered with a start the kiss she'd seen through the window. The apprentices had collapsed in celebratory exhaustion upon the barren furniture. Dorrie glanced around for Marcus, but he wasn't in the den.

He wasn't in his bedroom either.

"Where's Bang been anyway?" Dorrie asked Ebba a few hours later, trying not to sound bitter. A rainstorm had moved in over the whole of Petrarch's Library, and they had settled themselves on the floor in front of the den fire with the intention of finalizing their practicum choices.

"Manchuria," gushed Izel from where she sat working on

her embroidery again. "Finishing up his first assignment staffing at one of the Lybrariad's branch libraries. He's going to be made a lybrarian any second now."

She then treated them to a detailed enumeration of Bang's accomplishments and stellar qualities and the many ways in which he and Egeria were perfect for each other, stopping only when Mathilde threatened to use the pulley to send her down for a visit with Roger.

Thinking she'd better have the basics covered and wanting to spend time with Hypatia, Dorrie finally settled on Principles of Lybrarianship. Ebba decided to take that as well. For her second practicum, Ebba chose:

Burros, Horses, Camels, and Yaks: How to Ride
Anything with Four Legs. Taught by Yeshi Khan,
riding master. Meets Tuesdays and Thursdays.

"I've been meaning to tell you," Ebba said, her eyes shining. "My parents are taking me out to fourteenth-century Mali to visit their old city next interim."

"So it's safe out there for your family now?" asked Dorrie, knowing that Ebba's parents had come into the library as refugees many years before.

"The Lybrariad thinks so," said Ebba. "We'll get to travel from the Timbuktu Spoke Library across the Sahel on camels."

Dorrie grinned at Ebba. Before last quarter, Ebba had been too afraid to go out into any of the wherens.

For her second practicum, Dorrie felt pulled in fifty directions. "I'm thinking about taking Staying Afloat on Rafts, Sailboats, and Logs."

"Not Swords, Daggers, and Coffee Can Tops: A General Survey of Sharp Edges and Their Uses?" said Ebba. "I've heard Lybrarian Khan is a wonderful teacher. Scary but wonderful."

"I've got Savi to teach me sword," said Dorrie, her hand itching to hold a rapier again. She looked at the Staying Afloat teacher's name. "What's Mistress Daraney like?"

"Well," Ebba said, considering. "She lives in the cove on a boat. She hates coming inside Petrarch's Library. Gets lost every time, which is funny because she can navigate beautifully on the sea. I think she once worked as some king's librarian in Siam."

"Had to pretend she was a man, of course," added Mathilde from where she sat curled in one of the fatter armchairs. She had already chosen her practicums and was flipping eagerly through one of the books Lybrarian Davis had assigned. "The king sent her on a voyage to pick up some new manuscripts, and on the way back, pirates attacked and kidnapped her. *They* didn't care that she was a woman, and she liked the freedom. She's even missing part of a leg."

"But that happened before the pirates," said Ebba. "A bookcase fell over on her during an earthquake."

Dorrie considered the irony of that for a pleasurable moment and then circled the Staying Afloat practicum.

Giving up on Marcus returning to the Apprentice Attics before dinner, Dorrie and Ebba hurried down to the circulation department to get their practicum supplies and new clothes for Dorrie.

"And don't forget, you can check out a practice rapier too," said Ebba, which made Dorrie break into a run.

When Dorrie and Ebba arrived, Mistress Lovelace was standing behind the long counter, her face impassive, listening to a sun-burned lybrarian apologize repeatedly as she handed over a pair of pantaloons with a spectacular tear in the seat.

"I wonder what *that* mission was all about?" whispered Ebba.

Besides the counter and a lot of flowered wallpaper, the only things in view were a few poufy armchairs with lacy bits on the arms, a curtained doorway behind the counter, and a row of wooden booths for trying on clothing. However, Dorrie knew that through the curtained doorway lay a maze of cavernous rooms that held all the supplies and disguises necessary for the Lybrariad's missions. Shelves held zealously organized bins of mustaches made from real hair in every style ever conceived, boxes of belt buckles, barrels of boots, and great buckets of coins from every time and place. Capes and caftans and coats and chitons hung from long racks that reached to the ceiling. Dorrie knew about the rooms because she'd once had to spend a good many hours among the barrels and boxes, ironing undergarments to work off a fine for an overdue item.

Ebba led Dorrie to one end of the counter, where a fat folder lay. "The practicum supply lists are in here."

After a bit of shuffling, they found the right ones. Hypatia's list was written in a neatly flowing hand on a piece of papyrus.

Principles of Lybrarianship
One copy of The Twelve Principles of the Lybrarian
One copy of The Foundation: Essential Dictums
One writing implement (please, no chalk)
Material on which to take notes (please, no pottery shards)

Dorrie and Ebba's eyes met briefly, shining with excitement. Dorrie picked up Mistress Daraney's list next. It was written in thick, blotchy ink on what looked like a weathered wooden shingle, which smelled faintly of dead fish.

- Compass
- Rigging knife with marlin spike
- Telescope
- Six feet of manila rope

- Thirty-seven feet of bandage
- None of those newfangled bathing suits. You swim in what you sail in or nothing at all.

When they staggered out of the circulation department a half hour later, Dorrie was pleased. Along with her practicum supplies, she had acquired a pair of leather boots that made her feel instantly invincible, a soft, striped sailor's shirt, a many-layered skirt in a shocking shade of orange that hung to just below her knees, and a frock coat worthy of the most foppish pirate. Best of all, she now wore at her side a practice rapier with an ornate hilt that she felt compared favorably to King Arthur's own Excalibur. One pocket jingled with her apprentice's allowance of Filthy Lucre, the currency used in Petrarch's Library for small purchases between its residents, and in her satchel was a battered pocket watch.

Later at dinner, distracted by the fact that Marcus hadn't shown, Dorrie nearly missed Mistress Wu's announcement that she'd be visiting the attics the following evening to take nominations for the first field trip destination. "And please," she begged, "don't propose any wherens in which the Black Plague is active. I'll only have to say no."

Immediately, the apprentices began to argue about where they should go.

"How are we ever going to all agree?" asked Dorrie as,

under Ebba's supervision, she filled out her apprenticeship request form, carefully writing her name on the line beside the word "Apprentice" and then "Hercule-Savinien de Cyrano de Bergerac, Keyhand" beside "Requested Lybrarian."

"Oh, it's impossible," Ebba said. "We always just end up picking out of a hat."

Since Saul and Amo seemed about to come to blows on the question of whether they'd have more luck spotting a vampire in sixteenth-century or thirteenth-century Transylvania, Dorrie thought that was probably for the best.

Dorrie blew carefully on the drying ink. "So Petrarch's Library has two archways that lead into Transylvania?"

"No, just one," said Ebba, picking apple cores off the other apprentices' plates and wrapping them in a handkerchief. "It leads out to thirteenth-century Transylvania. If you want to get to seventeenth-century Transylvania, you have to exit Petrarch's Library through the Paris, 1643 CE archway and then do some traveling."

Hearing the archway that led to Savi's home wheren mentioned, Dorrie felt another surge of impatience for his return. She watched Ebba shove the apple cores in her satchel. "What do you want with those?"

"For Roger. I've got to go fill his water trough." She clambered off the bench.

"What about dropping off our registrations?" Dorrie asked.

"Don't they have to be in Mistress Wu's mailbox by eight o'clock?"

Ebba slung her satchel across her shoulder. "We've got plenty of time. I'll meet you at the Celsus in a half hour." She hurried off, leaving Dorrie to wonder why she hadn't asked her to come along.

"Well, I guess we won't be allowed to go out to twenty-first-century Passaic," said Izel.

Dorrie snapped her head around. "Why not?"

"After you brought so much attention to the Passaic Public Library getting caught in that newspaper photograph?" She leaned toward Dorrie. "I shouldn't even say anything, but—"

"Oh, since when has that ever stopped you," said Mathilde without looking up from her food.

Izel glared at her. "I just wanted to warn Dorrie that Millie told me that Francesco is furious about it."

Dorrie's stomach dropped. She tried not to show her dread. "Well, thanks. Good to know." She turned to Fatima, eager to change the subject. "You haven't seen Marcus today, have you?"

"Not since the cleanup," said Fatima. "We were supposed to play a little music together before dinner."

Dorrie surveyed the Sharpened Quill once again, uneasy. "It's not like him to even miss a snack."

"Hope he didn't decide to eat at the Inky Pot instead," said

Amo in the cheerful way he seemed to say everything now that the inspection was over.

The argument about Transylvania abruptly ended.

"What's the Inky Pot?" asked Dorrie.

"A terrible place!" whispered Fatima.

"A coffeehouse," said Mathilde in a sepulchral tone.

Dorrie let out a breath, relieved. "Petrarch's Library has a coffeehouse?"

"You *don't* want to go there," said Fatima. "It's run by this guy named Fedya, and he *hates* apprentices. A couple years ago, he *poisoned* some kid."

Dorrie's eyes widened.

"And the worst part?" said Mathilde. "He pretends to be friendly."

Fatima nodded. "It's true! Fedya tries to get me to eat something every time I deliver *Gouty Ben's Weekly Digest* there. 'Come on now, eat a little baklava,'" she said in a wheedling voice that made the other apprentices laugh. "'How are you going to grow strong enough to drive a chariot if you don't put some flesh on your bones. What, you don't like a little baklava? What is it about you apprentices not liking my baklava!'"

The other apprentices snickered.

"I don't trust myself to even walk near the Inky Pot," said Mathilde. "It smells too good. It's like Fedya is casting a spell and trying to pull in unsuspecting apprentices."

A friend of Amo's leaned down the table from where he sat nearly at the other end. "Hey, did you say you were looking for Marcus?"

Dorrie nodded, hopeful.

"I saw him walking past Master Casanova's office before dinner."

"Thanks," said Dorrie, relaxing. Marcus really liked Master Casanova. It made sense that he'd go to talk to him if he was feeling upset.

"Uh...Dorrie," said Fatima slowly "The Inky Pot is right near Master Casanova's office."

Fifteen minutes later, Dorrie skidded to a stop beneath a small swinging sign with a picture of a steaming copper kettle on it. Below it, black letters spelled out "The Inky Pot." She wrenched open the door. The heady delightful aroma of coffee wafted past her.

Where the Sharpened Quill was low and snug, the walls of the Inky Pot soared to a lofty height. Instead of worn, warm wood, the Inky Pot glowed with brass and silk. Along one wall, floaty red-and-orange drapes made little private tents around gatherings of carpeted benches and low wooden tables. More of the benches ran along the opposite wall, in front of which stood more tables. Along a third wall ran racks hung with newspapers, mud tablets, scrolls, and pieces of parchment.

Dorrie glanced wildly among the few lybrarians at the little tables but couldn't spot Marcus. She drew back when she noticed a man with a stiff upbrush of graying hair behind a marble counter in the center of the room. He was filling a plate from tiered platters piled high with cakes and pastries. Two glistening copper canisters with bronze taps steamed gently on either side of him. Heart hammering, Dorrie wondered if the man was Fedya. She had turned to leave when she heard Marcus's voice.

"—Fedya! You shouldn't have."

Dorrie whirled back in time to see Marcus's hand sticking out from inside the endmost curtained tent and Fedya standing nearby, the plate he'd been filling extended. The pastries dripped tantalizingly with something sweet and sticky looking. Dorrie was horrified to feel her mouth watering.

Marcus took the plate, and Fedya moved on. Dorrie wasted no time. Sprinting across the room, she swatted at the pastry Marcus had lifted to his mouth, sending it sailing across the table and onto the floor.

He stared at her, outraged. "What is wrong with you?" He reached for another.

"You can't!" said Dorrie, trying to bat that one away as well.

"Cut it out!" he hissed, fending her off. "You are a guest in a civilized establishment."

"You don't understand!" Dorrie hissed back urgently.

"What? That Fedya's baklava is delicious?" Marcus took an enormous bite.

"No!" whispered Dorrie. "That Fedya is trying to poison you!"

At Dorrie's words, Marcus's face went slack. The rest of the pastry dropped from his limp hand onto the plate. His eyes rolled back in his head, and his back arched.

"Marcus," cried Dorrie, wondering if she should punch him in the stomach.

Marcus's fit stopped as abruptly as it began. He shook his hair out of his eyes, reached for the pastry again, and stuffed the rest of it in his mouth. "You kids. With your crazy stories. I've been eating these all day. Fedya thought they might help my ennui."

"Your what?"

Marcus stared out at the darkening sea through a nearby window. "My ennui, my feeble zestlessness."

Dorrie snorted. "What are you talking about?"

Marcus took another bite of the baklava, showering the newspapers spread all over the table in flakes of pastry. "Fedya's given me some books. I'm exploring a life of nonattachment."

"You look pretty attached to that baklava."

"Please. Me and my shredded heart have turned our backs on the world."

"I," said a hulking lybrarian in a feathery headdress who was sitting nearby, without looking up from his mud tablet. "*I* and my shredded heart."

Marcus shot the lybrarian a dirty look and then looked back

106

out the window. "*Marcus* and his shredded heart are going to spend all our time here from now on. Drink coffee, breathe, maybe write a short poem now and then, stare at things."

He looked farther out to sea than Dorrie had thought possible.

"What *is* a wave?" Marcus said hoarsely.

"I hope that's not your first poem."

He glared at her. "You should get a job writing sympathy cards. Really. You have a knack."

"Look, I'm sorry about Egeria having a boyfriend. But she was way too old for you anyway. She's sixteen!"

"I'm almost fifteen!"

"Marcus, your birthday is in eight months."

"Bang!" Marcus said in disgust, crossing his arms and sinking back into the cushions. "With his hair and his shoulders and his face!"

"He can't really help having a face," said Dorrie.

"And did you notice he chuckles? Who *chuckles*? And did you see the way he put his arm around her?"

"Well, she is his girlfriend."

"Another great card in the making. How do you do it?" Marcus lifted another piece of baklava to his mouth.

Halfway there, it jerked sideways out of his hand and plopped onto the table.

Ebba slid onto the bench opposite them, breathing hard, one hand clutching her slingshot. "Don't eat the—"

"Can a man not eat his ninth piece of baklava in peace?" bellowed Marcus, reaching for it again.

Ebba dove to intercept him.

"Cakes? Coffee for the newcomers?" said Fedya at Dorrie's elbow, smiling pleasantly.

"No!" said Dorrie and Ebba far too loudly, their eyes wide and Ebba's hands splayed over the slingshotted piece of baklava.

Fedya raised his eyebrows slightly.

"No…no…thank you," gulped Dorrie.

Fedya bowed slightly and strode away whistling, doing a good job—Dorrie thought—of hiding his dark intentions.

She turned back to Marcus. "You can't just sit here for the rest of your life."

"Even if it will be really short," said Ebba.

"I'm not 'just sitting here,'" said Marcus. He refocused his gaze. "I'm gazing out the window despondently."

"That doesn't even sound fun," said Ebba.

"Plus, we all have to turn in our practicum registrations by eight o'clock," said Dorrie. "If we don't leave soon, we'll be stuck taking library building maintenance!"

Marcus suddenly lunged for one of the newspapers on the table and held it up in front of his face. It was a copy of *Gouty Ben's Weekly Digest*.

Turning her head, Dorrie saw that Bang, Egeria, and a

couple other young lybrarians were seating themselves at another table.

Marcus's finger poked through the newspaper page—and then Marcus's eyeball appeared. "Is nowhere safe from him!"

"Um…Marcus," said Ebba.

"Really?" came Marcus's voice. "This is the time to shout my name?"

Dorrie saw that Ebba was staring at an illustration just below Marcus's darting eyeball.

"Sorry," Ebba said, "but I think you should look at this side of the newspaper."

Marcus snorted. "Haven't I seen enough already?"

Dorrie peered at the illustration. It showed a thin, mournful young man in a chiton holding a drum.

She read the headline below it out loud. "Philosopher Cries Foul on Newfangled Music. Lawsuit Filed Against Timotheus."

"Disgusting!" said Marcus. "Bang totally meant to do that with his hair."

"Did you hear me?" said Dorrie. "That drummer you taught how to play seventies rock music is in trouble."

"I can hear him chuckling from here!" choked out Marcus.

"Would you pay attention," said Dorrie. "Charges of theft, assault, and something called hubris have been lodged against musician Timotheus of Miletus, currently a resident of the outskirts of Athens."

"Yeah, yeah, yeah. So he has to spend a night or two in ancient jail," said Marcus. "Can't you see I'm coping with bigger problems here?"

Dorrie felt a tick of guilt. She, Marcus, and Ebba had been at the party in ancient Athens where Marcus had met Timotheus. They'd been there looking for the torn-out *History of Histories* page that had gone missing there. "Don't you feel responsible?"

"No, I feel like I need to get out of here," said Marcus standing, the newspaper still in front of his face. "Cover me."

They had just made it to the door, Marcus having smashed into only two chairs along the way, when it was thrown open.

A woman entered, dressed in black-and-yellow running shorts and a black, sleeveless shirt with "Messenger" embroidered across the front in yellow gothic letters. She waited until she had the full attention of the room. "One of our mission lybrarians has found Mr. Gormly. Dead."

Dorrie's heart seemed to contract. Though she'd been furious with Mr. Gormly for betraying her and the Lybrariad, she'd never wanted him dead.

"Where was he found?" said Egeria.

"In a culvert that dumps into the Passaic River," replied the messenger. "One of his pants pockets was slashed open and the other not, which Hypatia is certain means—"

"The Foundation found Petrarch's Star in the first pocket

they tried," the lybrarian who'd corrected Marcus's grammar finished grimly.

The messenger nodded. "Hypatia has called an emergency meeting of the staff."

Dorrie felt ill as an image rose before her of Mr. Gormly dying alone and scared.

As the lybrarians scattered, Dorrie, Marcus, and Ebba hurried to the Celsus, stuffed their practicum requests into the little bit of room left in Mistress Wu's mailbox, and then raced for the attics.

Though the fire burned as cheerily as ever in the brick fireplace, clearly the news had preceded them. Many of the apprentices hunkered around the flames looked frightened. Even Millie's usual glower had a nervous edge to it.

"I was sure the Lybrariad would find it first," Saul said from where he sat slumped in one of the armchairs.

"I heard Lybrarian Della Porta talking to another lybrarian in front of the mailboxes," said Izel. "Before they all went into their meeting. He said if the Foundation has already rebuilt Whim's Gift, it could start causing reversals any day now."

All the apprentices stared at her.

"What's a reversal?" asked Dorrie, slowly lowering herself onto a sofa.

"It's when a mission the Lybrariad has accomplished gets undone," Mathilde said.

"How does that happen?" asked Marcus.

"Well, the Lybrariad is active in over four hundred centuries. Even small changes in the past can have unintended consequences for the future," said Mathilde. "Every once in a while, something a lybrarian does in an early century changes some small detail that affects a mission in a more future time, and suddenly, the history books say the mission didn't happen."

"Reversals are really rare," said Saul.

"Accidental ones have been rare," said Izel. "But Lybrarian Della Porta's talking about the Foundation causing them on purpose. They could cause hundreds of them. He said if the Foundation travels to the right time, it could even undo a crux mission."

There was a murmuring among the apprentices.

"What's a crux mission?" asked Dorrie.

"A mission that changed history in a huge way," said Saul.

Izel hugged herself as if cold. "All the Foundation would have to do is go back in time and prevent one of the crux missions that seriously diminished its power and it would be back in business."

"But that's, that's…cheating!" said Dorrie.

"Well, wasn't the Lybrariad sort of cheating first?" said Marcus.

Dorrie's thoughts whirled. "But not to gain power for themselves or hurt anyone!"

"So now can the Foundation punch a hole in Petrarch's Library and turn us all into zombies?" asked Kenzo, sounding equal parts afraid and excited at the prospect.

"They don't turn people into zombies, nitwit," said Millie.

"Well, not the kind with flaking faces anyway," said Mathilde. "Though come to think of it...when the Foundation was in power in our wherens, they did do their best to make anyone who wasn't in their special circle sort of brainless. People had no written history, and memory is only so long, so it was easy for the Foundation to insist that having the Foundation in charge was best for everyone and that everyone would be destroyed by the Four Wolves if the Foundation wasn't there to protect them."

"Who were the Four Wolves?" asked Marcus.

"Hunger, Pestilence, War, and Whim." Mathilde ticked the names off on her fingers.

"Whim?" repeated Dorrie.

"Giant invisible being the Foundation claimed made the universe," said Mathilde. "Fond of smiting people. Most people believed it lurked around waiting for a chance to catch them breaking the Foundation's rules or forgetting to leave out the right amount of blood or gold for a midnight snack."

"Whim," Dorrie repeated, her thoughts winging back to when the lybrarians had visited her in Passaic. "As in Whim's Gift."

"Exactly," said Mathilde.

"How do you know so much about that Foundation stuff anyway?" Fatima asked Mathilde.

Mathilde waved her hand vaguely. "I might have taken the Archivist's History of the Foundation practicum once."

"*You* took a practicum with the Archivist?" said Dorrie. "Last quarter, you told me he was crazy."

"He is." Mathilde blushed ever so slightly. "I circled the wrong practicum on my registration form."

Dorrie pressed closer to Ebba. "What are the lybrarians going to do now?"

"Missions. Lots of them," Izel said importantly. "Every available lybrarian is being pressed into service. Lybrarian Della Porta said—"

"Does Lybrarian Della Porta ever stop talking?" broke in Marcus.

Most of the other apprentices laughed, but Izel merely flicked a long, dark strand of her hair over her shoulder, a knowing little smile on her face.

"Maybe Mr. Biggs will tell them something useful at the Lybrarians' Council tomorrow," said Saul.

Dorrie's heart suspended operations for a moment. She'd almost forgotten about the Council. And Mr. Biggs. And the fact that she'd have to see him again. Her gaze drifted to her thumbnail. She stared, sure now. The blackness was definitely retreating.

That night, Dorrie rode the ragged edge of sleep for hours, unable to fall in. Again and again, the image of Mr. Biggs's little vial at the bottom of her backpack made her heartbeat quicken. She had no doubt that Savi was going to be given an important mission, like hunting out an entrance to the Stronghold. What if he needed her power to succeed? What if they needed to get somewhere that only she could take him? Listening for a moment to Ebba's even breathing, she got out of her bed and crouched beside it to pull out her backpack.

After digging out the vial, she padded out to the den. By the light of the fire, she unscrewed the vial's little cap and peered inside. A few drops of liquid still clung to its walls. For a moment, she had the urge to upend the vial and drink them down.

Quickly, she replaced the cap and looked around. Izel's embroidery basket still sat by the fire. Dorrie helped herself to a length of heavy red embroidery thread. She looped the floss through the chain that connected the vial to its cap and knotted the ends into a loop large enough to slip over her head. She hesitated. The little metal vial dangled before her, dull even in the firelight. Quickly, she dropped the loop of floss over her head and tucked the vial into the neck of her pajamas.

She glanced out the window. In the far distance, she could just make out the dark hump of Crackskull Island.

CHAPTER 9

LYBRARIANS' COUNCIL

T HE NEXT DAY, FIFTEEN minutes before the Lybrarians'
Council was set to begin, the Celsus's main meeting room
was already jam-packed. Seated in the back of the room on
narrow wooden benches with the rest of the apprentices, Dorrie
thought that for lybrarians, the room's occupants were doing a
pretty good job of making a lot of noise.

She glanced at Marcus. He had his arms crossed and was
staring moodily at the spot where Egeria and Bang sat together
several rows ahead. Though Dorrie had hoped Savi would return
to Petrarch's Library for the Council, he hadn't yet appeared.

Up in the front of the room near the towering statue of
Athena, Hypatia sat behind a long table, facing the crowd with
Mistress Wu at one elbow and Francesco at the other. Another
dozen people sat with them.

Dorrie nudged Ebba. "Who are those other people up front?"

"Petrarch's Library's Board of Directors," said Ebba, turning her slingshot over in her hands.

"What'd you bring that for?"

"In case Mr. Biggs tries anything."

"Mistress Wu better not see you aim that anywhere," warned Mathilde.

Hypatia stood, her blue silk chiton rustling, and the din of conversation subsided. "Welcome, all."

Dorrie listened avidly as Hypatia told the lybrarians who had journeyed from distant branch libraries about the Foundation's rise in the future wherens to which Petrarch's Library was not yet connected and the Foundation's plan to colonize the past again.

"According to keyhand Kash," said Hypatia, describing the Foundation's epicenter, "the Stronghold is no library. It's made of…darker places."

The apprentices eyed one another.

Hypatia went on. "Now that the Foundation has Petrarch's Star, it's imperative that we learn what exactly Whim's Gift is and prevent the Foundation from remaking it."

There was a wave of subdued murmuring.

"Though we don't yet know why, Kash reported that Whim's Gift cannot be remade in the Stronghold—or in any of the future wherens to which it alone connects. The Foundation must remake Whim's Gift in the older wherens. In that fact lies our opportunity to stop the Foundation from succeeding.

"Our research lybrarians are doing everything they can to find out exactly what Whim's Gift is and where the Foundation might be working on it. We know the Stronghold now opens into at least four centuries connected to Petrarch's Library: fourth-century BCE, possibly in Athens; fifteenth-century BCE Egypt; twentieth-century Washington, DC; and the twenty-first century, possibly Passaic, New Jersey.

"We are running intelligence missions out in these centuries and in other likely wherens."

Dorrie felt a surge of excitement, wondering where Savi might be asked to go, and her along with him.

"Though Petrarch's Star is out of our hands for now," said Hypatia, "we must still learn all we can about it as well." She picked Petrarch's journal off the table. "We have two potential sources of information in our hands right now. The first is Petrarch's journal." She pulled a piece of paper out from between its pages, covered over with writing. "The second is the inscription on Petrarch's Star, copied down here. Both bear words written with the same set of symbols. Unfortunately, neither will auto-translate."

Dorrie and Ebba exchanged glances.

"They may be written either in code or in a language." She gestured to the big-boned lybrarian with the sharp, black point of a beard that Dorrie had seen eating with Hypatia in the Sharpened Quill. "We have asked Branch Lybrarian Della Porta, who has extensive knowledge of code making and breaking, to spend this quarter with us, and he has kindly agreed." She pivoted and gestured to the other side of the room. "We've also—"

"I am honored to do what I can in service to Petrarch's Library," interrupted Lybrarian Della Porta.

Hypatia, her brows slightly raised, turned back to Della Porta.

He had risen. "I have every confidence that we are dealing with a code and that it will yield its secrets in a matter of weeks. I look forward to sharing what I find."

As he sat again, Dorrie heard the faint complaint of a hinge as a nearby door opened. A heavily armed lybrarian slipped inside and signaled to Hypatia.

Hypatia nodded, then turned to where the Archivist sat, looking haunted. "Our own Archivist will continue in his efforts to determine if the symbols express a language that has been lost to the world, as he has long theorized."

The Archivist slowly rose—gaunt and uncertain, his robes in some disarray—to nod briefly.

"No wonder the Archivist has been looking so miserable," murmured Ebba. "If Della Porta succeeds, it'll prove that the Archivist has been wrong all these years."

"Well, maybe that's for the best," said Saul. "I mean, the Archivist's reputation has really suffered for clinging to that idea."

Another movement at the door caught Dorrie's eye.

Mr. Biggs had entered, surrounded by three armed lybrarians. Dorrie felt the blood rush from her face. Her hands went cold. Incredibly, Mr. Biggs was wearing the same dark suit and red bow tie she'd last seen him in, though they had lost a good deal of its crispness. He took in a deep, slow breath through his nose and then slowly turned his head until his dead-ice eyes found Dorrie's.

Memories of the horrible day when he'd attacked her and Marcus and Great-Aunt Alice and Elder closed in around her, their colors and sounds drowning out everything else. Dorrie began to tremble but couldn't make herself turn away. The little vial on the string around her neck suddenly seemed large and cold and obvious against her chest.

Like a shadowy figure intent on hurrying by a set of windows unseen, Dorrie thought she saw hunger flit through Mr. Biggs eyes. She leaned back out of view, her pulse racing.

"I'm glad Darling's not here to see him," Ebba whispered fiercely as the lybrarians led Mr. Biggs down to the front of the room. "Think how much it would upset her."

Marcus shot Dorrie a dubious glance, which she could just barely return. The room quieted again as the lybrarians escorted Mr. Biggs to a seat and arranged themselves behind him.

Hypatia spoke. "Mr. Aldous Biggs, you have thus far declined to give answers to the questions we have put to you about the Foundation's intentions."

Mr. Biggs crossed his legs. "I have not spoken because I do not know or trust you. You brought me here against my will."

"Yes. After you behaved with brutality toward a keyhand of the Lybrariad, an elderly woman, and two young apprentices."

Dorrie felt herself color.

"Do you not defend your people?" Mr. Biggs asked coldly, casting a disparaging eye on the crowd of lybrarians before him. "I only attempted to retrieve property valuable to those who depend upon the Foundation."

"I presume you mean Petrarch's Star."

"The Stone Star," said Mr. Biggs.

Hypatia nodded slightly. "The keyhand you imprisoned in the Stronghold reports that the intentions of the Foundation of the future, like those of the Foundation of the past, run counter to those of the Lybrariad. According to Kash, the Foundation wishes to once again hold humans in bondage and criminalize reading and writing among all but a chosen few."

Mr. Biggs's eyes locked onto Hypatia's. "You say we wish to hold humans in bondage. I say we wish to rebuild for them the safe fold you destroyed. We have history books in the future. You flatter yourselves with the thought the Lybrariad has made the world a sweeter place. From our perspective, you are destructive meddlers."

Protests rose from the crowd.

Hypatia held up her hand for silence.

"The future under the guidance of the Foundation is serene," said Mr. Biggs. "Her people live in peace and security. They have what they need." He leaned back and laced his fingers together. "Your wherens are a mess."

There was another chorus of protests—louder this time.

Hypatia again asked for quiet. "We have reason to believe that the Foundation intends to undo the work of the Lybrariad."

A mirthless smile appeared on Mr. Biggs's lips. "Your belief is entirely correct."

Dorrie gasped. A number of other lybrarians leaped to their feet and had to be pulled back into their seats by their neighbors. Francesco's chair fell with a crash to the ground behind him as one hand went to the pommel of his sword. Only Hypatia remained still.

It took Mistress Wu ringing a bell rather wildly for people to settle down again.

Mr. Biggs recrossed his legs. "We might start by—oh, I don't know—reversing your intervention in the case of one Algernon Sidney."

The name caused another stir.

"Who's that?" said Dorrie, looking urgently up the row of apprentices.

"This guy from 1600s London," hissed Amo.

"We studied the mission to rescue him in one of Casanova's stealth and deception practicums last year," said Saul. "He wrote this book called *Discourses Concerning Government.* Someone in charge didn't like his book and had him arrested, and then a judge sentenced him to a beheading."

Dorrie recoiled at the image. "Why?"

"The judge said, 'To write is to act.'"

"What's that supposed to mean?" said Marcus.

Amo gave Marcus a suffering look. "That criticizing the government with words was the same as attacking it with weapons."

"They're nothing at all alike!" protested Dorrie.

"The rescue was spectacular," Saul said. "It involved a basket of fresh baked crumpets and a catapult."

Dorrie pulled on Mathilde's sleeve. "How could Mr. Biggs know about the Lybrariad's missions?"

"No idea," said Mathilde as Mistress Wu swung the bell and the room quieted.

"Please go on," said Hypatia.

Mr. Biggs smiled at Hypatia in a way that made Dorrie think of old fish. "Return me now, and perhaps I can convince the Foundation that it's not entirely necessary for Mr. Sidney to go to the chopping block. Perhaps the Foundation, in its gratitude for my return, would even allow you to choose a few other favorite missions to keep intact." His smile disappeared. "Fail to return me, and the Foundation will surely reverse Mr. Sidney's mission and every other one of which we're aware."

124

"And just how many are you aware of?" Francesco asked, his one visible eye black with restrained fury.

Mr. Biggs's answer was to lazily wave away a fly.

Francesco surged toward Mr. Biggs, and Dorrie was sure he would have kept going if Hypatia hadn't put a restraining hand on his arm.

"I will make a different proposal," said Hypatia.

One of Mr. Biggs's eyebrows rose ever so slightly.

Hypatia fixed him with a steady gaze. "It may interest you to know that the Foundation possesses Petrarch's Star again."

Mr. Biggs's eyes filled with veiled triumph. "I'm not at all surprised."

Hypatia nodded slightly. "Tell us where Whim's Gift is being remade and what we need to do to acquire it. With Petrarch's Star in the possession of the Foundation and Whim's Gift in the Lybrariad's, neither will have the advantage, and you can go free."

Cold rage replaced the triumph in Mr. Biggs's eyes. His lips pursed so tightly that the pale skin around them turned even whiter. "Never."

The word hung in the air.

"Thank you, Mr. Biggs," Hypatia said, turning away from him. "You'll be taken back to Crackskull Island for now." She gestured to Mr. Biggs's guards.

Before they could move, Lybrarian Della Porta leaped from

his chair. "With all due respect, Hypatia, this brute just told us the Foundation plans to reverse some multitude of our missions. Is the Lybrariad just going to let him go back to sunbathing when it's likely he possesses all the information we need to stop the Foundation in its tracks?"

There was a whirring sort of silence.

Lybrarian Della Porta turned to face the room at large. "I think circumstances require that we hear more from Mr. Biggs."

Flocks of whispers traveled through the packed room, circling and spreading, separating and reforming. Dorrie looked from Hypatia to Lybrarian Della Porta.

"Just what are you suggesting?" asked Hypatia.

Lybrarian Della Porta hesitated, moving his lower jaw from side to side. "That we employ force."

A hundred gasps flew up from the crowd, but Dorrie thought she heard a few "Hear, hears" mixed in as well.

"Torture, he means!" the Archivist cried shrilly, standing.

Dorrie stared at him and then back to Lybrarian Della Porta, shocked, as the apprentices around her murmured.

Della Porta pulled himself up to his full impressive height. "Use the worst word for it you can choose. I won't flinch. I don't suggest it lightly, but in this case, I believe the end justifies such a means."

"If we measure the means by the worth of the end, then we might as well be the Foundation," said Hypatia.

"Not true," Della Porta said. "Were we ever like the Foundation because we both used parchment? Ink? Do we have so little faith in our discipline as lybrarians that we can't trust ourselves with the careful application of our strength? We would be lybrarians about the process through and through."

"That is a logical impossibility," said Hypatia. "The principles we pledge ourselves to specifically forbid lybrarians to do harm except in the most extreme, clear, and immediate moments of danger to others or to ourselves."

"Principles are fine things," said Lybrarian Della Porta. "But desperate times call for desperate measures. How many lives might this man's silence cost? Is there no place for consideration of the greater good?"

The room shook again with talk. Mistress Wu looked entirely discomfited and was patting her face with her handkerchief with such energy that Dorrie feared she might strain her arm. Francesco looked at war with himself.

Hypatia held up her hand again. "The Board of Directors will confer." The lybrarians at the table went into a sort of huddle.

The apprentices did the same.

"Maybe Della Porta's right," said Izel. "What Mr. Biggs knows could save a lot of people! Definitely that Algernon guy."

"Could," said Sven.

Dorrie felt unsettled. She trusted Hypatia, but Mr. Biggs

was an awful man who'd done awful things. What did I matter if they hurt him a little if that saved Algernon Sidney's life.

Hypatia stood. Her gaze swept the room. "It is tempting to use any and all effective means when we only want a just end and innocent lives are on the line." She paced the length of the table. "If we agree to inflict pain on Mr. Biggs, it's true that we may be rewarded with information that could help us stop the Foundation from carrying out the reversals Mr. Biggs has threatened. The information could perhaps save many lives." She glanced at the statue of Athena. "But then again, we many learn nothing and cease being lybrarians in the process. Dark means have a dangerous way of becoming dark ends." She nodded again to Mr. Biggs's guards. "For now, the Lybrariad will stick to its principles and pursue other strategies."

"What luck for me that I'm dealing with shrinking violets," said Mr. Biggs as his guards escorted him back up the aisle. "What luck for me that I'm dealing with shrinking violets. You'd do well to start composing a speech begging for the Foundation's mercy now. My people will not be pleased at my imprisonment, and they fear no means."

Dorrie felt rage course through her as well as a keen desire to knock Mr. Biggs's legs out from under him. He stopped short at the door and flicked his eyes from the Archivist to Lybrarian Della Porta and back again. "As for the writing on the Stone Star..." He gave a slow lizard-like blink. "Code or language? An interesting puzzle, indeed."

"He knows," said Izel, her eyes avid. "He knows how to make sense of the writing!"

A look of fury crossed Lybrarian Della Porta's face. The Archivist went visibly gray. To the sound of a great, angry buzzing among the lybrarians, Mr. Biggs and his guards disappeared.

"Please!" called Mistress Wu, ringing her bell with desperate zeal. "Come to order, please." She cleared her throat. "We have a last piece of business. Mission lybrarian Layla Al-Zarqua has sustained injuries that will prevent her from completing her reconnaissance mission in Constantinople, 1397 CE. It's an important mission, and we need a replacement. The mission will be long and dreadfully arduous, with much time spent in the field. Do I have any volunteers?"

A hand shot up in the crowd. "I have experience in the 1397 CE wheren well."

It was Bang. Beside him, Egeria was gazing up at him admiringly. Dorrie glanced at Marcus, whose eyeballs seemed to be swirling around in their sockets.

"A bit of a newly minted lybrarian to be taking on such a mission," said Francesco appraisingly.

Mistress Wu looked to Hypatia.

"He's going to chuckle amiably any second now," muttered Marcus wretchedly. "I know it."

With a glance at Francesco, Hypatia gave her assent, and the room erupted in applause. Bang grinned and did indeed chuckle amiably as a lybrarian in a sari clapped him on the shoulder.

"That is all the business for today's Council but for one thing," said Mistress Wu. "I need to see the apprentices up here, please."

The apprentices eyed one another curiously and made their way through the departing lybrarians. Bang taking on the mission had made Dorrie wonder again what exciting thing she and Savi would be asked to do.

Reaching Mistress Wu, Dorrie saw that she'd pulled out a fresh handkerchief and had begun to pat the back of her neck with it.

"As you heard," Mistress Wu said, "the Lybrariad is under terrific pressure. There are more missions to run than lybrarians available to take them on!" Forgetting herself, she patted her underarms. "I'm very sorry to have to break the news to some of you that not all your apprenticeship requests can be honored this quarter."

Cries of "What?" and "No!" and "I don't believe it!" rose up around Dorrie.

"It's been necessary to assign some of you to alternative staff lybrarians, who, having extra work themselves, could really use your help."

Blood pounded in Dorrie's head with punishing force.

Clearing her throat a bit desperately, Mistress Wu began to read off the names of the apprentices and the lybrarians they were to serve. Dorrie heard Millie assigned to Master Callamachus and Marcus to Master Casanova, as they'd requested. Ebba gave a great sigh of relief when she was assigned to Mistress Hamsa again. But then things started going wrong. Mathilde make a choking sort of noise when her name was paired not with Lybrarian Davis as she had requested but with Lybrarian Della Porta. Izel and Sven were assigned to him as well.

"He felt he needed a great deal of help," Mistress Wu said, responding to the apprentices' confusion and looking not entirely gracious. "And who's left. Yes." She looked up and smiled weakly. "Our Dorrie. She will serve Master Ishaq."

For a moment, everything seemed hazy around Dorrie except for the clear, sharp, terrible shape of her disappointment. Savi had promised. She had fought at his side and earned the chance to be his real apprentice. She didn't trust herself to speak, didn't trust her disappointment not to swallow her whole.

Mistress Wu looked pityingly at the apprentices who had been switched. "It must be horrible to have your hopes for the quarter dashed like that. Simply horrible!" She pulled out more handkerchiefs. "If anyone needs to cry, I won't think any the less of you."

Dorrie had been furiously building a wall against just that

131

urge, but Mistress Wu could talk her into any emotion, and horribly, tears began to form. She fought them back by glaring at one of Athena's knees. No way was she going to give Millie the satisfaction of seeing her cry.

"Oh, I'm feeling dashed to bits all right," said Mathilde, "but I don't want to cry about it. I want to throw something very heavy through a window."

"I quite understand," said Mistress Wu.

Mathilde glowered. "Hopefully, the feeling will go away before I find an anvil sitting around."

"That's the spirit," said Mistress Wu, beaming brightly and giving Mathilde a bracing squeeze on the shoulder before bustling off.

"Who's Master Ishaq?" Dorrie forced herself to ask.

"Oh, Dorrie," Ebba said, her hands over her mouth.

"What?" demanded Dorrie.

Slowly, Ebba turned and pointed across the room to a table where the shaken-looking Archivist stood gathering up his papers.

Chapter 10
THE ARCHIVIST'S APPRENTICE

A T BREAKFAST THE NEXT morning, Dorrie battled the lowest of spirits. The tables and corridors were alive with talk about Mr. Biggs's threats and theories about how the Foundation could have gained knowledge of the Lybrariad's missions. Dorrie felt ashamed that even with things gone so wrong for the Lybrariad, she couldn't shake her deep disappointment about her reassignment to the Archivist. Eating her eggs and sausage, she tried not to feel left out of the excited chatter of those heading off to the apprenticeships they wanted.

At last, following Mathilde's instructions, Dorrie made her way to the Archivist's office with dragging feet, sure it would be a horrible dank place filled with molding orange peels and spiders and dripping pipes. Her practice sword, which she hadn't at all got used to wearing, caught on innumerable table legs and tapestries along the way. She felt an angry resentment toward Savi growing beneath her disappointment. Dorrie scowled. Why hadn't he told her about the change in plans himself?

Arriving at the Archivist's office, Dorrie sighed deeply and knocked.

The door was opened promptly.

"Come in, come in," said the Archivist, who looked as though he'd made some attempt to tame his hair. He ushered Dorrie in awkwardly. She avoided his eyes. The room was bright with white plaster walls and one unadorned window. A long bench draped in carpets ran along one wall. A low, extravagantly carved table stood in front of it. A long plain table with a few neat piles of books and papers upon it was pushed up against another wall. The only other furniture was a great bank of floor-to-ceiling wooden cupboards. Clean and orderly, the room smelled pleasantly of the spices Dorrie's mother liked to put in her coffee.

The Archivist went to the low table and lifted a steaming teapot in a proffering manner. "Tea?"

Dorrie shook her head, feeling stubborn, despite the pleasant surprise of the absence of dripping pipes. "No, thank you."

He hesitated for a moment and then gestured to the bench. "Please. Sit." He poured hot amber liquid into one of the two small cups on the table.

While the Archivist stirred sugar into his tea, Dorrie noticed three tidy rows of symbols had been painted above the work table. They did not waver beneath her gaze, and Dorrie recognized them from the pages of Petrarch's journal.

The Archivist set her to work organizing a tall stack of mission reports into seven different piles based on the continent in which the mission had been run. The reports were so filled with tantalizing details that Dorrie had to keep forcibly reminding herself to stop reading them and focus on the task.

Halfway through the morning, the Archivist paused in his own work at the other end of the table and offered Dorrie tea again—this time with a little plate of gingersnaps. She again refused it—on principle and out of pique—though her stomach was growling. He set the plate down softly with an apologetic nod, and Dorrie felt a little ashamed.

When he saw her to the door at lunchtime, he paused before closing it behind her. "I know working with me wasn't your choice, but I shall try to make it worthwhile."

Dorrie felt her face going red. She forced herself to meet his gaze. "It's...I...if..."

He smiled with sad humor. "Would you believe that once upon a time, young people *chose* to apprentice with me?"

"No, I actually can't," Mathilde said a little while later when Dorrie told her about the conversation over lunch. "And I can't believe anyone would voluntarily apprentice with Lybrarian Della Porta either."

"I think he's brilliant," Izel said, buttering a piece of crusty bread.

"He has three apprentices, and all morning, he complained about how he really needs five," Mathilde said, stabbing a meatball.

"Well, his work is important." Izel lowered her voice to a stage whisper. "Lybrarian Della Porta says he's going to crack the code before the quarter is half done."

Millie clambered off the bench, taking a piece of bread and cheese with her and slinging her satchel onto her shoulder.

"You just sat down," complained Izel.

Millie slung her satchel onto her shoulder, her bangs in her eyes. "I said I'd give Master Callamachus extra help before practicums."

Dorrie began to carefully move a chunk of carrot around in her stew. "Great," she muttered, intending only Ebba to hear. "Everyone else is doing work that will really help the Lybrariad, and I get to be the idiot's apprentice."

"Hard to believe the Archivist is a keyhand, isn't it?" said Mathilde.

"He is?" said Dorrie, astonished.

Mathilde nodded. "Tyre, 327 BCE. The Lybrariad hasn't asked him to take on a mission in ages. The only reason his skipkeys don't have cobwebs on them is that he still travels out to the wherens to look for stuff 'written' in Petrarch's language."

"What's a skipkey?" asked Marcus dolefully. Though he'd resumed eating meals in the Sharpened Quill, he still couldn't seem to string together two words without an enormous sigh in the middle.

"The lybrarians use them to get around out in the wherens," explained Ebba. "They're made of a little bit of two libraries. Every keyhand has a whole set of them. They can travel from their Spoke Libraries to any of the branch libraries in their centuries."

"What, like instantly?" said Dorrie.

"I think it's faster than that actually," said Sven.

"If you're lucky, Dorrie," Izel said, gathering up her things, her eyes sparkling with malice, "maybe the Archivist will take you on one of his expeditions to look for proof of his language theory."

"Yeah. Maybe," Dorrie said, not wanting to give Izel the satisfaction of seeing her look appalled at the prospect.

"Which reminds me," said Mathilde. "The field trip pick is tonight"—she raised her voice to reach Amo—"and I'm just saying it once. If anyone even thinks about choosing another wheren in which I have to wear wooden shoes, I will take my revenge. With a wooden shoe."

Dorrie was happy to set off with Ebba for the courtyard of the Dharmaganga Library, where Hypatia had decided to hold her Principles of Lybrarianship practicum.

As they passed the open door of a room full of vases on which Chinese characters danced, Ebba stopped short.

"That's it," she said gleefully, pointing at an archway on the far side of the room. "That's the archway that leads out to Timbuktu. The one my parents and I are going to use for our trip."

At that moment, a keyhand with a sky-blue cloth wrapped around her head strode through the archway, making them jump.

"Keyhand Obaji," said Ebba. "You scared us."

"Oh, good," she said and bopped them both on the head with the leather packet she carried, as she passed.

Ebba giggled and Dorrie was reminded of all that was wondrous about Petrarch's Library, even for an Archivist's apprentice.

In the courtyard, they found Hypatia already seated at a large, square wooden table, along with a half dozen other lybrarians-in-training. Hypatia welcomed them with one of her calm smiles and gestured to the two remaining empty chairs. Dorrie sat down beside a woman who appeared to be the oldest human on earth. Her back bent, a set of glaringly false teeth in her mouth, she had to turn her head sideways like a bird to see anything. Regarding Dorrie, she gave her a wink. The other lybrarians-in-training had copies of *The Twelve Principles of the Lybrarian* sitting on the table in front of them. Dorrie quickly pulled hers out as well.

Leafing through it, she saw that the chapters had names like "The Extra Mile," "The Stayed Hand," and "A Place for Everything, and Everything in Its Place." She was just beginning to read about a principle called "The Preserving Shield" when Hypatia spoke again.

"In this practicum, we'll focus on the twelve principles of the lybrarian. Your books contain beautiful descriptions of each of them written by Petrarch himself not long before he died." She began to pass around sheets of paper. "However, even Petrarch's thoughtful ruminations will only take us so far in developing our understanding of the principles. For that reason, I am going to ask each of you to plan and execute at least one mission of your own out in a wheren and to attempt to apply the principles of the lybrarian as you do so."

An hour later, Dorrie and Ebba left the courtyard clutching the pieces of paper Hypatia had given them, their eyes glowing. Dorrie peeled hers off her chest and looked it over again.

Each Principles of Lybrarianship student will plan and execute a mission designed to assist an individual or organization facing the suppression of his/her/its thoughts, ideas, or opinions. You will hereafter refer to this person or organization as the "imperiled subject" of your mission.

"We get to go out on a real mission!" crowed Dorrie. "On our own! To help anyone we want! In any wheren!"

"Well, not exactly," said Ebba. "Look farther down."

**IMPORTANT*: Mistress Wu would like me to specify that apprentices taking the practicum may only choose to assist imperiled subjects facing Class Three threats. These threats include: destruction of written artifacts of which there are no other copies, social ostracization, minor injury, ridicule, and financial hardship. Apprentices are strictly forbidden from choosing imperiled subjects facing Class One or Two threats of impending assassination, imprisonment, loss of home, loss of family members, loss of livelihood, loss of limbs, or loss of copious amounts of blood.

***Apprentices are expected to work in pairs.

"Fine with me," Dorrie said, grinning at Ebba. She thought of Mr. Biggs's threat of a reversal. "I don't suppose Hypatia would let us choose Algernon Sidney."

Ebba gave Dorrie a side eye. "I'm pretty sure a beheading counts as"—she consulted Mistress Wu's addendum again—"a Class One threat." She folded up the paper. "Anyway, Petrarch's Library doesn't even open up into Algernon Sidney's time anymore. I mean, time's moved on in that wheren since that mission was run."

Dorrie stopped walking, feeling stupid. She'd been thinking that even if the Foundation did cause Algernon's beheading to happen, the Lybrariad might be able to re-reverse it.

They decided to get to work right away on choosing an imperiled subject. They headed to the main reference room. The two long lines of study tables with their green-shaded lamps were packed. A good number of lybrarians were even sitting at the one that held the *History of Histories* books, which itself stood inside a strange birdcage-like enclosure in the center of the room. The dozen sets of mahogany doors were in constant motion as lybrarians entered and exited. After looking up some promising-sounding history book titles in a strange cupboard full of tiny drawers that Ebba called "a card catalog," Dorrie and Ebba copied them down on slips of paper and headed for the great oak reference desk, where a line had formed.

At last, Ebba turned over their slips of paper to the harassed-looking lybrarian managing the desk. Almost instantaneously, a man dressed very much like the messenger Dorrie had seen in the Inky Pot materialized beside the lybrarian, the words "Reference Runner" embroidered across his shirt. He wore a close-fitting leather pack covered in pockets of various sizes. The reference lybrarian filled them with a load of scrolls, a damp-looking mud tablet, and a bundle of book request slips, including Dorrie and Ebba's.

"They're tremendously fast," Ebba said as the man sprinted away.

It was only after she and Ebba had sat down at one of the crowded tables to wait for their books that Dorrie noticed Millie a few seats down, scribbling madly, books open all around her. Before she could look away, their eyes met, and Millie's fountain pen went still. Hurriedly, without acknowledging Dorrie and Ebba, she stuffed her books in her satchel and left the table.

"Ever since she found out about that stupid picture in the newspaper, she's been treating me like some kind of leper!" said Dorrie, looking after Millie.

That evening, when Mistress Wu came up to supervise the field trip pick, she looked distracted and anxious.

Marcus looked positively gloomy. Saying he had no desire to visit any particular destination or any desire to do anything at all really, he offered to write down the other apprentices' suggestions and toss them into Mathilde's admiral's hat.

The apprentices began calling out their choices, which were subject to Mistress Wu's approval, based on her knowledge of current conditions in the various wherens.

"Tenth-century Dublin," called out Fatima.

"There's intense fighting going on there at the moment," Mistress Wu said, sighing.

"But no Black Plague…" wheedled Fatima.

"I suppose not," said Mistress Wu, gesturing to Marcus, who scribbled it down. "But if that gets chosen, you'll need to wear armor under your clothes."

Marcus folded up the scrap of paper and tossed it into the hat.

"Ninth century, Morón de la Frontera," called out Saul.

Marcus snickered and then apologized and got very serious as he put pen to paper—but then ruined his apology by snickering again. He folded the suggestion and threw it in.

"Next."

"Tyre, 327 BCE," Sven said slowly from where he sat carving a slingshot for Kenzo.

"Lovely choice," said Mistress Wu approvingly.

"If you don't mind depending on the Archivist to get through the archway," said Mathilde under her breath.

"Twelfth-century Constantinople," said Saul.

"Such an elegant city and time," said Mistress Wu. "The chariot races are a must-see, but I must insist that no betting take place. Riots, you know."

As angry as Dorrie was at Savi for utterly abandoning her, Dorrie still nominated Paris, 1637, his home wheren.

Finally, only Ebba was left. First, she said Nubia, then quickly changed that to Mexico City, and then Lapland. She opened her mouth again.

"Lapland it is!" said Marcus, scribbling hurriedly.

"Are you sure you don't want to suggest a destination, dear?" Mistress Wu asked Marcus, looking at him with motherly concern.

"No," he said. "I've decided not to want anything anymore."

Looking a little alarmed, Mistress Wu danced her fingers among the strips of paper while the apprentices waited with bated breath, and she finally plucked one out. "Tyre, 327 BCE it is!"

A buzz of excited chatter broke out, except from Marcus, who merely sighed heavily and threw himself on the sofa with Fatima's balaban.

Mistress Wu patted him on the shoulder. "Do go on the field trip at least. Always fun to use the Tyre archway. It leads to our only Spoke Library located on a boat!"

Most of the next morning passed more or less like the first with the Archivist, with Dorrie continuing to organize mission reports into piles. This time, however, the Archivist took one of her piles of mission reports and began to enter the details of the completed missions into various large, red books stacked on his end of the worktable.

Watching him out of the corner of her eye, Dorrie gave a start. The spines of the books bore the words *History of Histories*. The books were all volumes from the set she and Marcus had accidentally ripped the page out of the previous quarter. Remembering again how she'd left the Archivist to take the blame, her insides squirmed.

A wave of irritated justification followed. It hadn't been her fault that the Archivist had left open the door of the little room that held the *History of Histories* books, and if he hadn't startled them, the accident never would have happened. Closing her mouth tightly, she went back to her task.

That afternoon, the first thing Dorrie learned at her Staying Afloat practicum, besides the annoying fact that Izel and Millie had signed up for it as well, was that Mistress Daraney was not a fan of talk. Within the first five minutes, everyone taking the course had jumped or been thrown off a short pier fully clothed to assess their swimming skills. Anyone who couldn't swim back to the beach without assistance would be limited to plying their boats close to shore in the shallows.

"Couldn't we just wear life preservers?" asked a rather timid lybrarian-in-training with a bobbing Adam's apple. "They've been invented, you know."

"And you know what they're good for?" scolded Mistress Daraney. "Keeping you from ever feeling that you'd better learn to swim a good distance."

Dorrie did well. Swimming back to shore was no problem, and she was faster than many of the adults.

Back in the attics after dinner, Dorrie and Ebba settled in adjoining armchairs to decide on their imperiled subject.

Nearby, Mathilde had her nose in *African American Women in the Struggle for the Vote, 1850–1920*, occasionally looking up to sputter things like "fish's gizzards" and "How could they!"

At last, after an hour of noisy debate, Dorrie was pushing for John Stubbs, who'd had his hand chopped off for writing a book about Queen Elizabeth I that she didn't care for, and Ebba was quite sure they needed to assist a Cherokee named Buck Deer who was going to have his newspaper, the *Cherokee Phoenix*, shut down for criticizing the government. Neither Ebba or Dorrie would budge.

"You're going around in very annoying circles! And the threat against Stubbs is at least class two." Mathilde finally declared. She smacked a page in her book. "Here's one for you."

Dorrie leaned over and peered at the page. It held a photograph of a group of women in dark dresses and coats. They wore odd star-studded poufy hats and carried pennants that read "Suffrage." All of them had light-colored skin except for one woman in the center of the picture. She had her chin raised high. A scarf printed with the word "Illinois" hung around her neck.

Ebba read the caption. "'Ida Wells-Barnett marching with other suffragists in a parade in Washington, DC, in 1913.'"

Mathilde snorted with disgust. "Yeah. After she had to force her way in. The white suffragists who organized the parade told her and the whole Alpha Suffrage Club she'd organized—black women who came all the way from Chicago—that they couldn't march with the white women from Illinois. No, they had to march by themselves at the end of the parade."

"But why?" asked Dorrie.

"The parade organizers didn't want to scare the racists away from voting for women's suffrage."

"That's awful," said Ebba.

"So what would the mission be?" asked Ebba.

"Well, the way history is now, Ida B. Wells and the Alpha Suffrage Club members decided to fight their way through the crowds with a plan to join the parade when the Illinois suffragists walk by, but only Ida makes it through. The others were kicked and punched and had their banners destroyed, and that was that."

"Totally fish's gizzards," Ebba said indignantly.

"Disgusting," said Dorrie.

"Perfect," Dorrie and Ebba said together, satisfied.

"Enjoy it while you can," said Marcus listlessly from where he'd been idly plucking on the balaban over by the window. He stood and yawned hugely. "I guess I better go and get my beauty rest." He shambled toward his bedroom, stopping at his door for a moment to sigh heavily. "For nobody's sake." He disappeared and closed the door behind him. The apprentices spread around the room glanced at each other.

"He's just wrecked, isn't he?" said Mathilde.

"I guess so," Dorrie said uncertainly.

"I am never falling in love," Fatima said, looking up from a game of solitaire.

Chapter 11

Potato, Potah-to

AT BREAKFAST ANNOUNCEMENTS THE next morning, to Dorrie's disappointment, Mistress Wu made no mention of any news connected with Whim's Gift.

"You know," Dorrie murmured to Ebba as they were leaving the Sharpened Quill, "there's another good thing about choosing the Alpha Suffrage Club."

"What?" Ebba asked as she stuffed a napkin full of leftover toast crusts into her satchel. She'd taken to doing this every morning, always claiming the bits were for Roger, but whenever Dorrie offered to go with her to feed them to him, Ebba always put her off. Dorrie had begun to suspect that Ebba was searching for Darling in her spare time.

"We know that the Stronghold definitely opens up into Washington, DC."

Ebba closed her satchel. "At least it did in the 1950s, when Kash escaped into it from the Stronghold."

"Well, maybe it had already been open for a while."

Ebba looked dubious as they walked out into the Commons sunshine. "Since 1913?"

"I'm just saying…" Dorrie looked around furtively. "Maybe we could be useful to the Alpha Suffrage League *and* the Lybrariad there. You know, keep our eyes open for signs of Foundation activity or any mentions of Whim's Gift."

Marcus, who had caught up with them, pressed a biscuit into Dorrie's hand.

She tried to hand it back. "No thanks."

"You should eat it," Marcus said pointedly, backing away with one eyebrow raised. He turned and shot off down the oyster-shell path in the direction of Master Casanova's office.

"What, is he Fedya now?" Dorrie asked, looking after him. She took a tentative bite, tasted paper, spat, and pulled a small roll of paper from the biscuit. She smoothed it out and read: "Major development. Meet me at the Inky Pot at lunch. Bring Ebba."

"Again?" Ebba wailed. "We barely escaped with our lives last time."

When Dorrie and Ebba sidled into the Inky Pot after their apprenticeships, Marcus was sitting in the same booth where they'd found him before. His sighing ennui appeared to have vanished. He waved them over impatiently, all business. After a quick, suspicious glance at Fedya, they hurried across the room.

"You got my message," said Marcus.

"If by 'got' you mean did I eat some of it," said Dorrie, "then yes."

He smiled broadly. "We've been working on inconspicuous handoffs in Everyday Stealth and Deception. Man, I love that practicum!" He leaned forward. "You need any documents forged? Locks picked?" He sat back again. "What's with the appalled face? Those are legitimate areas of lybrarian study."

"I'm only appalled that you made us come here again," said Dorrie.

Marcus pounded his fist on the table. "I hereby call this meeting to order."

"You didn't say it was a meeting," said Dorrie. "You said to meet you here."

"Potato, potah-to," said Marcus. "Order in the court!"

"We're not in—" began Dorrie, but she ended her sentence abruptly as a plate of pastries was lowered to the table in front of her.

Dorrie felt Ebba squeeze her hand under the table. Slowly, she looked up to see Fedya leaning over them, his lips pulled back in a grin. "For my friend's friends."

Dorrie tried to look grateful.

As soon as he'd gone, Marcus pushed the plate toward her. "Dorrie…we've been siblings for a long time now."

"Yeah," she said warily, pushing the plate back toward him and trying to ignore the fact that her mouth had begun to water without permission.

"I need a favor," said Marcus.

Dorrie slapped at Ebba's hand as she reached for one of the more glistening pastries. "What kind of a favor?"

Marcus pulled out the copy of *Gouty Ben's Weekly Digest* that Dorrie had last seen wrapped around his head. He spread it on the table. "I read that article about Timotheus—mostly because I found myself in a prolonged outhouse situation."

"Good to know," said Dorrie.

"He is in way worse trouble than I thought." Marcus read from the newspaper. "The defendant in the suit, Timotheus of Miletus, maintains a zither repair stall at the Athens agora. A ribbon maker who has the stall next to his commented that though she can't stand Timotheus's music either, the suit brought by Aristotle of Stagira seems extreme. Any fines or imprisonment will hit Timotheus's family hard. He is the sole caretaker of four younger siblings. They have no other living relatives."

"Oh, how terrible!" said Ebba.

Marcus sighed heavily. "Obviously, this is all my fault, and it's up to me to right this travesty of justice!"

"Wait a minute," said Dorrie, suddenly suspicious. "You didn't care a bit about him a few days ago."

"Well, that was before I read that his three sisters suffer respectively from blindness, a clubfoot, and a fainting condition, and his younger brother lost a hand in a fishing accident in the Athens harbor."

Dorrie regarded him shrewdly. "This is about impressing Egeria, isn't it?!"

Marcus reared back, seemingly appalled. "Total slander."

"Total truth," said Dorrie.

"Okay!" Marcus took an enormous bite from one of the pastries. "Did you see Egeria look at Bang like he was the most disgusting kind of fat-chested hero when he volunteered for that mission?"

"So you want her to think you're some kind of disgusting, fat-chested hero?" asked Ebba in confusion.

"If acting like a disgusting, fat-chested hero is what it takes to make her be my girlfriend, then I'll sacrifice myself. I've been doing a little research."

"Really?" said Dorrie, genuinely surprised.

Marcus gave her an injured look. "Timotheus cannot—I repeat, cannot—stand trial. The history books say he ends up as total toast. Fines, imprisonment because he can't pay the fines, exile. His siblings get sold into slavery."

"Oh no!" said Ebba.

"See, in Athens, you have to speak in your own defense at your trial, and Timotheus's defense was just pitiful. He couldn't convince a frog to croak. Complete fail. The trial *has* to be called off before it happens!"

"But how are you going to stop it?" asked Dorrie. "The Lybrariad is never going to let you go back to 399 BCE right now. That was one of the last places Mr. Biggs was seen. The Stronghold entrance is somewhere out there."

"I don't have to," said Marcus. He pointed at the newspaper. "Look at the quote from Timotheus."

Ebba read out loud. "'I'm not a fan of dog sacrifice'—oh, he sounds nice."

"Farther down," said Marcus impatiently.

Dorrie took a turn. "I asked the soft-spoken musician how he'd invented his criminal style of music. 'I didn't invent it,' replied the musician. 'It's a style of music I learned from my grandfather back in Miletus as a boy.'" She looked up. "But I thought…"

"Keep going," urged Marcus.

Dorrie found her place again. "'My grandfather told me he learned the drumming style from a stranger while playing at an Athens party with his first band.'" Dorrie looked up. "So you taught those rhythms to this Timotheus's grandfather—also named Timotheus?"

"Wild, right?" said Marcus.

154

Dorrie gave him a beady eye. "I thought you didn't care about anything anymore."

"Oh, that's just my cover," said Marcus. "We're working on misrepresenting ourselves in Everyday Stealth and Deception. I'm getting credit for it."

"What?" cried Dorrie. "Casanova lets you practice that stuff on *us*?"

"Well, how else am I going to learn?"

"How are you going to help Timotheus?" asked Dorrie.

"It all comes down to Aristotle. He's the one who brought the charges against Timotheus. I've been reading up on him and talking to some of the lybrarians who've met him. Apparently, he's a total sucker for logic. I think I can show him that he's in the wrong in pressing these charges. I've got a speech all made up."

Dorrie was impressed that Marcus had figured out so much, even if it was just to impress Egeria. "But how are you going to deliver a speech to Aristotle?"

"Well," said Marcus, leaning closer. "The field trip we're going on is to Tyre, 327 BCE. I checked the calendar on the wall next to the archway. The timing is perfect. Timotheus's trial will be happening out there in a couple months."

"But Tyre is miles and miles away from Athens," said Ebba. "In Persia."

"Which is why I need that small favor," said Marcus. He

delicately removed a few crumbs from the corners of his mouth. "I need you to borrow one of the Archivist's skipkeys and take me to Athens."

"What?" Dorrie roared, unable to control her volume. "I can't do that! Francesco would…would…dismember me!"

"No, he wouldn't," said Marcus. "Think about it. Francesco didn't say you couldn't use your multitool keyhand power to skip from one library to another. He just said you weren't allowed to use it to get through archways."

"And how am I supposed to take you to Athens in 327 BCE without going through an archway?"

"Because on the day of our field trip, one of the Tyre keyhands will be getting us through the archway."

"Oh, that's true," said Ebba.

Dorrie shot Ebba a reproving look.

Ebba reached for the plate again. "Well, it is, technically."

"Like any of that would make a difference to Francesco if I got caught! He's already angry about the newspaper picture. No way."

"I'm not saying you should take him to Athens, 327 BCE," said Ebba. "But it does seem kind of fated for Marcus to help Timotheus. I mean, how perfect that Tyre, 327 BCE got picked for the field trip."

"That was pretty amazing," Dorrie conceded.

Marcus licked his fingers clean one by one. "You two are so

quaint. You don't think I just lucked into the right field trip, do you?"

Ebba stopped pulling the plate toward herself. "You didn't?"

"Of course not." Marcus snorted. "Every time someone shouted out Tangiers, 1729 or Arapata, 1140, I just wrote down Tyre, 327 BCE."

Dorrie goggled at him. "So you cheated!"

"Well, if you're going to call giving Sven a little Filthy Lucre to suggest Tyre, 327 cheating."

"You paid him off?" said Ebba.

"Well, it's not like anyone else had a pressing mission," said Marcus. "Like I said, Timotheus needs my help."

"You mean you need to help Timotheus so Egeria will fall in love with you."

"To-mato, to-mahto," Marcus said airily.

Dorrie rolled her eyes. "Well, sorry. You'll have to think of a different scheme." She glanced at the pocket watch she had tied to her satchel. "We're going to be late for our practicums." She and Ebba slid out of the booth.

"That's right," said Marcus, trailing them across the room. "Take all the time you need to think about it."

"Not happening," Dorrie said as she pushed through the door. "Ever."

"Exactly," said Marcus as they parted ways in the corridor. "No need to make a hasty decision."

Chapter 12
The First Principle

I T WAS WITH GREAT anticipation that Dorrie arrived at Hypatia's practicum at the end of the week, the mission proposal she and Ebba had finished that morning in her satchel.

During her morning with the Archivist, Dorrie had been so full of daydreams concerning when and how the mission would begin that she'd almost nodded yes when he offered her tea.

Hypatia began the practicum by asking about the imperiled subjects the practicum students had chosen. All went well, with Hypatia nodding approvingly at the choices until the very elderly lybrarian-in-training reported she had chosen someone named Sophie Scholl. Hypatia had to point out that since current history showed Sophie as having been killed by the Gestapo in Hitler's Germany, the nature of the threat she faced would have to be considered Class One and not inappropriate for training purposes.

"Hitler, Schmitler," railed the elderly lybrarian, nearly losing control of her false teeth. "Who cares if I die in the line of duty? I'm old. I've had a good life. A bad oyster could take me out tomorrow."

Beyond the problem with the nature of the threat to Sophie, Hypatia also had to explain that the Lybrariad did not yet connect with Sophie Scholl's time.

Just then, a research runner appeared beside Hypatia with such startling suddenness that the elderly lybrarian-in-training's false teeth did fall onto the table with a clatter.

Hypatia gathered up the students' proposals and handed them to the runner, who disappeared as suddenly as she'd appeared.

Before Dorrie could ask Ebba what she thought that was all about, Hypatia asked them to take out their copies of *Twelve Principles of the Lybrarian* and open to Section One: "The Even Eye."

"So," Hypatia said after a half hour of reading and discussion, "would someone be willing to summarize the Principle of the Even Eye for us?"

Dorrie experienced the uncomfortable realization that daydreams of her upcoming mission had blotted out parts of the discussion.

A nearly bald lybrarian-in-training spoke. "If I had to take a wild stab at an answer, I would say that lybrarians must serve any and all persecuted writers and protect any and all written artifacts without regard for the opinions expressed therein. Even if the opinion induces sensations of anger, fear, loathing, or nausea in the lybrarian."

"That's his wild stab?" Ebba asked out of the corner of her mouth.

"Imagine if he'd been aiming," Dorrie whispered back.

The reference runner reappeared, bearing what looked like the same stack of files. This time, the elderly lybrarian-in-training managed to hold on to her teeth.

"Perfect timing," said Hypatia as the runner put the folders down in front of her and evanesced again. She looked carefully at each folder and then laid one before each of the practicum members.

Dorrie and Ebba exchanged curious glances as she laid theirs to rest between them.

"Yes. The Even Eye," said Hypatia. "One of the most challenging principles to put into practice." She sat back. "Please open your folders."

Eagerly, Dorrie and Ebba complied. In each lay an identical piece of parchment, and on each, a tidy hand had written "Training Mission for Dorrie Barnes and Ebba Ghambo" at the top. Her heart hammering with excitement, Dorrie skimmed over the words.

Mission Category: Protection of Printed Material

All right, she thought, that'll be the banners carried by the Alpha Suffrage Club…

Wheren: London, England, February 1913

Dorrie read the words again. She frowned slightly. The parade that the Alpha Suffrage Club would try to march in was to take place in Washington, DC. And then her frown cleared. Hypatia must have listed the wheren that held the Spoke Library they'd have to go through to get to Washington, DC. She read on.

Imperiled Subject: The National League
for Opposing Woman Suffrage

She read it again. Who were they? And opposing! That couldn't be right. There had to be a mistake. She glanced at Ebba, who was frowning and squinting at her own page. Dorrie skimmed down farther.

Nature of Threat: Copies of the Anti-Suffrage Review
have been taken repeatedly from the doorstep of the
National League for Opposing Woman Suffrage
before they can be distributed.

Mission: Prevent any further disappearances.

Dorrie nudged Ebba. "*Anti-Suffrage Review?*"

"This isn't what we proposed at all," Ebba said.

"Excuse me," said Dorrie, looking up, "but there must be some mistake. Our mission proposal was to help Ida B. Wells and the Alpha Suffrage Club at the suffrage parade in Washington, DC, but this says our mission is to assist the..." She looked down at the piece of paper again. "The National League for Opposing Woman Suffrage."

"Indeed." Hypatia smiled. "I hope you'll forgive the subterfuge. To give you an opportunity to put the Principle of the Even Eye into practice, the research department looked at the opinions and ideas your chosen imperiled subjects were trying to express and found each of you a substitute imperiled subject."

"A substitute?" Dorrie repeated, not liking the way this was going.

"Yes," said Hypatia. "An imperiled subject who holds opinions opposite to those held by your chosen imperiled subject."

Ebba gaped at her. "You mean...someone who *doesn't* want women to vote."

"Precisely," said Hypatia.

"But...we're girls!" said Dorrie. "We don't want to help people who want to convince other people not to let women vote!"

"And that's exactly why you must practice doing so."

At dinner, Dorrie and Ebba cornered Mathilde.

"Why'd you tell us to pick the Alpha Suffrage Club?" Ebba demanded furiously.

"I'm sorry," said Mathilde. "I forgot about the whole bait-and-switch part of that practicum. I was just thinking about how rotten things were for the Alpha Suffrage Club."

Dorrie banged her satchel down on the table in a resentful temper. "Well, if you had remembered, we could have proposed a mission to help those obnoxious anti-suffrage people and gotten one to help Ida B. Wells!"

Mathilde chased a butter bean around her plate. "Somehow, I don't think you would have fooled Hypatia."

That evening, Dorrie and Ebba and about half the other apprentices trooped down to the Gymnasium to take part in the first of the quarter's weapons tournaments organized by Mistress Mai.

In the corner set aside for the rapier tournament, Dorrie and the other competitors donned pads and helmets. After assigning them to pairs for their first bouts, Mistress Wu moved among them, watching their form and calling out corrections and encouragement. They were expected to keep track of when they were touched. Dorrie was assigned to take on Kenzo. Mortifyingly, despite the work she'd done with Savi the previous quarter, she found herself fighting hard to beat the eight-year-old and, in the end, only did so by one touch.

After being beaten handily by two lybrarians-in-training, Dorrie came close to beating Fatima but couldn't really celebrate since directly after the bout, Fatima had run outside to throw up in the shrubbery and had then been sent up to see Ursula in the human preservation and repair department due to a raging fever.

Finally, Dorrie found herself facing Millie. If Dorrie was at the bottom of the heap in terms of sword skill, Millie was very near the top, even among the adults. Exuding a stiff, simmering sort of hostility, Millie defeated Dorrie in a humiliating thirty seconds to the sound of Izel's admiring giggles and her taunt of "What do you expect from the Archivist's apprentice?"

Tearing off her pads and helmet, Dorrie stormed from the Gymnasium without even waiting for Ebba. Rapier still in hand, she charged through room after room, feeling she might bite the next person who strayed into her path.

As Dorrie ducked through another doorway into a graveled yard, her rapier was sent flying. It landed with a clatter.

Filled with sullen fury, she spun around. "Hey—" she cried but broke off her exclamation. Savi was sitting on a wooden bench, his own rapier aloft.

"Mademoiselle, either march blindly or hold a rapier

unsheathed before you but not both at once. It's very poor manners."

"Savi!" she cried, a grin splitting her face. About to throw her arms around him, she stopped short as the murky feelings of resentment and abandonment she'd been keeping stuffed away swelled inside her.

"I'm experimenting with sitting and doing nothing," said Savi, looking at the bench upon which he sat as though it were a strange curiosity. "Phillip tells me it's a wonderful thing to do. Would you like to join me?"

"Why didn't you write me or find me or something?" Dorrie hated the strain and squeak in her voice. "Why did you just disappear like that? Like you didn't even care about me!"

"Of course I care. But in the last few weeks, circumstances have dictated I be far away and not in a position to send messages, however much I might have liked to."

"I didn't even sign up for any sword-fighting practicums," said Dorrie hotly. "I've got to help a bunch of anti-suffragists in my principles practicum, and they've stuck me with the Archivist! It's terrible."

"*Non*, mademoiselle," said Savi, grimacing as he shifted his position, his hand going to his side. "Bad puns and dead friends are terrible."

For a moment, the memory of the glorious, terrible day when she'd watched Savi sink wounded to the ground after fighting off at least six attackers at Porte de Nesle flashed loudly and frighteningly before her.

Dorrie's bitterly felt disappointments collided with perspective, and she dropped onto the bench beside Savi. "But that's just it. The Lybrariad is in trouble. The *world* is in trouble. Algernon Sidney is definitely in trouble, and I'm just sorting papers for the Archivist while other apprentices..." She broke off the thought. "I don't want to be his apprentice. I want to be yours! I wanted to help you with your missions the way I did at Porte de Nesle! I want to help you find out where the Foundation's making Whim's Gift and help stop them."

"Is the important thing that you and I are the ones who stop them?"

"No!" said Dorrie, feeling herself scowling.

Savi looked down the entirety of his nose at her, which took a while.

"Okay, yes!" she cried. They stared at one another for a moment, and then she kicked out a leg. She groped to explain. "I want it to be impossible for anyone to ever think for a second that the Lybrariad offered me my apprenticeship just because"—she took a deep breath—"because I'm an 'accidental keyhand,'" she said, curving her fingers into angry air quotes.

Savi stared at her. "I have no idea what you are trying to convey with your fingers, but this I know, and mark me well."

Something in his tone of voice made Dorrie give him her full attention.

"One could waste a lifetime trying to prove one's worth to others rather than developing the worth itself." He stood. "Now as far as I'm concerned, you are indeed my apprentice, and I am simply loaning your services to the Archivist. In the meantime, I will offer you this. While missions will keep me away from Petrarch's Library for much of this quarter, I will still make it my business to give you rapier lessons as I can."

"You will?" Dorrie asked, her spirits lifting.

"No," he said, adjusting his hold on the hilt of his sword. "I just said that to hear myself speak."

"When can we start?" she stammered, jumping up.

"When I'm sure you intend to bring your best effort to helping the Archivist."

Dorrie stared at him, feeling needled. "Would *you*?"

"At your age?" He looked thoughtfully at the little pond full of goldfish nearby. "Probably not. But then again, I didn't have such a fine mentor as myself who will now tell you that the Archivist is no more a fool than any of the rest of us. It's likely that he's as wrong as wrong can be about Petrarch's alphabet, but his efforts are not necessarily any less worthwhile than Della Porta's, for all that Della Porta likes to tell the world that story. Hypatia wouldn't have assigned you to the Archivist if she didn't think he deserved an apprentice."

"She assigned three to Della Porta," mumbled Dorrie.

"I'll pretend I didn't hear that," Savi said.

"All right. Fine," Dorrie said, scurrying to retrieve her sword from the gravel.

"Fine, what?"

"Fine, I'll do the whole best-effort thing," she said, advancing on Savi with her rapier aloft.

"You haven't even thought about it properly yet," flamed Savi as he offered a slow thrust for her to parry. "How can I possibly take you seriously?" He left himself open, daring her to take advantage. Dorrie attempted a feint, which he parried in a flash, and then in some way she didn't understand, he caused the rapier to fly out of her hand for a second time.

"Can you teach me to do that?" she asked.

"Perhaps in a year or two," Savi said as she retrieved her sword again.

"A year or two!" Dorrie exclaimed, feeling like that was so far away as to not be real.

"That's if you put in an enormous amount of practice time."

"All right. What are we going to start with?"

"Well, I have found that aim is of some importance in swordsmanship."

CHAPTER 13
TURN OF EVENTS

OR THREE GLORIOUS DAYS, Savi remained in Petrarch's Library, and true to his word, he gave Dorrie a lesson on each of them. Right off the bat, he ordered her to retire the rapier she'd checked out from the circulation desk.

"But...but..." Dorrie had said, finding it difficult to part with the fine-looking sword with its ornate hilt and shiny blade.

He had plucked it out of her hand with a disgusted thumb and forefinger. "It's an ostentatious, unbalanced hatpin." He handed her a terribly plain-looking rapier, the bell of which was dented and scratched, but Dorrie had to admit it felt better in her hand as she practiced the footwork Savi had shown her the previous quarter.

Rather than invite her to cross blades with him in any of the lessons, Savi had talked her through the fundamentals of aim and then had her lunge at a spot inked on a pad he had hung on the Gymnasium courtyard wall. Repeatedly. So many times, in fact, that Dorrie thought she might expire from the pure tedium of it.

Savi spent the lessons sitting on his favorite bench, his quill busy on a piece of parchment in his lap.

Midway through the lesson on the third day, she staggered toward the well and poured a dipperful of water into her mouth, not caring how it splashed on her hot face and neck.

"There are no water breaks on the field of battle," said Savi.

"There aren't any quills either," Dorrie replied grumpily, splashing the dipper back into the bucket.

"Ah, you believe I should be sweating along with you," Savi said, scratching out a line with a flourish. "That I am too comfortable here in the shade with my blistered feet up and a cushion beneath my poked and lacerated frame?" He scratched out a sentence. "Believe me, apprentice, I'm doing my own sweating here. It takes excessive amounts of energy to aim for the perfect word, to deliver the perfect verbal thrust, to parry in advance the lurching and threadbare objections that will be made by my most clever readers, to employ the sure footwork of one splendid analogy after another. Trust me when I say that my brain is laboring ten times as hard as your arm." He glanced up at Dorrie, who was just finishing the dipperful of water. "Make that a hundred times."

"Is that your very long way of asking for a drink of water?"

"Yes. Would you mind?"

Dorrie grinned.

"The hole in my side still complains."

Dorrie's grin faded, remembering how much blood had stained his shirt. Quickly, she scrambled to her feet, scooped up another dipperful, and brought it over to him. "What are you writing?" she asked cautiously as she sat beside him, trying not to look over his shoulder in case she'd see a new round of love poems.

"It's an essay entitled 'Against Witches.' In it, I aim to lay out the whole, logical, beautiful, and certain case against the existence of witches, warlocks, warty devil spawn, the gibbering possessed, and any number of other absurd creations of the human mind." He dipped his quill in a pot of ink. "And if it's all the same to you, I think it's time you got back to your own aiming."

Before Savi left Petrarch's Library again, he extracted a promise from Dorrie at the Paris, 1647 CE archway. "Practice your footwork, and practice your aim for at least a half hour a day—more if you'd like to be able to hit your target with any kind of consistency before you need your own set of false teeth." He had raised her chin and then looked down his nose at her. "And don't forget. Best effort for the Archivist."

She jerked her chin away and given Savi an exasperated look.

The weeks that followed were busy ones as Dorrie and Ebba

prepared to launch their Principles mission in London, 1913. Hypatia had given them the task of thoroughly researching the wheren's politics, technology, music styles, food, and entertainment as well as popular pastimes, manners, and lifestyles of the very rich and very poor and everyone in between—and a hundred other topics, it seemed.

Each student had to meet with Master Casanova in his luxuriously appointed office. He handed Dorrie and Ebba dossiers containing the details of the false identities they would claim in London.

"Ebba." He tossed the end of one of the scarves he always wore smartly over one shoulder. "Your father, William Risien, is a successful lawyer of the South African bar and practices in Bulawayo in the area currently known as Rhodesia. You have been sent to London for a visit with your uncle, Dr. James Risien Russell. He is the personal physician of Mrs. Humphrey Ward, who happens to be a member of the National League Opposing Woman Suffrage, hence your knowledge of the organization and your fervent wish to lend your energy to their sterling efforts."

Ebba made a face of which Mathilde would have been proud.

He turned to Dorrie. "Dorothea. Your parents exist on the outskirts of the aristocracy but have fallen on hard times. Your father is Rathcliffe-Exleys, lately of Rhodesia. Opportunity to pillage and claim treasure in the name of civilization and all that. Your mother and Ebba's father are acquainted, hence you have been included in the trip to England. You're both looking forward to living lives full of proper deportment at tea parties and marrying well."

Master Casanova picked up Sophocles, one of the two small terriers that accompanied him everywhere he went. "Now we must talk about something unpleasant."

"More unpleasant than anti-suffragists?" said Dorrie.

"In London, 1913, the majority of persons have light skin. Most of them labor under the illusion that they are superior to anyone with darker skin."

Dorrie and Ebba gave each other sidelong glances.

"Based on that, Ebba, you'll need to prepare yourself for insulting theories, superciliousness, and most likely flagrant disparagement and discrimination."

Sophocles growled.

"Like Ida B. Wells?" asked Ebba.

"Precisely."

"That doesn't sound fair at all," said Dorrie.

"Well, if you want to experience it yourself, you'll have to go to seventeenth-century China."

Dorrie reared back. "I didn't mean—"

"However," said Casanova, getting up from behind his desk, "you can both enjoy the male chauvinism. Plenty of that to go around."

After that, there were arrangements to be made for the clothing they'd wear, which necessitated a trip to the circulation desk and a meeting with one of Mistress Lovelace's staff members.

She had stroked her chin as she had first looked over Casanova's dossiers and then Dorrie and Ebba with a hard, evaluative eye, remaining silent for a good minute. "Linen blouses and skirts. Simple yet smart," she'd finally declared. "Navy coats. Leather boots. Wool tights. No shouty trimming. Ridiculously large hats." She cocked her head to one side. "Not quite old enough for corsets, which is unfortunate."

"Why?" asked Dorrie.

The assistant stared at her as if she'd asked why humans eat. "Nothing says 'wealthy' more than personal discomfort. Rich people positively insist upon it. Think of the scads of people it takes to care for your needs when you can't bend over. Comfort, my dear, is for bootblacks."

In Mistress Daraney's practicums, Dorrie and the other students had been introduced to the parts of the dinghy and the basics of maneuvering it in the surf. They had spent hours rowing around in a large circle, many of the students crashing into one another and losing oars, while Mistress Daraney stood effortlessly balanced in a rocking boat in the center of the circle and called out instructions and insults by turn. Dorrie found she had a knack for the rhythm of rowing and felt marvelously at home in the boats.

When they'd practiced standing in their boats and moving from bow to stern in rough water, only Dorrie had managed to stay upright and in her dinghy. During one pleasurable practicum, Mistress Daraney had grown annoyed enough with Izel's squeaks of protest about the blisters forming on her hands that she'd thrown a haddock at her.

As the weeks passed, Dorrie found it more and more difficult to hold on to her resentment toward the Archivist. Not because of Savi's opinion on the matter, but because no matter how much stiff indifference she displayed, the Archivist never altered in his patient kindness toward her. She knew in her bigger moments that it wasn't his fault that Savi had been called to other duties. Finally, one morning, she could resist no longer and ate one of the cookies he left beside her elbow. On the next, when he offered her tea, she nodded, and on the third morning, her resistance crumbled altogether, and she took both tea and cookies.

One day, knees creaking, the Archivist bent awkwardly and began to pull a small wooden trunk out from under one of the benches. Dorrie left her work and went to help him.

"One of the other Tyre keyhands broke her Tyre-Persepolis skipkey," he huffed as together they lifted the trunk and set it on the table. "I said she could use mine until it's repaired."

He blew off a thick layer of dust and lifted the lid, letting it fall back on its hinges. "Oh, but I did love the constant key-skipping back when I spent more time out in the wherens! Sometimes, I'd go from Khampur to Guinea to Kish all in one day. Maybe stop at a dozen branch libraries to pick up news and check on the progress of our missions, and still get back in time for a late-night hot toddy at the Inky Pot."

Dorrie peered inside the trunk and saw a shallow tray. It was broken up into compartments, each of which held a rectangle that reminded Dorrie of her sister's dominoes. The two halves of these rectangles were made of completely different materials joined with a hinge. A metal prong the length of the hinge stuck up at an angle from one end. No two of the "dominoes" looked quite alike.

"These are the skipkeys?" she said aloud, immediately reminded of her talk with Marcus in the Inky Pot.

The Archivist gave a wheezy laugh. "Not what you were expecting?"

In fact, they weren't. Since she'd first heard of their existence, she had imagined them as very ornate, heavy brass keys like the one that stuck out of Great-Aunt Alice's old-fashioned desk back in Passaic.

He lifted one out. "Here's the one we want." One half was made of dark, highly polished wood and the other of some kind of stone. He turned it over in his hand. The backs of the squares of wood and stone had a thin layer of deep-brown leather tightly affixed to them. Each square of leather was embossed with a series of letters and numbers. One read PSPLS 327B and the other, TYRE 327B.

"Here," said the Archivist, dropping the skipkey into Dorrie's hand.

The two squares wanted to fold toward each other, leather side out, but were kept from meeting by the metal prong.

"Just don't move the stop stick," said the Archivist, pointing to the prong. "That's the first thing you learn about handling a skipkey."

"What's it do?" asked Dorrie, pulling her fingers away.

"It keeps the two halves of the skipkey from touching until you want them to." He took the skipkey from her and bent the stop stick slightly upward. "It's flexible, see? When the time is right, you push it out of the way and let the skipkey fold completely. Tyre touches Persepolis and"—he leaned toward her conspiratorially—"you hope you don't land on somebody's grandmother."

They both laughed.

On the evening before Ebba and Dorrie were due to head out to London, 1913 at last, right before dinner, Roger broke out of his yard and got wedged in a narrow alleyway nearby. This was unfortunate for several reasons. For one thing, he'd startled the very elderly lybrarian-in-training when she turned into the alley, and her false teeth had flown out again and this time broken into bits on the cobbles. For another thing, rumors had been flying all day that Mistress Lovelace's famous chicken potpies were going to be served at dinner. Dorrie and Ebba knew they wouldn't last long.

Under duress, Marcus agreed to help Dorrie and Ebba ease Roger back out with the help of a bucket of lard.

"If all the chicken potpies are gone when we get to the Sharpened Quill, I'm personally sacrificing Roger," Marcus announced when they'd finished freeing the aurochs.

"Don't worry," Ebba said when they'd finally succeeded in freeing the aurochs. "I know a shortcut up to the Commons." She led them through a door in the alley wall and across the slippery floor of the Biblioteca Marciana. In the far wall, Ebba pushed through another door. Instead of another room, Dorrie saw sky and sea and a very narrow ledge of rock onto which Ebba skipped.

"What is that?" Marcus asked, staring at the ledge.

Ebba looked surprised. "It's the Middle Shelf. Didn't you ever go out on it last quarter?"

"No," said Marcus, peering past Ebba at the precipice just beyond her toes. "And I didn't do any sword-swallowing either."

"It goes all the way around the outside of Petrarch's Library," said Ebba, starting down the ribbon of stone as though she had goat hooves rather than feet. "It's perfectly safe as long as you stay away from the edge." She disappeared from view.

Cautiously, Dorrie and Marcus inched out after her.

"There's also a Bottom Shelf and a Top Shelf," Ebba called over her shoulder. "They're very useful for getting around if you don't mind a little weather."

"Or death!" said Marcus, clinging to the Biblioteca Marciana's outer wall.

When they'd gone a few yards, Dorrie heard the sound of violently splashing water. Ahead, the ledge disappeared into one of the Library's perpetual rainstorms.

Dorrie paused. "It looks kind of wet."

"Don't worry," said Ebba, who had stopped at a row of hooks. "We keep umbrellas on both sides of the rainstorm." She handed them around.

About fifteen feet into the storm, Ebba turned into the dark mouth of a stone tunnel. Dorrie followed. Initially relieved to get off the slick precipice, she soon wondered if the tunnel was a real improvement. It sloped steeply downward, lit only by candles that flickered wanly on the walls. Greasy-looking puddles stretched over much of the floor, and the air smelled horrible.

"Tallow candles," said Ebba as Dorrie and Marcus both covered their noses.

Soon, the smaller puddles became one big puddle that quickly became ankle-deep.

"There's no earthly way of knowing," Marcus started singing in a creepy monotone, "which direction we are going."

"Cut it out," said Dorrie, unnerved.

"I don't know why more people don't use this shortcut," Ebba said from up ahead.

Dorrie heard a squeak and then a splash that seemed to speak clearly of the presence of rats.

"That's one reason," said Dorrie.

"There's no knowing where we're rowing," sang Marcus, "or which way the river's flowing."

Dorrie elbowed him hard in the ribs.

At last, Dorrie saw brightness ahead. It came from a break in the tunnel wall. They stumbled up a few wet steps into a nice, dry whitewashed corridor.

It ended abruptly at a door painted blackest black and covered in cobwebs. Ebba stopped, looking confused. "There used to be an iron staircase here with a piece of the National Library of Peru at the top."

Dorrie stared at the bug-eyed gargoyle with a lolling tongue that served as the black door's knocker. "You think it's a new Ghost Library?"

Ebba nodded. "It must have squished in sometime recently and changed things around."

"Chicken. Pot. Pie," said Marcus with some urgency.

Dorrie realized the door was slightly ajar. Against the protests of the hundreds of little hairs on the back of her neck, Dorrie pushed it. The hinges made a horrible grating sound.

Cautiously, she stuck her head inside. Dark wooden bookcases ranged around the walls and brooded over velvet moth-eaten furniture set some distance from an immense stone fireplace. A dark chandelier lit the place with its dirty-looking, guttering candles.

Marcus and Ebba poked their heads in as well.

"Cozy," said Marcus, eyeballing a moth-eaten stuffed vulture. "In a gravediggers' clubhouse kind of way."

Dorrie saw that the room held four other doors: one on either side of the fireplace and another two flanking a portrait that hung on the wall opposite the fireplace. "Maybe one of those will take us toward the Sharpened Quill."

"Ugh," Ebba said fiercely, catching sight of the great, shaggy head of a bison that hung over the fireplace. "Someone had better have eaten every bit of him!"

"I don't think that would make me feel any better if I were him," said Marcus.

Dorrie walked farther into the room, the others shuffling along behind her. She felt a rush of cold air, and the door slammed behind them. They screamed and clutched one another.

"The tunnel wasn't so bad," Marcus choked out.

"It was just a draft," Dorrie said firmly, talking to herself as much as the others. Slowly, they disentangled themselves. Despite the allure of chicken potpie, the odd room made her want to linger

The books on the shelves were some of the most mildew-ridden, blackened, crumbly ones Dorrie had ever seen in Petrarch's Library. "These look positively ancient," she said, pulling down one of the tomes. She read the title: "*Poisons with Which to Wither Your Enemies.*"

"Definitely matches the decor," said Marcus, pulling down another. A reddish-brown blotch on its cover looked terribly like a bloodstain. "*The Executioner's Art.* Cheery."

Ebba reached for one as well beside the fireplace. "*True Spine-Tingling Ghost Stories from around the World.* I *love* ghost stories." She sank onto the floor to give the book a closer look, nearly sitting on the head of a polar bear. Its lips were pulled back in a fierce snarl, and the flames from the fire flickered eerily through its yellow teeth. The rest of its pelt was spread out as a rug. "Poor creature!" cried Ebba, jumping up again.

Dorrie wandered toward the portrait. A set of dark, hooded eyes stared at her from beneath a top hat, one eye looking slightly more protuberant than the other. The man's eyebrows were fixed at such a sinister angle that Dorrie wondered if anyone had ever had the nerve to talk to him when he was alive. On a shelf below the portrait, two fat, grinning brass toads sat keeping a row of books upright. Dorrie peered more closely at the face in the portrait. There was something else in it, something…

"What's with the stuffed stuff in this place?" asked Marcus, staring at something sitting on top of a pipe organ. "Look at this one." Dorrie turned to see Marcus opening his jaws wide near the snout of what looked like a small crocodile.

"Darling!" sang out Ebba as the creature opened one eye and launched herself at Marcus with a great gurgling snarl.

He windmilled backward. Darling hit the ground with a heavy thud and scurried after him on her powerful, stubby legs.

Dorrie grabbed hold of Marcus's arm and raced for the nearest door, seizing Ebba with her free hand on the way.Letting go of them, she wrenched the door open. A skeleton, heavy with chains, erupted from the darkness beyond the doorway, its arm and leg bones dancing madly and its jaws clacking.

In a storm of shrieks, Dorrie, Marcus, and Ebba retreated clumsily, getting in one another's way and overturning a hollow elephant leg. Weapons spilled across the carpet. As Dorrie dove for a broadsword, the skeleton withdrew, and the door it had erupted from slam closed.

"What kind of maniac puts a spring-loaded skeleton in a closet!" yelled Marcus as he and Dorrie clambered up on the sofa, dragging Ebba along with them as she made soothing sounds in the direction of the advancing lizard. Darling clawed her way up onto the sofa after them, forcing the apprentices to climb higher onto a long table that stood behind the sofa.

"Watch the candles!" warned Dorrie as Marcus nearly knocked over a candelabra. The lizard's tail lashed. Panting,

Dorrie held the sword out in front of her, trying to keep the animal at bay.

"She's scared!" said Ebba.

With another mighty lunge, Darling chomped down on the sword blade. It broke off in her mouth like a breadstick.

"Oh, no you don't!" Marcus cried as Darling crouched to spring again.

He kicked the candelabra toward her. Rather than sailing off the table, it simply bent over under his foot and then sprang back up again as though on a hinge, its flames dancing. The lizard shied away from it and fell onto the floor. Before Dorrie could think what to do next, a creaking sort of cracking sound from above made them all look up. The chandelier was trembling. A great web of cracks appeared in the ceiling.

"The suspense is terrible," whispered Marcus. "I hope it lasts."

Dorrie heard a snap. The three apprentices leaped off the table in different directions as the chandelier plummeted. Sprawled on the floor, Dorrie watched it jerk to a jangling, bouncing halt about where their heads had been. A low growl made her look toward the end of the couch. Darling was advancing around it in a slow, toothy, purposeful way. Dorrie scrambled to her feet and raced for the door beside the portrait. It refused to open. Desperate, she grabbed hold of one of the brass toads on the shelf below the portrait, intending to throw it at Darling. Instead, Dorrie felt herself swung around violently as the wall spun. Before she could make a sound, Ebba, Marcus, and the slobbering monitor lizard disappeared from view.

CHAPTER 14
THROUGH A THREADBARE HOLE

DORRIE FELT HERSELF LOSING her grip on the toad. In another moment, she'd fallen hard on a flagstone floor. Panting, she raised her head and looked around.

She was lying on a landing at the top of a flight of curving stone steps. On the wall that had spun, two torches in iron brackets cast their flickering light on another portrait, this one of a woman with russet hair, sky-blue robes, and much nicer eyes. Directly across from the portrait stood a wooden door set in a stone wall, its top curved to a peak. Dorrie turned back to the portrait, wondering if behind it, Ebba and Marcus were still in one piece.

From down the stairway came the sound of another door opening, followed by ponderous footsteps, and suddenly, Dorrie knew exactly where she was. Her heart nearly stopped.

She was outside Master Francesco's tower office. For a moment, she considered explaining the situation to him but then dismissed the thought immediately. As angry as Izel had said he was about Dorrie making the Passaic Public Library front page news, Dorrie felt certain that if he found her lurking outside his door, he'd assume she was up to no good.

Fervently hoping Ebba had been able to work her animal magic on Darling and that she and Marcus were safe, Dorrie darted behind a moth-eaten tapestry and tried to make herself as thin and as silent as paper.

Through a threadbare hole, she saw Lybrarian Della Porta come into view. He knocked on the door. After a moment, Master Francesco threw it open. Stronger light illuminated the landing.

"Oh, it's you," said Francesco, looking haggard and slightly unsettled. "Any breakthroughs on the code-breaking?"

"Not quite yet," said Della Porta, "but soon, very soon. No, I've come about another matter."

"Yes?" said Francesco.

"As you may know," said Della Porta, "I have made something of a study of ancient Athens during my life."

"Because you desire to serve as the next Athens keyhand," said Francesco, his voice impatient.

Della Porta gave him a sharp look. "Keyhand Diadora is not going to live forever, and I don't care if it offends you that I say it. The role will have to be filled, and yes, I would like to be considered, but that's not why I've come." He pulled a piece of papyrus from a book he held and handed it to Francesco.

Dust tickled Dorrie's throat, and she suppressed a cough.

"I realize the Foundation could be remaking Whim's Gift just about anywhere, but here is a list of locations in Athens, 399 BCE I think the Lybrariad should prioritize investigating." Della Porta poked at a place on the papyrus. "I believe a house owned by one Critius warrants special interest. He would have been just the sort of person to appreciate the Foundation's goals and throw in with them."

"Thank you," said Francesco, sounding anything but grateful. "Keyhands Aspasia, Leandro, and, yes, Diadora have also provided me with extremely long lists of suggestions, and I assure you that my overtaxed, overstretched, under-rested mission lybrarians will get to yours just as soon as humanly possible." He began to withdraw into his office.

"One more thing," said Lybrarian Della Porta.

The tickle in Dorrie's throat now a clawing tiger, she despaired of the lybrarians ever leaving the landing.

"What?" demanded Francesco.

"It's about Hypatia's ill-considered decision at the Council."

"It wasn't Hypatia's decision," Francesco said.

"Hypatia, the Board of Directors, what does it matter," said

191

Della Porta. "The point is that it was a bad decision. Mr. Biggs as good as told us that the Foundation has that missing *History of Histories* page."

Dorrie drew a sharp shocked breath. There was a moment of silence.

"And yet he is treated like a guest!" continued Lybrarian Della Porta.

Francesco stared at him icily. "He's being treated like a prisoner in accordance with Lybrariad principles."

"For Petrarch's sake, Francesco," cried Lybrarian Della Porta. "Algernon Sidney's fate aside, there is a crux mission on that *History of Histories* page. A crux mission!"

Dorrie's thoughts raced, trying to remember what the other apprentices had said about crux missions. They were missions that changed the world in huge ways.

"If the Foundation manages to reverse it," sputtered Della Porta, "thousands upon thousands of lives will be lost, countless others will suf—"

"—I am acutely aware of the possible consequences," Francesco said through gritted teeth.

"And yet, Mr. Biggs still sits on his island free to withhold the location of Whim's Gift." Della Porta's voice rose. "Free to keep the means to break the journal's code to himself!"

The two stared at each other for another long moment. The *History of Histories* page. The words echoed awfully in Dorrie's head. She felt as though she were falling faster and faster into a bottomless pit.

"The Board of Directors has made its decision," said Francesco, his voice tight.

"And we must force them to reconsider," said Della Porta, clutching at his arm.

Francesco stared at Della Porta's hand, a dangerous light in his eye. "I have work to do."

Della Porta released his hold. "I will leave it there for now."

He turned and descended the stairs, Francesco staring after him. When the door at the bottom closed with a sonorous boom, Francesco shifted his gaze to the portrait of the woman. To Dorrie's astonishment, a sound of animal anguish escaped him. He plunged his hand into one of his black tailcoat's pockets. When he drew it out again, his fingers cradled a circle of silver set with a black stone that glinted in the torchlight. For a moment, Francesco stared at it along with Dorrie. Then, with a savage cry, he hurled it against the wall. As he stormed down the stairs, the armband bounced and skittered, finally coming to a rest near Dorrie's feet.

As soon as the door below slammed again, Dorrie staggered out from behind the tapestry and began to hammer at the wall beneath the portrait. "Ebba! Marcus!"

She stopped and listened intently. Nothing. Desperate to get off the landing before Francesco returned, her gaze roved over the wall. "There has to be some way back in." She felt along the bottom of the frame and in the cracks between the stones. Just when she was going to give up on one of the torch brackets, it bent to one side and the wall lurched into motion again, Dorrie holding on for dear life. She tumbled onto the carpet at Marcus and Ebba's feet in a cloud of dust.

"That was one hundred percent Scooby-Doo," said Marcus.

"Are you all right?" asked Ebba.

Marcus helped Dorrie up. "Where'd you go?"

"To the landing outside Francesco's office," said Dorrie, relieved that Ebba and Marcus were alive but unnerved by the sight of Darling tucked under Ebba's arm like a long, scaly, drooling football.

"Did he see you?" Ebba asked, giving the lizard's underside a stroke.

"I hid," Dorrie explained, a feeling of overwhelming horror welling up in her as she recalled what she'd overheard. "But I found out something terrible."

Dorrie quickly relayed what Lybrarian Della Porta had said about the crux mission and the *History of Histories* page.

"Who was the imperiled subject of the crux mission?" asked Ebba.

Dorrie frowned. "Della Porta didn't say."

"I'd say let's go check the *History of Histories* books in the main reference room to find out," Marcus said, "but…"

Dorrie groaned. "That's not funny yet." She hurled herself on the tattered couch. "Stupid *History of Histories* page! Stupid Foundation. Stupid Athens! Stupid us for losing it."

"We weren't stupid," said Marcus, joining her. "Just surprised. Then clumsy. Then blundering. Then unlucky."

Ebba tried to sit down as well, but Marcus shot her such an outraged look that she reversed course and headed for the closet they'd discovered. Standing well back, she opened the door. When the skeleton was done erupting, she stuck Darling in with it and closed the door.

"If that crux mission gets undone, it'll be our fault," said Dorrie, wrapping her arms around her knees. Her thoughts skittered in panicked circles. The *History of Histories* page. In the Foundation's hands. How could such a terrible thing have happened?

"I hate that we lost it and they've got it," said Marcus, "but it was an accident."

"So you don't feel guilty?" asked Dorrie.

Marcus's face took on a thoughtful look as he felt around his chest with one hand. "Nope."

"Well, I do!" said Dorrie as she experienced an unpleasant vision of Algernon Sidney's head rolling around all by itself.

A thick silence took hold, broken only by the sound of Darling chewing on what Dorrie was sure was one of the skeleton's femurs.

"Francesco got so mad after Lybrarian Della Porta left," murmured Dorrie. "He threw some keyhand's armband at the wall."

Ebba, who had been reaching down to pick up the book of ghost stories she'd dropped the first time the skeleton had erupted, straightened with a jerk. "You're sure it was a keyhand's armband?"

"Positive," said Dorrie.

"I guess he kept it," said Ebba. "I mean, after he got in trouble and couldn't be a keyhand anymore."

"Francesco used to be a keyhand?" asked Dorrie.

Ebba nodded. "Years and years ago."

Marcus looked as though he'd gotten a dream birthday present. "What did he get in trouble for?"

Ebba lowered her voice as if Francesco might be listening. "I don't know exactly what he did, but I heard it was really bad."

As Dorrie tried to take this in, another thought oozed through her. How long would it be before everyone in Petrarch's Library knew that, courtesy of Dorrie and Marcus, the Foundation had a blueprint for undoing a crux mission? She'd go from being thought of as "the Idiot's Apprentice" to "Mr. Biggs's Apprentice."

She felt for the hilt of her sword. She was pretty sure Savi wouldn't waste time worrying about people's reactions. He'd think about what to do next to keep the Foundation from getting any use out of the *History of Histories* page.

She scrambled to her feet and faced the others. "I want to find Whim's Gift."

"And I want a bean feast," said Marcus.

She ignored that. "Do you still want the Archivist's skipkey to get to Aristotle?"

Marcus raised his eyebrows. "Possibly."

"Okay," Dorrie said. "I'll get it, and we'll go to Athens, 327 BCE—just like you said."

Ebba stared at Dorrie. "You want to look for Whim's Gift there?"

"Lybrarian Della Porta wanted the Lybrariad to see if the Foundation was remaking Whim's Gift in the house of this guy out in Athens, 399 BCE named Critius, but Francesco sort of shot Della Porta down."

"But we'd be going to Athens, 327 BCE," said Ebba. "That's about seventy years later."

Dorrie took a deep breath. "I know, but—"

"Why should Francesco listen to Della Porta?" interrupted Marcus.

"I know, but it's the best I can do. Athens, 399 BCE is crawling with lybrarians. I doubt I could ever get through undetected. Plus I'd be breaking my promise about not going through any of the archways on my own."

"Okay," said Ebba. "But if the Foundation is rebuilding Whim's Gift at Critius's house in 399 BCE, what would there be to find in 327 BCE?"

"I don't know," said Dorrie. "Proof that the Foundation had been there in the past so the Lybrariad will put it at the top of the list?"

"What makes you think Della Porta knows what he's talking about?" asked Marcus.

"Because he knows a lot about ancient Athens," Dorrie said, not feeling it necessary to explain why exactly that was.

Ebba frowned. "If there are good reasons to look at Critius's house, how come Francesco doesn't want to do it?"

"Francesco has a really long list of places to check on," said Dorrie. "More places than lybrarians. Plus, I don't think he likes Della Porta very much."

"Because Della Porta wants to go all Torquemada thumb-screws torture on Biggs?" asked Marcus.

"I think so," said Dorrie. "But Della Porta might be right. It's a lead anyway."

"I guess it wouldn't hurt to look," said Ebba.

Dorrie beamed. "You'll come?"

Ebba snorted. "Instead of going souvenir shopping in Tyre? I'll make the sacrifice." She began to flip through *True Spine-Tingling Ghost Stories from around the World*.

Dorrie felt a rush of relief. Though a part of her felt like she should try to talk Ebba out of getting involved, she couldn't bring herself to try.

"Well, I think we have our plan-making lair," said Marcus, looking approvingly at the smirking portrait and the stuffed vulture.

Thinking about the flooded, stinking, rat-filled tunnel that had gotten them here, Dorrie had to agree.

"Even with Francesco so close?" Ebba asked, nervously looking up from her book.

"If this Ghost Library just squeezed in, he probably doesn't even know about it yet," said Marcus.

Ebba's eyes lit up. "Could we hide Darling here?"

"I'm sorry, but all questions must be submitted in writing," said Marcus.

After a long argument about Darling's fate, during which Marcus finally agreed to share the lair with Darling on the condition that Ebba build the lizard a fortress to live in, they backtracked through the tunnel and along the Middle Shelf. Sloshing past one of the torches, Dorrie caught sight of her thumbnail and nearly stopped walking. The patch of black had shrunk further.

"Let's see if there are any crumbs of crumbs left at the Sharpened Quill," said Marcus after they'd slipped back into the Biblioteca Marciana.

"You guys go," said Dorrie. "I'm not really hungry. I want to start looking stuff up about Critius."

When they'd disappeared up a stairway, Dorrie took a deep breath and fished Mr. Biggs's vial out from under her shirt. She couldn't lose her ability now. Not with the *History of Histories* page in the Foundation's hands. Not with the plan to get to Athens, 327 BCE depending on it. With a rapidly beating heart, she unscrewed the cap, and before she could have second thoughts, she let the remaining drops fall on her tongue. Just in case.

Chapter 15

To London, 1913

D URING HER NEXT STAYING Afloat practicum, Izel, to Dorrie's dismay, couldn't stop talking about how Lybrarian Della Porta had said that Algernon Sidney's head was going to roll again any second now.

This didn't go over very well with Mistress Daraney, who was trying to show them how to raise the sail on a little gaffe-rigged sloop.

"Once you've got your sail up, it'll be under a lot of tension," she said after sending Izel away to press sticky, black pitch into the hull of a beached boat. "You must tie off the halyard end so it stays put but can be released quickly if need be." She looped the end of the halyard rope deftly over two thick, wooden pegs embedded in the side of the boat, one pointing up and the other down. "Three times minimum. Fewer than that and you'll find the whole weight of your sail and gaffe boom falling on your head when you least expect it."

As Dorrie and Millie raced in dogged silence to see who could get her sail up first, Dorrie tortured herself with the thought that Francesco had already told Millie about the kind of danger Dorrie and Marcus had put the Lybrariad in— probably as they sat sharpening daggers together or whatever they did for father-daughter fun.

But to Dorrie's perplexed relief, Millie gave no indication she was sitting on any explosive piece of information. As the days passed, Dorrie grew less wary. Hypatia, Phillip, and Ursula treated her with the same kindness and consideration they always had, and none of the other apprentices behaved differently toward her.

The Archivist continued to pour tea. He told Dorrie stories about the many years he'd spent keeping the *History of Histories* updated, but he said nothing about the lost page. He did show Dorrie rubbings of symbols from some old caves on an island in the Mediterranean Sea that resembled a few of the symbols in Petrarch's alphabet. He explained how unknown alphabets were deciphered when no one was left who used them. "It's a Rosetta stone I need."

"What's that?" asked Dorrie.

"An artifact that has the same thought expressed in one known and one unknown language. For our purposes, one written in Petrarch's language and one in a known translatable language." He sighed. "If it exists."

By the time another week had passed, Dorrie had begun to half believe that the Archivist wasn't completely crazy.

Master Francesco and Lybrarian Della Porta were a different matter. Whenever Dorrie passed Francesco on the oyster-shell paths, he stiffened, avoiding her gaze. Though he never said a word, Dorrie sensed a shaking anger in him that made her want to run in the opposite direction. Often, when she looked up from eating in the Sharpened Quill, she found Della Porta's gaze sliding away from her. Dorrie had the distinct feeling he was keeping silent about the Foundation's possession of the page against his will.

At her next lesson with Savi, he showed her a sand-filled glove suspended from a rope that he'd rigged up against the courtyard wall. Savi's job was to release the rope and send the glove plummeting. Dorrie's job was to pin it to the wall with the point of her sword as it fell. Which she failed to do. Repeatedly. As she labored, Savi continued with his writing, stopping only to shout things like "deplorable!" and "underwhelming!" when Dorrie's aim went especially wide.

Not sure which lybrarians knew about the Foundation's possession of the *History of Histories* page, Dorrie couldn't bring herself to bring the matter up even with Savi, certain she wasn't meant to know.

Busy as she was helping Ebba build a pen for Darling in the Scooby-Doo Library, planning the trip to Athens, 327 BCE, and searching Petrarch's Library for any documents that mentioned Critius, Dorrie hardly had a thought to spare for their upcoming trip to England.

The more time Dorrie spent in the Scooby-Doo Library, the more she felt strangely at home in it, despite the killer chandelier. Rather than genuinely scary, the library now seemed more like someone's odd joke.

Ebba, who now spent all her spare moments lost in *True Spine-Tingling Ghost Stories from around the World*, didn't want to hear about Dorrie's theory. "Don't ruin it. I like it scary."

At last, the day to embark arrived, and Dorrie found herself standing side by side with Ebba in front of the London, 1913 archway wearing the clothing that Mistress Lovelace's assistant had chosen and carrying an umbrella and a drawstring bag.

Mistress Wu nervously checked them over as one of the keyhands, a tremendously tall keyhand with stooped shoulders and a shock of white hair, waited for her to complete her interrogation.

"You've got your map? Your money? Your letter of introduction?" Mistress Wu said, making little checkmarks on a wax tablet.

Dorrie and Ebba nodded vigorously.

Mistress Wu looked up. "The addresses of the seventeen branch lybrarians of England in case of emergency?"

"Regulation battle-ax? Yak-hide tent? Emergency hatbox full of beef jerky?" inquired the keyhand, tapping his foot.

Mistress Wu shot him a look. "Well, off you go then."

The keyhand held out an arm each to Ebba and Dorrie. Dorrie took it, feeling too shy to say she didn't need help. They walked toward the invisible barrier. Anticipating the warmth and the momentary sensation of being lost in a staggering amount of space, Dorrie glanced at Ebba, but she looked eager.

"Remember!" Mistress Wu called. "You are English ladies of the early twentieth century! Don't hit anyone with your umbrellas." There was a pause. "Unless absolutely necessary."

A few steps into the London Library, the keyhand released them.

"I didn't even begin to panic!" crowed Ebba, looking utterly transported.

They were in a windowless, stuffy room full of packed bookshelves with narrow aisles between. The keyhand led them down four flights of stairs every bit as narrow as the aisles and then steered them through the public reading room, where Dorrie tried not to give herself away by gawking at the patrons.

"You know where you are, I assume," said the keyhand once

205

he'd shepherded them through the library's front door and out onto the cold street.

"St. James's Square," said Dorrie, her breath a little faint as a large pair of dappled horses, their nostrils whooshing steam, pulled a lorry into view.

The keyhand readjusted the umbrella in Dorrie's hands. "A little less like a sword for best results." He disappeared back inside.

Their route to the headquarters of the National League for Opposing Woman Suffrage took them along several broad streets filled with honking motorized trucks and horse-drawn vehicles. At last, they came to the large park they'd need to cross. At its edge, a group of children played with a piece of rope, the soles of their bare feet flashing black when they ran.

They had almost made their way across the park to the street on the other side, when over the sounds of traffic, Dorrie heard a raised voice.

Ahead, a woman stood on a wooden crate, her arm lifted in a passionate gesture, a few people gathered around her. "I should no more have to explain to you why women want the vote than you should have to explain to me why you don't want a piano to fall on your head!"

Curious, Dorrie pulled Ebba closer.

"Have you not heard Lord Curzon say that the vote 'is the imperishable heritage of the human race?'" the woman cried.

"Well, I believe him on that point, and interestingly, I happen to be a human! Yet our laws ignore this truth. Right now, women who demand the vote are being held as base criminals in the Brixton and Holloway jails."

"Well, the harpies broke windows, didn't they?" shouted a young man passing by in a group of shoving, jostling friends. They all laughed uproariously.

"If someone holds your head down in a pail of water and you scratch their hands to escape, does that make you a criminal?" The woman raised a newspaper high in the air. "Mrs. Emmeline Pankhurst—lately jailed as a criminal for dealing out such scratches—intends to tell all about her experience in the next issue of the *Suffragette*!"

A cabbage sailed through the air from out of the group of laughing young men and glanced off the woman's shoulder.

"Hey!" shouted Dorrie, taking a step toward them, her hands balled into fists and her umbrella up before she could stop herself.

"Don't trouble yourself," said the woman. She raised her voice so it reached the young men who were moving on, clapping their arms around one another's shoulders and guffawing. "They throw cabbages because they don't have the brains to make arguments."

The woman winked at Dorrie. "They're frightened by what they don't understand." She plucked a flyer from an open valise at her feet and held it out to Dorrie and Ebba. "Come to a rally at Hyde Park to end the jailing of suffragists as criminals!"

Dorrie and Ebba glanced at each other. Dorrie shook her head shyly, and then they hurried past the suffragist, out through the gate, and onto the wide avenue.

"Master Casanova would get apoplectic if he heard we showed up at the headquarters of the National League for Opposing Woman Suffrage with our bags full of suffrage flyers," said Ebba.

Dorrie stopped to consult their map. "It should be right across the street."

It was. A sign above a handsome bay window spelled out "National League for Opposing Woman Suffrage." In front of the building, a table stood covered with pamphlets and flyers.

Holding hands and dodging traffic, Dorrie and Ebba darted across the street. After taking a moment to smooth their clothing and readjust their hats, they pushed open the door.

The room that lay on the other side was large and carpeted and full of highly polished furniture. A banner hung across the back of the room. It read: *GIVE LADIES PROTECTION, NOT VOTES.*

A woman dressed in black rose from a group of people sitting at the back of the room and came to greet them. "I'm Mrs. Richardson, the manager here. May I help you?"

"I'm Dorothea Rathcliffe-Exley of Rhodesia," said Dorrie, feeling silly.

There was a faint stir at the table and a fluttery whisper of "'Rathcliffe-Exley' did she say?"

Ebba held out the letter. "We've brought a letter of introduction from Mrs. Humphrey Ward for Mary, Countess of Ilchester."

"Why, that's me," said a heavyset woman with a great number of rings on her fat fingers. She bustled over, giving Mrs. Richardson the choice of moving out of her path or being injured. The last thing she seemed to need was protection.

Dorrie groped for her next lines. "With our parents' permission, we've come to volunteer for the anti-suffrage cause."

To Dorrie's disgust, the Countess of Ilchester turned and beamed at those still sitting at the table. "Isn't that darling?"

"Inspiring," said a young woman at the table. She had a heart-shaped face, and her arms were encased in long, white gloves. "Two girls on the cusp of womanhood, firm in their abhorrence of women's suffrage."

"Well said, Lady Agnes," said the countess. She smiled at Dorrie. "We're happy to have your help. We have a benefit tea planned for next week and hundreds of rosettes to make for our supporters." She fluttered her hand toward a closed door. "Your lady's maid can hang up your coat."

Dorrie stared at the countess, shocked into speechlessness by her mistake.

Ebba rose to the occasion. She dropped a graceful curtsy and smiled prettily. "Oh, what a funny mistake. I'm not the lady's maid. I'm Ebba Risien, also of Rhodesia. I'm visiting my uncle James Risien Russell, a physician here in London. Ms. Rathcliffe-Exley is our guest."

Now it was the countess's turn to momentarily lose the power of speech. Her cheeks went pink. "Why, of course. I-I do beg your pardon."

Dorrie and Ebba soon found themselves sitting at a table between Lady Agnes and a man with the thinnest mustache Dorrie had ever seen.

"And this is Mr. Sacks-Sandbottom, our tireless secretary," the countess said, indicating the mustachioed man.

"Mr. Sacks-Sandbottom is wonderfully in demand," said Lady Agnes. "Besides acting as our esteemed secretary, he also acts as a financial advisor to Lady Whitcomb."

From the approving glitter in Lady Agnes's eyes, Dorrie got the sense that this meant something wonderful. She smiled as though impressed herself.

"My aunt is a distant cousin of the Rathcliffe-Biddles of Kent," said Lady Agnes. "Do you by any chance summer with any of the Upchuck-Ridmores?"

"Not that I remember," said Dorrie, in serious danger of bursting into laughter.

"Perhaps you see the Archley-Smeggs occasionally?" said

Mr. Sacks-Sandbottom to Ebba. "Fine family. Adore lion hunting. Every one a crack shot."

Not daring to look at Ebba, Dorrie silently hoped her friend hadn't packed her slingshot.

For several hours, Dorrie and Ebba worked dutifully at constructing rosettes. As Dorrie reached for a fresh sheet of paper, Lady Agnes suddenly jumped from her seat.

"Oh, that monstrous creature is back again!" she said, pointing through the window.

Craning her neck, Dorrie saw that across the street, the suffragist from the park had come into view, carrying her suitcase and box. She set them down.

"The nerve of her," said Lady Agnes, jerking the curtains closed. "Setting up right in front of our headquarters!"

"She deserves a turn setting up in Newgate Prison," said Mr. Sacks-Sandbottom.

"Why?" asked Dorrie. "What did she do?"

"Twice now," said Lady Agnes, sitting down with a sniff, "she's stolen freshly printed copies of our newspaper, the *Anti-Suffrage Review*, right off the doorstep."

Dorrie felt Ebba step on her foot under the table.

"We believe," said Mrs. Richardson as she filled a basket with rosettes.

"Oh, I'm quite certain it's her." Lady Agnes wrinkled her nose as though she'd just opened an outhouse door. "I found out she belongs to that lunatic window-breaking, building-burning, letterbox-destroying Women's Social and Political Union."

There was a great deal of tsking and head-shaking around the table.

"Did anybody actually see her take them?" asked Ebba.

"No," said Mr. Sacks-Sandbottom, the word seeming to come through his nose. "But the circumstantial evidence is quite compelling. Isn't that so, Mrs. Richardson?"

"Well…" said Mrs. Richardson as though she would really rather not say. "The printer always delivers the new edition of the *Anti-Suffrage Review* on Monday evenings sometime after I've closed up here. On two separate Tuesday mornings, I arrived and found the newspapers gone."

"And both times, that mad banshee had spent the Monday carrying on across the street," said Lady Agnes. "On the last several Mondays, she didn't make an appearance, and no one stole the newspapers."

Plying her pair of scissors crookedly, Dorrie glanced at Ebba.

"But no matter," said Mr. Sacks-Sandbottom. "Lady Agnes has explained the situation to her uncle and our benefactor, Lord Cromer."

"He's promised a proper response," said Lady Agnes. "Those WSPU outragers will be quite sorry for taking such an action against us."

Closing the door of the League's headquarters behind them

a few hours later, Dorrie and Ebba let out twin whistles of relief into the chilly dusk.

"Don't forget! Two weeks from Monday. 11:00 a.m. sharp to help us get ready for the benefit tea!" Lady Agnes had called out as they'd put on their coats.

Now as they waited to cross the street, Dorrie looked down at the pamphlet Countess Mary had pressed into her hand. *Against Women's Suffrage: Some Reasons* by Grace Saxon Mills. She looked at Ebba. "Not much of a title."

Ebba snorted and thumbed through her copy. Affecting Lady Agnes's tones, she read out loud: "'Because women's suffrage is based on the idea of the equality of the sexes and tends to establish those competitive relations that will destroy chivalrous consideration.'"

Now it was Dorrie's turn to snort. She tried one: "'Because past legislation in Parliament shows that the interests of women are perfectly safe in the hands of men.'"

"Ugh," said Ebba.

Seeing the suffragist on the other side of the street, Dorrie lowered her voice. "Do you think she took the newspapers?"

"I hope not," said Ebba. "I like her."

"Me too," said Dorrie, jamming *Some Reasons* into her bag. They crossed the street.

"Ah," said the woman, throwing back the hood of her cloak. Her eyes twinkled. "The young suffragists who watched me nearly lose my nose to a cabbage today!" She was repacking her valise.

Dorrie looked nervously back at the anti-suffrage headquarters, but the curtains were still drawn.

The suffragist waved her hand over the suitcase. "It's all free. Take one if you'd like." She pointed to a pamphlet called *Fourteen Reasons for Supporting Women's Suffrage*. "One of my favorites."

Dorrie took it. "Thank you."

"How about you?" she said, handing Ebba a newspaper. "Can't go wrong with the *Suffragette*." She closed the suitcase smartly. "I'm Annie Knox, by the way."

Dorrie and Ebba introduced themselves, sticking to first names.

"Off to earn my coppers and pence," said Annie, picking up the suitcase. "My way is through the park. Yours?"

"The same," said Ebba quickly. "Thanks for the newspaper."

"Hot off the presses," said Annie, grinning. "My sister helps edit it."

They turned into the park.

Dorrie took a chance. "Have you ever...ever read the *Anti-Suffrage Review*?"

"Ha," said Annie, swinging the valise. "Dull, infuriating drivel! But yes, I do read it. I like to know what the anti-suffragists are thinking. Or refusing to think."

"Hot chestnuts!" called a young boy coming down the

path from the other direction. A sweet, rich smell tantalized Dorrie's nose.

"Manna!" declared Annie, stopping. "We suffragists are chilled to the bone and want a pound, please!" She dug in her cloak pocket while the boy, his bare hands blue with cold, scooped a mess of chestnuts into a newspaper cone.

"Oh, we can—" began Ebba.

"My treat," said Annie.

"Thank you," said Dorrie and Ebba as they popped the first ones in their mouths, glorying in the chestnuts' heat as much as the rich taste.

Annie lifted the cone high. "To the vote! And long underwear!"

Dorrie and Ebba giggled.

"And the end of imprisoning suffragists," Annie added more soberly.

"Have you ever been to prison?" asked Dorrie.

"No," said Annie. "But I have another sister who's been to Holloway three times. She's there now."

Dorrie stared at Annie, thinking back to all that Lady Agnes had said. "She didn't…she hasn't…"

"Burned down any buildings?" said Annie. "Thrown an ax at a prime minister?"

Ebba's eyes widened. "Someone did that?"

"Yes, but not my sister. She's in prison for cutting a telegraph line. She did it because she feels women have waited too

215

long for our rights. Like Mrs. Pankhurst, my sister believes that petitioning our representatives for them has failed."

"I'm…I'm sorry," stammered Dorrie.

They had exited the park. Gas lamps winked in the darkness along the street.

"Women are going to get the vote," said Annie firmly as they crossed the street. "We just have to help the public understand why it's just and important. The next issue of the *Suffragette* is going to make a big splash, what with Mrs. Pankhurst telling her own imprisonment story."

They had stopped in front of a store window with "McAndrews Laundry" painted on it.

"To the ramparts," said Annie, opening the door. A bell jingled. "Lovely to have met you. Get home safe."

Slowly, they walked in the direction of the Spoke Library.

"Now I really hope she isn't the thief," said Ebba.

Dorrie swung her bag thoughtfully. "And I really want to know exactly what kind of proper response Lord Cromer has planned for the suffragists."

Chapter 16

Seals

THE DAY AFTER THEIR return from London, Dorrie and Ebba went back to the main reference room fully intending to get out materials that might help them discover the identity of the *Anti-Suffrage Review* thief, only to find themselves leaving with books they thought might help them find out more about Lord Cromer's intentions.

During the next week, they spent hours sitting in front of the attics' fire, looking through the indexes for "Lord Cromer" and "National League for Opposing Woman Suffrage" and "Annie Knox" and "the *Suffragette*."

"I don't believe it!" Dorrie said suddenly one quiet evening.

Ebba, shrieked, jumping as though she'd been shot. She closed *True Spine-Tingling Ghost Stories from around the World.* "Sorry. I was at a really creepy part."

"You're always at a really creepy part," Mathilde said irritably from across the room where she sat at a table, covered with the ink she'd just spilled. "Do you ever put that thing down?"

"Listen!" said Dorrie, her voice tight with excitement. "In 1913, the Home Office—"

Ebba set her book aside. "What's the Home Office?"

Dorrie scanned the page. "It doesn't say exactly. We'll have to look it up. It's some kind of department of the government, but just...listen... 'In 1913, the Home Office, at a suggestion from Lords Cromer and Curzon, made a formal threat against subscribers of the *Suffragette*, informing them that it was now illegal to subscribe to the newspaper and they'd be charged with a crime for doing it.'"

"For reading something?" said Ebba outraged. "Oh, those, those...!"

"Rats" said Dorrie. "Just say it. They're—"

"—poison ivy leaves," Ebba said firmly.

"But this part's the worst," said Dorrie. "'In late winter of 1913—'"

Ebba's eyes widened. "That's now, out in the London, 1913 wheren!"

"'—The Home Office tried to suppress the *Suffragette* entirely. Sidney Granville Drew, the managing director of Victoria House Printing Company, the newspaper's printer, was arrested.'"

Dorrie and Ebba stared at one another.

"That's got to be what Lady Agnes was talking about when she said Lord Cromer had promised a 'proper response,'" said Ebba.

"There's more!" said Dorrie, excitement making her hands shake.

"Another printer was engaged, but the Home Office arrested the second printer. In the end, no printer in London was permitted to print the *Suffragette*."

Dorrie threw the book aside. "Okra slime sandwiches!"

"I've tried to warn you," said Mathilde primly.

"Can you believe it?" cried Dorrie. "We're supposed to protect their stupid newspapers from being stolen while they're off figuring out how to keep the *Suffragette* out of print."

"Maybe we should tell the Lybrariad what we've found out," said Ebba, reaching for one of the baked potatoes Mathilde had read out for them earlier.

Dorrie felt a surge of excitement at that idea, which then fizzled. "The Lybrariad hardly has enough available lybrarians to take care of the most urgent missions." She imagined the suffragist on her soapbox. "But maybe we could at least warn Annie."

As the field trip drew closer, Dorrie and Ebba and Marcus spent more time in the Scooby-Doo Library, working out their respective plans to visit Critius's house and talk Aristotle into dropping his charges against Timotheus. It didn't take much reading about Critius before Dorrie realized that she was not

a fan. He had been one of the Thirty Tyrants who had terror-
ized Athens, killing people left and right during the year they'd
taken power in 404 BCE.

Their lair continued to surprise them. One day, when Ebba
lifted the stuffed vulture up, intending to place it near Darling's
pen for company, another of the locked doors had flown open
to the sound of a blood-curdling scream. Beyond it, they'd
found a decrepit bathroom with a fake mummy sprawled in
a claw-footed tub, along with a sink faucet that dripped something that looked convincingly like blood.

"How exactly are you going to convince Aristotle to drop
his lawsuit?" Ebba asked Marcus later in the week, while she
and Dorrie pored over a large map of ancient Athens they'd
opened on the wide expanse of empty floor between the back
of the couch and the spinning wall.

"I will use the word 'ergo.' A lot," Marcus said from where
he sat making a racket at the organ while Darling, banished
from her favorite napping spot atop the keys, glowered at him
from her pen.

"Ergo?" repeated Dorrie.

"It's a logical argument word," said Marcus, crashing his
fingers among the keys. "He'll love it. When are you going to
get hold of that skipkey?"

Dorrie stared at the little square on the map that represented the Lyceum, Aristotle's philosophy academy, where

the skipkey would land them. "I can't take it *too* soon or the Archivist will be more likely to notice." Even as she said the words, Dorrie knew that she hadn't yet taken it because she was feeling increasingly uncomfortable about going behind the Archivist's back.

Their conversation had ended when Marcus played a particularly funereal chord, and a very large piece of the floor had simply dropped away on a hinge, nearly pitching Ebba into the dark fathomless depths of a stone-walled chute. After he'd found another chord to make the trapdoor rise into place again, Marcus was also banished from the organ.

In the midst of all the planning and researching, the time Dorrie spent on the water became even more of a relieving pleasure. She loved the feeling of skimming over the waves in one of Mistress Daraney's little sailboats. She loved swimming from one side of the cove to the other, lost in the simple pleasure of making her way through the water. And it didn't hurt that Dorrie learned all of Mistress Daraney's knots faster than Millie did.

Two days before the field trip, sitting in Hypatia's practicum, Dorrie was entirely preoccupied. Near the close of their time together, Hypatia called her name. With a start, Dorrie looked up to find the other students staring at her and Hypatia holding up a worn white book with a picture of three diamonds balanced atop one another on its cover.

"I was saying, now that we've discussed the first six principles of the Lybrariad, you might want to look at *The Foundation: Essential Dictumsand* and compare."

Mortified, Dorrie nodded.

At last, the day of the field trip arrived.

"I can't believe the Lybrariad's still letting us go," Izel said as the apprentices waited at the Tyre, 327 BCE archway for one of the keyhands to arrive. She lowered her voice so Mistress Wu couldn't hear. "Lybrarian Della Porta says things are much worse than the lybrarians are telling us."

Dorrie pretended she hadn't heard and calmed her nerves by putting her hand on the little leather pouch she'd been issued. Tied around her waist, it held a few coins for lunch and the skipkey she'd taken from the Archivist's chest.

After warnings from Mistress Wu about the unsteady footing in the Tyre Spoke Library due to the fact that it was in actuality a worn-out Phoenician merchant's ship called the *Hura*, the keyhand took them through in pairs. There was a regrettable bit of shoving, pushing, and treading on borrowed chiton hems as the apprentices tried to stay upright on the tilting floor, but at last, they were all in.

A woman, her dark wig askew, stood beside a hatch ladder, an electric sort of delight on her face.

"Welcome! Welcome!" she called, holding out a tray full of fruit chunks stabbed through with what looked like a rough version of toothpicks. "I'm Jalileh, the Tyre Spoke Lybrarian. I'm so *very* glad you're here to peruse our small but important collection."

Dorrie, Marcus, and Ebba eyed each other. They hadn't factored a tour into their plans.

Mistress Wu looked caught out. "Ah…hello there, Jalileh. I'm afraid we're just passing through today. Must row directly over to Tyre."

Jalileh's face all but collapsed on itself. "Oh, I see…"

"I don't think she gets many visitors," whispered Mathilde.

"Are you sure?" pleaded Jalileh. "The *Hura* is really a beautiful Spoke Library, even if she is small and isolated. Not that I'm unhappy with my assignment here. I mean, you find things to appreciate." She laughed a little maniacally. "Let's see, there's the total freedom I enjoy from the petty demands of patrons, the unrelenting smell of fish, the unremitting silence…"

"Jalileh…" began Mistress Wu.

"Not that I don't have adventures," Jalileh interrupted brightly. "One night, the anchor came free in a storm, and I drifted a good ways across the Mediterranean Sea. I heard later that inside Petrarch's Library, the Tyre archway temporarily became the Kourian archway, then the Paphos archway, and then the archway to a whole string of other town the *Hura* passed while I slept. Her shoulders shook with laughter. "I didn't wake up until we got to Xerxesville." She looked dreamy for a moment. "I should have gone ashore and visited. I really need to get out more and—"

"Jalileh," Mistress Wu shot out more forcefully, "we really must move on."

Jalileh plunged her hand into an urn and pulled out a scroll. "Not even time for a read-aloud of *The Odyssey*?"

"Everyone up the ladder," said Mistress Wu firmly.

"You simply must let me show you the deck cleats," said Jalileh, hurling herself at the ladder and beginning to climb. "Did I mention that the *Hura*'s prow is carved in the shape of a bird?"

Dorrie, Marcus, and Ebba hung back until Izel, the last one up the ladder, had disappeared.

"Hey!" Marcus called up the ladder. "Dorrie's not feeling well."

Instantly, Mistress Wu's head appeared in the hatchway, framed in blue sky.

Dorrie did her best to look sickly.

"I told her not to eat that mushroom," said Marcus.

"What mushroom?" asked Mistress Wu sharply.

"A *Gyromitra esculenta*. Looks sort of like a purple brain. I learned about it in Egeria's foraging practicum last quarter."

"I ate some of it too," Ebba said with an impressive tremor in her voice, "and I feel kind of faint."

Mistress Wu looked of a mind to possibly leap back down into the ship's hold.

"They'll be fine!" said Marcus quickly. "But they should go lie down before the confusion sets in." He turned to Dorrie. "Do. You Have. The. Strength. To. Get. Us. Back?"

Dorrie nodded.

Marcus looked back at Mistress Wu. "I can take them to Ursula." He sighed. "I'm not really in the mood for a field trip anyway."

"Oh, you poor ducks," said Mistress Wu. "Well, all right then."

The moment Mistress Wu's head disappeared, Dorrie dug the skipkey out of her pouch. She took hold of the metal pin the way she'd seen the Archivist do. "No matter what, don't let go of me."

Marcus and Ebba each caught hold. Stilling her breath, Dorrie flicked the metal pin upward.

The two halves of the skipkey came together with the faint click of magnets meeting, and the sound of the ocean ceased as though it had been unplugged.

Dorrie didn't feel as though she'd moved—more like while she had stood perfectly still, the world had slid a new stage set around her. The ship was gone, and they were standing in a cool room full of scrolls arranged neatly in cubbyholes on the walls. "We made it," she said with relief.

"Step one. Locate Aristotle," said Marcus. "And remember," he said with far too much satisfaction, "I'm a thoughtful young man doing some philosophy school shopping, and you are my slaves."

Dorrie and Ebba rolled their eyes.

"Yes, well, since it's ancient Athens and we're girls, we can't be much else if we want to walk around freely during daylight hours, can we?" said Ebba.

They peeked through the nearest door and saw that it led out to a courtyard lined with colonnades with a plashing fountain in the middle. A young man was walking slowly toward them, with his nose in a scroll.

"Excuse me," said Marcus. "Where can I find Aristotle?"

"He's lecturing in the auditorium," he replied and pointed to a half-open door across the courtyard. Dorrie, Marcus, and Ebba settled themselves on a bench beside it to wait. From inside the auditorium, Dorrie heard a deep, sonorous voice talking, then appreciative laughter. A man in a short, dirty chiton was lounging against a nearby wall. He eyed them curiously.

"Aristotle," he called a moment later as a man with thick, dark hair streaked with gray and a mounding beard emerged from the auditorium, along with a flood of students. Dorrie looked nervously from Ebba to Marcus as Aristotle gave the lounging man what looked like coins and took a large sack in exchange. Turning, he started down the colonnade.

Marcus sprang off the bench and hurried after him. "Excuse me, sir," he called as Dorrie and Ebba jumped up to follow.

"Yes?" Aristotle shot out without stopping.

"May I talk to you for a minute, please?"

"Ha!" Aristotle said without stopping. "No one ever talks to me for a minute. Especially not on a day when I have a rare hour to spend on my categorizing project before my next blasted lecture."

"It's about a musician named Timotheus."

Aristotle put on the brakes hard, and they all nearly plowed into him.

"Timotheus, the banger-outer of cacophonous rhythms?" said Aristotle, his face mottling. "Robber of sleep? Thief of serenity?"

Marcus blinked. "Er...possibly."

Aristotle pushed through a door into what Dorrie took to be some kind of study or laboratory. The shelves held scrolls and tablets, carefully organized collections of shells and rocks and skulls and feathers, and what looked like thin sections sawed out of trees. There were teeth and horns, dried grasses arranged by height, and a whole tray of things that looked like pinecones.

He dropped the sack on a table. "And?"

Marcus was most of the way through his very logical argument as to why Aristotle should drop his charges against Timotheus—and had just used the word "ergo" for the fifth time—when out of the sack poked a small, sleek head with protuberant brown eyes and a set of twitching whiskers.

"A seal," Ebba cried out. It wiggled the rest of itself out of the bag and barked sharply. "A baby seal!" Quite forgetting herself and their situation, she fell upon it. "Oh, what's its name?"

Aristotle lifted a wooden basin from beneath the table and set it down with a clatter. "You might as well ask me where the rays of yesterday's sun have gone." His face took on a faraway look. "I wish someone would ask me that."

"Right," said Marcus, "but about Timotheus. As a citizen of Athens, I have to protest your suit against him. Your charge of hubris is based, in fact, not on the volume of Timotheus's drumming but on the fact that you don't happen to like his *style* of drumming, ergo—"

The seal barked again and nuzzled at Ebba's face.

She stroked its head. "I think it's hungry."

"Not for long," said Aristotle, rattling the contents of a cupboard as he searched for something.

"Oh, may I feed it?" Ebba cried.

The rattling stopped, and Aristotle stood with several knives in his hands. "I'm afraid you've gotten the wrong impression."

Ebba's eyes widened as understanding seemed to dawn on her. "Nooooo!"

"Come, come," said Aristotle, dropping the knives on the table and beginning to rummage in a basket of scrolls. "I want to know how a seal is made and in what ways it is like and unlike a man. I must go inside to find out."

"Well, go inside a dead one then!" cried Ebba.

"That's what I intend to do, you silly girl. It won't feel a thing."

"She's not silly!" said Dorrie.

"And you know what else isn't silly?" said Marcus. "The rest of the very logical argument I'd like to make about why you should drop your charges against Timotheus."

"Timotheus will have ample opportunity to make his arguments before the jury," Aristotle said.

"And I want to go on record saying that I think it's completely unfair that he has to go up against you in the courtroom. You're a philosopher! You're used to making arguments. Timotheus is a musician."

"And this seal has a right to a life," said Ebba, her eyes blazing.

Aristotle raised an eyebrow. "I see your point."

"You do?" said Ebba, her face brightening.

Aristotle shot her a look. "Not yours." He jerked his chin toward Marcus. "His." He pulled down a tray of empty bowls from a shelf. "If Timotheus is incapable of making sound arguments, then he should hire an orator to write up a defense of his position. Surely he can memorize something someone else has written."

"That's a thing?" said Marcus.

"Sounds like more cheating," muttered Dorrie.

"Well, I think it is," said Aristotle, now rummaging through a basket full of clay pots. "But it's perfectly legal. Surely you're aware that half of lazy Athens does it." He gave up his search. "Zeus alive, I specifically told my assistant I needed a jar of green ink."

He headed for the door.

Out of the corner of her eye, Dorrie saw Ebba's hands creeping toward the seal.

"Well, where can Timotheus find an orator then?" Marcus asked, chasing after Aristotle.

Ebba's hands dropped to her sides as Aristotle spun around to look sharply at Marcus. "In the Courts District. Where else?"

"Of course," said Marcus. "But what I really want to know, Aristotle of Stagira, is do *you* know the exact location of the Courts District?"

Aristotle raised both eyebrows this time. "Adjacent to the agora, oh citizen," he said putting an undue amount of emphasis on "citizen." "And a piece of advice: If you decide you must have a fried fish sandwich while you're there, do *not* buy it from Tacitus of Macedonia." He shivered as if recalling a horrendous experience and disappeared into the colonnade.

Marcus chased after him as Ebba scooped up the seal.

"No!" Dorrie hissed at Ebba. "What are you doing? We can't just…take him! We're supposed to be inconspicuous! We still have to find Critius's house."

"Well, I can't leave him here," Ebba said fiercely as she shoved the little seal down the front of her chiton.

"All right, all right," said Dorrie. She pulled Ebba, now considerably more plump, over to the door and peered out. Aristotle and Marcus were arguing a little farther down the colonnade. Not too far away in the other direction, Dorrie saw a gap in the wall that encircled the Lyceum's buildings. Beyond it, she glimpsed the bustle of a street and headed for it, towing Ebba along.

"I think we should go, *master*," Dorrie yelled back at Marcus.

"Fine," he said, backing away from Aristotle. "But I'm not going to let Timotheus be the baby seal under your philosophical knife. Did I mention that he's the sole support of six younger siblings and one of them lost a hand in a fishing accident?"

"Three times," said Aristotle.

Dorrie, Marcus, and Ebba tumbled into the street. Marcus stuck his head back through the gap. "I'm going to find him the best orator money can buy!"

CHAPTER 17

DEALS

WHAT DO YOU MEAN you're going to find an orator?" Dorrie asked as soon as they were out of earshot.

"Well, you heard Aristotle," said Marcus. "It's the only way to save Timotheus. Did I mention he's the sole provider for—"

Dorrie punched him in the shoulder, unable to restrain herself. "We don't have time! The whole point of coming was to find Critius's house."

"Your whole point," said Marcus. "Mine is to help Timotheus."

"So now we're supposed to go shopping for an orator!"

"Relax," said Marcus. "Those old maps showed that Critius's house is just on the other side of the agora. Two birds, one stone." He looked darkly at Ebba. "Anyway, I think that's the least of our problems."

"I'm sorry!" she cried, holding on tightly to the shifting bulge inside her chiton. "But I couldn't leave it there to be carved into pieces!"

After a twenty-minute walk, they found themselves at the outskirts of the open square where people were selling goods and services from various stalls shielded from the sun by cloths stretched tight over poles. A heady smell of cooking garlic wafted toward them. Everywhere, crowds of people eddied basketfuls of vegetables, bread, and other purchases.

Marcus shaded his eyes and peered around. "I better find Timotheus's stall and see if he'll go for the orator idea."

Dorrie took a deep breath. "Okay, but—"

The seal barked sharply and stuck its whiskery nose out of the top of Ebba's chiton.

Ebba adjusted her hold. "I think he really is hungry."

Dorrie closed her eyes. "All right, Ebba and I will look for milk or sardines or something for the seal. Marcus, you go talk to Timotheus." She saw a man hauling a bucket of water out of a well. "We'll all meet back at that well."

Dorrie, Marcus, and Ebba had thought that the clothing they'd checked out for the Tyre field trip looked close enough to the pictures they'd found of clothes worn in Aristotle's Athens, but people eyed them curiously as they walked past stalls full of ribbons, honey, strongly scented myrtle wreaths, and great sacks of wool.

"That's what we need," said Ebba, stopping. Above a stall, a painted cloth banner showed a picture of a goat and her kid frolicking. A woman brushed by them with a jug full of frothy white liquid.

The seal began to struggle again. Dorrie and Ebba joined the line in front of the stall.

"Next," said a voice. It was their turn. An old man, his eyes bright in a mass of wrinkles, looked at them expectantly.

"Some milk, please," said Ebba, trying to keep the seal still.

"Put your jug up here."

Dorrie stopped digging for her coins. "Our jug?"

The goat-milk seller sucked on his teeth. "Unless you want me to pour the milk into your hands."

"Here," said a voice from the next stall over.

Dorrie turned. A woman about her mother's age was holding out a jug with a piece chipped out of the rim. In her other hand, she held a wax tablet—the kind that Master Callamachus preferred for taking notes. She passed the jug to the goat-milk seller. "They can have this one."

"Thank you," said Dorrie and Ebba together.

The woman jabbed a stylus into the messy knot of her hair, where several others stuck out. She smiled wryly. "Oh, with that chip, I was never going to sell it anyway."

Dorrie looked more closely at the woman's stall. A sign hanging above the woman's head read "Kalliope's Erstwhile

Treasures." The stall was choked with piles of dusty baskets, chairs with missing bits, and sagging tables. Broken crockery covered the floor and tables. A stack of wooden bowls looked as though they were actively rotting.

Ebba appeared at Dorrie's elbow, trying hard not to spill the jug of milk as the seal thrashed and made mewling noises.

Kalliope stared. "Whatever is going on in your chiton?"

Before Ebba could answer, the seal poked his whole head and a flipper out.

Kalliope laughed out loud.

"He's lost his mother," Ebba explained as some of the precious milk spilled.

"Wait a minute." Kalliope rifled through the crate of rotting bowls. "Aha!" She held up a leather bag with a little wooden spout coming out of it. "I knew I had one. Here, give me the milk."

In a moment, she had filled the bag. "You can come out of the sun and feed it in the stall if you'd like."

"Oh, thank you!" cried Ebba.

Dorrie quickly helped Kalliope unearth a stool and a chair, which required finding new places for an empty dagger scabbard, a bronze platter with a big dent in it, and half a marble head. Dorrie took an instant dislike to the bust's one white, staring eyeball and vaguely cruel lips. "Glad I don't have to look at your whole head."

"Ah, Critius. Not someone I'd want to have to dinner either," said Kalliope, shifting a bucket of pottery shards.

The head nearly tumbled out of Dorrie's hands. She glanced at Ebba and then back at Kalliope. "Did you say Critius?"

Kalliope gaped at Dorrie. "You know who I'm talking about?"

Dorrie set the bust on a small table. "One of the Thirty Tyrants and all that."

Kalliope ushered Ebba and the seal into the excavated chair. "You must have very enlightened parents to have taught you any history."

"Very," said Dorrie quickly, remembering that in ancient Athens, formal education was only for boys.

Kalliope pointed to a crate. "I bought a whole pile of things that a tramp dug out of the ruins of Critius's house. Never should have. Haven't been able to unload any of it. Not once customers hear about where I got it. I really have to stop telling them."

Dorrie stared at the crate. "Critius's house is ruined?"

"Oh, yes, it collapsed ages ago. It's that pile of stone near the sandal shop on Panathenaic Way. There's been legal squabbling over the property for approximately forever, and about five years ago, the house just got tired of its sad, empty life and gave up."

Just then, Dorrie spied Marcus wandering by, looking panicked.

"Over here!" called Dorrie.

Marcus charged over. "You said to meet at the well!"

"We had a feeding emergency," said Dorrie. "Did you find Timotheus?"

"Oh, yes," said Marcus. "And he'd be willing to use an orator-written defense, but he's flat broke. Also? He's an emotional mess. He could barely hold on to the zither he was trying to repair. No wonder he was going to fail so..." He broke off, noticing Kalliope for the first time as she rose to help a customer.

Dorrie was hardly listening, impatient to look through the crate of Critius's things.

"I checked out the orators over at the courts and they're super-expensive. We're talking piles of drachmas. But listen to this." He lowered his voice. "I heard a rumor about a woman who writes orations under a fake name who might do one for cheap."

"Why a fake name?" asked Ebba.

"Because only men are legally allowed to write them or something, yada yada, like that," said Marcus. "I say we try to find her."

Kalliope, who'd finished with her customer, turned back to them. "I hear she sells secondhand junk on the side."

While Marcus explained the situation to Kalliope and Ebba tried to rock the seal to sleep, Dorrie pounced on the crate again. It wasn't until she'd taken nearly everything out that something interesting caught her eye. It was a stone box with the jagged-edged remains of a hinged lid.

A piece of an etched design or word could be traced on the remaining bit of the lid. It looked like the top of a letter *A* or the outline of a steeply pitched roof. It tugged at Dorrie's memory. Suddenly, she remembered Hypatia holding up her copy of *The Foundation: Essential Dictums*. Dorrie sucked in her breath. Three stacked diamonds had adorned the cover. She traced her finger along the etched lines, stopping at the rough edge created by the break. Judging from the size of the box and the bit of design left, she thought three stacked diamonds would have fit on the lid perfectly when it was whole.

"Can I buy this?" Dorrie blurted out.

They hurried out of the agora a few minutes later.

Marcus was beaming. "I can't believe Kalliope is letting us pay her later."

"I can't believe we found something that might connect Critius and the Foundation," said Dorrie.

When they reached the Lyceum, the paths were empty of people, and they scuttled quickly back to the door that led to the Spoke Library. They were congratulating themselves on their good luck when the seal woke and began writhing violently, forcing Ebba to bend over nearly double and clutch her middle to keep the seal from falling to the ground.

"C'mon," urged Dorrie, the skipkey in her hand. Marcus was already holding the door open.

As Ebba staggered toward them, Aristotle and the man

who'd given him the seal emerged from a room farther down the colonnade.

Dorrie's heart lurched. Grabbing hold of Ebba, she hauled her inside.

"She just had to have the fish sandwich," Marcus called out to Aristotle before diving in after them.

Chapter 18
Dirty Laundry

WOULD YOU QUIT TRYING to have the last word!" Dorrie said furiously as she fumbled with the skipkey. The ship's hold engulfed them again. From the deck above, Dorrie could hear the voices of the returning apprentices. Grabbing hold of one another, Dorrie, Marcus, and Ebba burst through the archway back into Petrarch's Library.

"We can't let them see us!" said Dorrie.

They made a dash for the Middle Shelf. No time to bother with umbrellas, they arrived at the Scooby-Doo Library, sweating, soaked, and smelling of seal.

They decided that simply walking up to Francesco and gifting him with Dorrie's discovery wasn't really an option. Not if Dorrie wanted to remain an apprentice.

"The box might not even have anything to do with the

Foundation," Ebba said, struggling with the seal as Dorrie lifted the vulture off its shelf. Darling's jaws snapped hungrily. Ebba stowed the seal in the tub. "You can't risk your apprenticeship on a guess."

"All right. Fine," Dorrie said. "I'll wait until the coast is clear and leave it by his office door with an anonymous note. When he sees it, he'll have to take Lybrarian Della Porta's suspicion about Critius's house seriously."

While Marcus and Ebba fetched buckets of seawater to fill it, Dorrie set to work. Marcus insisted she write the note with her left hand to disguise her identity.

In it, she explained that the box had once belonged to Critius, shared her theory that the lid might have once borne the symbol of the Foundation, and suggested that a search of Critius's house in Athens, 399 BCE might be a good idea.

When she finished, it was dinnertime. Dorrie tucked the note into the basket, grateful that the corridors would likely be empty. Not daring to use the spinning wall, she set off for Francesco's office the long way around. She had just turned into the corridor that led to Francesco's tower when she heard raised voices behind her. Though the box was hidden in the basket, Dorrie broke into a soft run, not wanting to be seen.

"I want to know now!" Millie's voice rang out before Dorrie was halfway to the tower door.

Panic shot through Dorrie, and she ducked into a narrow

opening marked by rough wooden posts. She found herself in a tiny room lined floor to ceiling with shelves full of great, carved wooden blocks. There was no door to close. The only place to hide was behind a tall stand upon which rested several of the carved blocks. Dorrie dove for it.

Dorrie dove behind a tall, narrow stand, upon which several of the carved blocks rested.

"Please stop harrying me," came Francesco's voice from the corridor.

From her new position, Dorrie noticed another narrow doorless opening. Francesco spoke again: "Petrarch's Library is facing a crisis right now, Millie. I don't have time to give you proper answers and explanations right—"

"I just want to know my real parents' names," said Millie.

A short intense silence followed, during which Dorrie tried not to breathe, too afraid of being found to sprint for the other door.

"Millie…" Francesco said, his voice strained with feeling. "By any measure that matters, you are my own true daughter. I am your own true father who loves you fiercely."

"Then answer me!" Millie demanded.

"I can't right now," Francesco said, a note of pleading in his voice. "I'm late to meet Hypatia, and I still need to find a few things in my office."

"You're always too busy to talk about this," said Millie.

"I've told you about your mother," stammered Francesco.

"Just the vaguest details!" cried Millie. "That she came from a small village. That her name was Sophia. That she had brown eyes and liked the woods. That she wrote poetry. I can tell you're hiding something from me!"

"Enough," barked Francesco. "After we find the Foundation's workshop. After we stop them from remaking Whim's Gift, there'll be time to talk properly. Now be my strong girl. Attend to your duties with Callamachus. Attend to your practicums." Dorrie heard the creak of leather as though Francesco had turned to go.

"If you love me, then you'll tell me," said Millie.

"Please, Millie, I don't—"

"They're my parents, I have a right to know about them. You can't keep me closer by pretending they don't exist," said Millie, her voice cracking. "You taught me to never answer a question with a lie, and I'm asking you. Who is my father?"

"Millie," said Francesco, a pained huskiness in his voice. "You're too young. You're too—"

"Tell me."

There was another moment of quivering silence, during which Dorrie could not stop herself from avidly listening, transfixed.

"Your father…your father in nothing but name is…Tomas de Torquemada."

Dorrie's mouth dropped open.

"I knew it," whispered Millie. "I've gotten quite good at research, working with Callamachus and—" she broke off, her voice trembling. "And I know why you didn't tell me. Because you're ashamed—"

"No!" cried Francesco. "You don't—"

"Because you think I might be like him deep inside, unfit to be a lybrarian!"

"Never!" cried Francesco.

"Go away!" snarled Millie, and Dorrie wondered if he'd stepped toward her.

"Millie," said Francesco. "It's not that way."

"I said 'go away'!"

Dorrie heard Francesco's footsteps retreat down the corridor and the door to the tower open and close. She let out a silent breath and leaned her head back in relief. It was a terrible mistake. The stand tilted, and the wooden blocks perched upon it toppled onto the floor with an echoing crash.

"Who's there?" barked Millie over the sound of a sword being unsheathed.

Dorrie closed her eyes in total and complete mortification and then gathered herself. "It's me." She hauled herself to her feet, heavy with the horrid embarrassment of having to reveal herself.

Millie appeared in the doorway, eyes blazing and sword

raised. A look of animal panic passed over her face, and then her eyebrows shot together. "You sneaking, horrible spy!"

"I wasn't spying! I swear!"

"Like in my bedroom you weren't spying? What did you hear?" Millie demanded, a tremble in her hand making her blade wobble.

Good, serviceable, wonderful lies began to offer themselves up to Dorrie.

"What did you hear?" Millie repeated, each word soaked in raw desperation.

Dorrie licked her lips, tempted to say she'd just walked in through the other door and hadn't heard a thing. But the words wouldn't come. "Everything," Dorrie said quietly, a wave of empathy for Millie washing through her. "I'm sorry."

Millie's face twisted with violent emotion and her eyes glistened. "I hate you, Dorrie Barnes!" Then she spun on her heel and was gone.

Dorrie waited a good long time after Francesco had descended the stairs from his office again to make her delivery. As she slowly padded up to his office, Dorrie thought back to the passage Marcus had read out of the book under Millie's mattress. Torquemada had planned the whole frightening Spanish Inquisition. "The architect," the book had called him. Dorrie shivered and for a moment felt full of raw longing for her parents and Miranda and then a strange, novel pity for Millie. *Torquemada! Her father! That couldn't feel good.*

Leaving the box and note beside Francesco's door, she was about to twist the torch to get back in the Scooby-Doo Library when her eyes caught on the portrait. The woman had brown eyes that radiated brave warmth. Like two banked fires. Francesco had gazed at her as he threw his armband. She wondered what the woman meant to him.

Dorrie let the wall spin her back into the Scooby-Doo Library.

"Anybody see you?" Ebba called over the sounds of splashing from the bathroom.

Dorrie hesitated, torn. "Nobody," she said at last.

✳ ✳ ✳

The next morning, Dorrie began to understand what it felt like to be dead to someone. Millie sat as far away as possible from Dorrie at the apprentices' table and absolutely refused to meet her eyes and no longer bothered to loft even scoffing, scornful words her way.

"What's up with your nemesis?" Marcus asked as Millie got up from a chair in the den and disappeared into her room a half second after Dorrie came in and sat down.

"She's not my nemesis," Dorrie said and left it at that.

Dorrie had other things to worry about. She began to watch

Francesco and the other lybrarians carefully, looking for some sign they'd heeded her note. There was also the matter of the principles mission. Dorrie and Ebba were soon due to return to London. They had been so busy planning for the trip to Athens and researching what Lord Cromer had in store for the suffragists that they'd spent next to no time researching who might be taking the *Anti-Suffrage Review*.

After sitting through a principles practicum in which every other member had reported making at least some progress in protecting their imperiled subjects, Dorrie and Ebba vowed to give their official mission attention.

They settled themselves in the Scooby-Doo Library one day with every intention of focusing only on the needs of the anti-suffragists. Despite this, they kept forgetting themselves and drifting into talk about how unjust it was that the *Suffragette* wasn't going to be printed.

It didn't help that Marcus kept interrupting them every two minutes to announce each new idea he had for raising the money to pay Kalliope. So far, he'd proposed a valet bicycle parking service, working off other people's overdue circulation department fines for cash, and getting Mistress Wu to offer a bounty for Darling, after which he'd turn the lizard in to her. The last idea had been rejected in most colorful terms by Ebba.

Dorrie watched Ebba feed the seal she'd named Spinoza,

after a philosopher who was rumored not to think much of Aristotle. "Let's just do a stakeout. Mrs. Richardson said Monday night is when the *Anti-Suffrage Review* gets delivered. The League's benefit tea is happening on a Monday. Let's ask Hypatia if we can stick around afterward to see who takes the newspapers. We can watch from the park."

"Obligation met," said Ebba, tossing the seal another sardine.

"FA-TI-MA!" crowed Marcus, as though he'd just won the lottery.

"Yes," said Dorrie, staring at him. "Her name has three syllables."

Marcus leaped up. "And she's the answer to our money-making needs!"

"Our needs?" said Dorrie. "Since when—"

"She's gotten really good on the ukulele," said Marcus. "We can play a bunch of songs together now. And she sings pretty well. I mean, she does that annoying teen girl warbly thing sometimes, but it's not a deal-breaker." He ran for the door. "We'll busk in the Inky Pot. Play for tips. I'll offer to give her half." He disappeared, slamming the door behind him.

Ebba stared after him. "Dorrie, I think I just had my own great idea for helping Annie and the suffragists."

"What?" asked Dorrie.

"FA-TI-MA!" yelled Ebba, just as Marcus had done. "She

apprentices to Lybrarian Franklin. She knows all about presses and how to make newspapers."

Dorrie grinned, understanding. "We can print up the next edition of the *Suffragette*."

The next morning, Dorrie rose before dawn. While Ebba and the other apprentices slept, she made her way to the mission room, where the lybrarians met to plan and prioritize their missions. As she had hoped, it was empty. Last quarter, when Dorrie had visited it, there'd only been one enormous blackboard, showing the list of missions the lybrarians were currently working on. Now blackboards covered every bit of wall space, including the fronts of the glass-doored bookcases. She raked her eyes over them one by one. An entry on the last one electrified Dorrie into full and total wakefulness . A mission to search Critius's house had been chalked in.

Jubilant, Dorrie sprinted back to the attics to tell Ebba and Marcus, but her joy was short-lived. At breakfast, Dorrie got her first indication that the silence the lybrarians had maintained about the fate of the *History of Histories* page was crumbling.

Dorrie had just lifted a ladleful of oatmeal at the serving table in the Sharpened Quill when she heard Lybrarian Della Porta's voice from a nearby table. "No sense, that apprentice.

Did you see that photograph of her in that newspaper from Passaic? Couldn't have focused more attention on our new Spoke Library if she'd led one of Hannibal's elephants through it."

A great gob of Dorrie's oatmeal fell from the ladle with a plop as a temporary sort of paralysis took over her.

"Well, no harm done really," said another lybrarian.

Lybrarian Della Porta swallowed noisily. "Can't say that about the *History of Histories* page, though you'd think from the inaction around here, it didn't contain the crux mission that kept that loathsome—"

"Kindly steward your words," cut in the Archivist's voice. Out of the corner of her eye, Dorrie saw that though he had spoken quietly, his hands gripped the back of an empty chair at Della Porta's table. His eyes were blazing.

Dorrie longed to sink into the floor.

"If you must assign blame for...'the situation,'" the Archivist continued, "then lay it entirely at my feet."

Della Porta slurped his coffee, deep disdain in his eyes. "As you wish."

Dorrie replaced the ladle in the pot and hurried back to the apprentices' table, grateful that it was far from Della Porta's.

After breakfast, Dorrie took her time walking across the Commons to the Celsus. She checked her mailbox in the hopes that Savi had left her another invitation—he hadn't—and then walked even more slowly to the Archivist's office. When she entered, he was bent over a rubbing of a monument stone from out in one of the wherens. "Good morning," he said, getting up to pour her a cup of tea.

Dorrie lingered in the doorway. "I'm really very sorry," she said, her voice catching.

The Archivist set down the teapot and blinked at her.

"For losing the *History of Histories* page last quarter and..." Dorrie felt tears in the corners of her eyes. "And for letting people think you had lost it and just couldn't remember. That wasn't right."

The Archivist quickly poured the tea and offered her one of the pretty blue cups. "There, there," he said, smiling. "It's not like people were fully confident in me before the page went missing."

Dorrie smiled back over the lump in her throat. "How... how is your work on the translation going?"

"Terribly," said the Archivist, settling himself on the bench. He sighed. "What's hardest is knowing that Mr. Biggs is sitting out on that island with the answers. I'm sure of it. If it weren't against every principle I'd sworn to uphold as a lybrarian, I'd be tempted to squeeze Mr. Biggs myself!"

The morning they were to leave for London, 1913 again, Dorrie at last received another invitation to practice with Savi. During the lesson, she did her best to focus, but by the end, she had begun to hate the sand-filled glove. Sweat dripped off the end of her nose as, for about the fiftieth time that hour, she took a ready stance, sword arm bent and rapier level. This time, she thought fiercely. *This* time!

Savi pushed the lever, and the glove fell. With a brutish grunt, Dorrie lunged forward—and missed.

"Can't I practice something else?!" she shouted in frustration.

"Why?" Savi replied, busy writing again. "Have you mastered aim?"

Dorrie glared at him, panting, desperate for a distraction. "What are you working on now?"

"I am writing another essay. It's called 'For Witches.' In it, I lay out passionately and in great extravagant detail my argument for their existence."

Dorrie stared at him. "But you just wrote a whole essay about how witches don't exist!"

He dipped his quill. "This is a satiric essay."

"Which means…?" asked Dorrie, relishing the fact that she wasn't busy for the moment failing to spear the glove.

"It means I'm writing the essay as though I *do* believe in witches. It means I'm writing it with such absurd vigor that the belief in them is shown to be ridiculous. In the part I'm working on now, I recount the words of a witch I say I met who shared with me the details of her typical day."

"Can I hear some?" asked Dorrie, hoping to prolong her rest.

"Only you would know," said Savi, blowing on the parchment.

Dorrie rolled her eyes. "May I? May I hear some?"

He gave the piece of parchment he held a shake. "In this essay, I claim I have met a witch and I've written down a description she gave me of her typical day." He hunched one shoulder and made his voice high and gravelly. "I cause the thieves to burne Candles of dead mens grease, to lay the Hoasts asleep while they rob their houses; I give the flying money, that returnes again to the pocket after 'tis spent; I make the witches seeme nothing but a troope of Cats; 'tis I that, invisible, tumble the dishes and bottles up and downe the house."

Dorrie giggled.

Savi spoke again in his own voice. "I've so far stacked about seventy-five such inane claims into a great teetering pile of lunacy."

"But what if someone thinks you're serious?" asked Dorrie.

"Then the person is too far gone to worry about." He began to write again.

"Please, can't we do something different?"

Savi looked up her. "Something fun, you mean?"

"Yes!"

"Something that involves crashing blades and long, satisfying runs of parries and thrusts, preferably while covering a great amount of territory with several changes of elevation, including, perhaps, a jump up onto the lip of the well?"

"Yes!"

"No," he said, cranking the glove upward again.

A few days later, dressed again as proper young English ladies and wielding a pair of binoculars for their stakeout, Dorrie and Ebba slipped through the archway with the keyhand again.

They went immediately to McAndrews Laundry to find Annie. A very sweaty, red-faced woman with a booming voice told them Annie wasn't there.

"We'll try again after the stakeout," Dorrie said as they hurried across Hyde Park toward the League's headquarters.

Fatima had told Ebba that Master Franklin was going to be leaving Petrarch's Library for a few days at the end of the week and that they could print the *Suffragette* on one of his presses then. Mathilde, Saul, and Marcus had also agreed to help. Now Dorrie and Ebba just had to talk Annie into entrusting them with the job.

The benefit tea dragged on for hours, with the headquarters choked with well-dressed guests.

Lady Agnes was in a state of perpetual apoplexy and insisted on filling Dorrie and Ebba's arms with stacks of anti-suffrage pamphlets, urging them to hand them out to one well-dressed guest after another.

"Oh! Mr. Sacks-Sandbottom!" said Lady Agnes at one point, her voice suddenly breathless. "Lady Whitcomb is here."

Dorrie followed Lady Agnes's admiring, if slightly terrified, gaze and saw that it was trained on a woman who'd just arrived. A maid took Lady Whitcomb's coat but left a long fox fur draped around her neck, the snarling head of which looked as though it might still bite someone. Elegant gloves ran up to her elbows. Beautiful in a cold, chiseled way, she was listening with all the vital interest of a fork to an older man standing beside her.

"She's immensely wealthy," said Lady Agnes. "Her family made a fortune in ginger beer bottling. Oh, my goodness. She's coming this way." Lady Agnes glanced hastily at herself in a nearby mirror, her hands restless on her dress, smoothing and arranging.

"Lady Agnes. Mr. Sacks-Sandbottom," said Lady Whitcomb, arriving in their midst. "How good to see you." She waved away a plate of watercress sandwiches as if they were gangrenous big toes. "I just wanted to thank you for your work on the *Anti-Suffrage Review*. So much wisdom and good sense in its pages. I'll be donating liberally."

Lady Agnes blushed deeply and dug her elbow sharply into Ebba's side to remind her to offer Lady Whitcomb a pamphlet, which she ignored.

"You have my appreciation," said Lady Whitcomb, playing with a thin necklace inlaid with tiny white stones that shimmered against her neck. "I must excuse myself as I've promised the Earl of Sandwich a conversation. Feel free to join us, of course."

Lady Agnes and Mr. Sacks-Sandbottom fairly ran to catch up with Lady Whitcomb, finally leaving Dorrie and Ebba to their own devices. They wandered to the front window, hoping to glimpse Annie, but the sidewalk in front of the park was empty.

"Mrs. Richardson said she hasn't been here all day," said Ebba.

"Then I hope the copies of the *Anti-Suffrage Review* do get stolen tonight," said Dorrie.

They suppressed laughter.

At last, dusk fell, and the room began to empty. Dorrie and Ebba hurried into their coats, intent on taking up their watch—first for the delivery of the *Anti-Suffrage Review* and then for the thief—from the park. They were about to leave when Mr. Sacks-Sandbottom grabbed hold of Ebba's arm. He looked angry. "Lady Whitcomb is missing her diamond necklace. It has a faulty clasp, and she believes it fell." He stared pointedly into Ebba's face. "Did you find it?"

Dorrie didn't like the hold he had on Ebba's arm—or the accusatory look on his face and the way little flecks of spit had gathered in the corners of his mouth.

Ebba must not have liked these things either because she jerked her arm free, looking angry herself. "No, I haven't."

Mr. Sacks-Sandbottom glowered at them. "Lady Whitcomb says that the last time she remembered it on her neck was when you, Ebba, Lady Agnes, Lady Whitcomb, and I were talking."

"Well, I didn't touch it," Ebba said, looking icily at Mr. Sacks-Sandbottom. They let themselves out.

On the sidewalk, coat collars up, Ebba spoke first. "So that's what Master Casanova was talking about. Mr. Horrible Hyphenated assumed I took the necklace because I have darker skin?"

"He didn't even think to ask me about it," said Dorrie.

"And he gets to vote?" Ebba jammed her hat on. "Glad I don't live in this wheren."

Since the bundles of the *Anti-Suffrage Review* weren't scheduled to be delivered to the League's headquarters for at least another hour, Dorrie and Ebba decided to check McAndrews Laundry one more time before settling in for their watch.

Luck was with them. Through the steamy window, they could see Annie behind the counter. They went in.

Annie looked up from where she was turning the crank on a great wooden drum and smiled. "If you're here to warn me about the numerous rotten fish that will be thrown at me today, you're too late. It already happened."

Dorrie and Ebba looked at each other.

"Actually," Dorrie whispered, "we came here to warn you about something worse."

Chapter 19

Waves

A NNIE HADN'T BELIEVED THEM at first. "How do you know this?"

Dorrie had been prepared. "My father has a cousin who has a friend who works in the Parliament building. He heard Lord Cromer talking about it in an elevator."

When they'd shared their second rehearsed fiction—that Ebba's uncle's hobby was printing and that he had a press in his basement and that he quietly supported the cause of women's suffrage and had offered to help print the next edition of the *Suffragette*—she'd positively gaped at them.

All the same, Annie had agreed to go find her sister—who helped edit the Suffragette— when her shift ended, tell her the news, and put the proposal to her.

Dorrie and Ebba had hurried to the park to shiver beside

one another on a bench. At 6:00 p.m., a motorized van had dropped off two tall bundles of newspapers on the doorstep, where they'd remained undisturbed for two hours. At 8:00 p.m., Dorrie and Ebba, cramped and cold, called it quits and hurried back to McAndrews Laundry to see what Annie and her sister had decided. A half hour later, they emerged, faces shining.

Though they ran all the way to the London Library after they emerged a half hour later, they were late to meet the keyhand but very glad he did not ask them what was in the battered valise Dorrie now carried.

Near midnight, when most of the other apprentices had gone to bed, Dorrie, Ebba, Marcus, Mathilde, Fatima, and Saul sat crowded on Dorrie and Ebba's beds.

"It'll take us hours just to typeset all this," said Fatima, looking at the contents of Annie's valise. "Never mind printing off the copies."

"But we can do it, right?" Dorrie asked.

"With six of us working on it?" said Fatima. "I think so."

"Beauregarde & Gloop, Publishers at Large," said Marcus.

Before breakfast the next morning, Marcus was given the task of informing Mistress Wu that he'd seen Darling slithering down the corridor near the room that held the printing presses. To the apprentices' delight, during announcements she declared the area off-limits until Master Yeshi, who handled all the animals kept in Petrarch's Library, returned from tenth-century Mongolia and could search for the creature.

As Mistress Wu asked the staff lybrarians to attend a short meeting in Hypatia's office, the members of Beauregarde & Gloop exchanged triumphant glances that made Izel's eyes dart with wild suspicion.

"Apprentices should go on with work as usual," finished Mistress Wu.

It occurred to Dorrie that this was the perfect time to return the skipkey, so she hurried down to the Archivist's office, relieved to finally have an opportunity to return the "borrowed" skipkey. After slipping it back in the trunk, she sat down to the work she hadn't finished the day before. At the usual time, she remembered to put the kettle on to boil, sure the Archivist would be surprised and pleased. However, when the Archivist finally returned, he didn't even notice. Barely acknowledging Dorrie, he went straight to one of the great cupboards and unlocked it.

When he swung open the door, Dorrie gaped. On the shelves within stood volume after volume of *History of Histories*. It seemed to be an entire set. Her heart beat a little faster. Ever since she'd overheard Francesco and Lybrarian Della Porta talking about the crux mission, Dorrie had assumed that only the lybrarians—or the page she and Marcus had lost—could tell her the identity of its imperiled subject. Yet, another source of the knowledge had been right under her nose for more than a month.

The Archivist pulled out a volume and brought it over to his end of the worktable, where he hunched over it. Having finished the work he'd given her the day before, Dorrie had to ask him three times what he'd like her to do next before he snapped at her to think of a job herself.

"Is something wrong?" Dorrie asked, her feelings hurt.

"No, no. Forgive me."

Dorrie saw that his eyes held grief along with some of the wildness she'd seen when he'd been upset at other times.

The Archivist gave her a weak smile. "I'm just… Why don't you…straighten up a bit."

Dorrie swept the floor, then steeped and poured a cup of tea. She set it by the Archivist's elbow.

He took it gratefully, and then, whether because Dorrie's eyes had drifted to the open *History of Histories* volume or for another reason, he marked his place with a feather, closed the book, and laid a pile of rubbings atop it.

For the rest of the morning, the Archivist bent over his translation work, lifting his head now and then to stare at the set of symbols on the wall.

Starting just after practicums and for the duration of the afternoon and into the evening, the six partners of Beauregarde & Gloop, Publishers at Large threw themselves into the task of producing one thousand copies of the *Suffragette*.

Once, returning to the printing press room with some water for the parched among the publishers, Dorrie nearly collided with Mistress Daraney. Luckily, the librarian, who'd been invited to play whist at Ursula's cottage, was too preoccupied with having gotten lost again to ask any uncomfortable questions about why Dorrie's face and hands were covered in ink.

Dorrie gave her directions, and she'd stumped off on her peg leg, muttering about the impossibility of navigating without stars.

Beauregarde & Gloop finished its task near midnight. There had perhaps been more tidy editions of the *Suffragette* produced, but it was doubtful that any of them had seen such copious amounts of sweat produced on its behalf.

After they'd stowed the newspapers in an empty trunk in the Abbey St. Gall, Marcus suggested a trip to the Inky Pot for some baklava. Only Ebba considered.

"What about Fedya?" Dorrie asked.

"He hasn't poisoned me," said Marcus.

"Yet," said Fatima ominously.

Only Ebba, citing near-starvation, agreed to go. The rest of the apprentices decided to return to the attics by ones and two for the sake of inconspicuousness. When Dorrie slipped in last, it was immediately apparent that something was wrong.

For one thing, despite the late hour, the den was packed. Izel stood with her fists on her hips, her mouth open as if Dorrie's arrival had interrupted her midsentence.

"What's going on?" Dorrie asked.

"What's going on?" repeated Izel, her eyes flashing. "Remember the reversal Mr. Biggs threatened? The one that would undo Algernon Sidney's rescue? Well, it turns out the Foundation didn't just choose that event randomly."

Dorrie's blood seemed to run instantly cold.

Izel marched toward her. "Lybrarian Della Porta says the mission is listed on the *History of Histories* page you and Marcus lost in Athens and it's now in the Foundation's clutches!"

"Clutches?" repeated Mathilde. "Who says *clutches*? Now you're just trying for drama."

Izel rounded on her. "Lybrarian Della Porta says the page has an extremely important crux mission listed on it!"

"Well, which one already?" Saul said.

Izel swept her gaze around the room. "The one that cut the size and power of Tomas de Torquemada's Spanish Inquisition in half."

There was an outbreak of hot, urgent talk.

"Torquemada is a monster," Izel said, raising her voice over the hubbub. "Lybrarian Della Porta says he had thousands of people burned at the stake. He's just the most evil of evil humans." She turned back to Dorrie. "This is all your fault!"

Dorrie felt as though Izel had punched her. Around her, she sensed the accusing stares mounting in number. Her eyes caught on Millie's. Instead of judgment, the other girl's held panic, and Dorrie realized Millie was afraid. Afraid that Dorrie would spill her secret in the face of Izel's attack.

Mathilde whistled shrilly through her fingers. The talk died down. "Even if the Foundation does terrible things with that *History of Histories* page, it's not Dorrie and Marcus's fault. They made a mistake. They didn't give the page to the Foundation, and they tried to get it back. If the crux mission does get reversed or Algernon Sidney loses his head again, that's on the Foundation."

"But if they hadn't been so selfish and sneaky last quarter, the page wouldn't—"

"Izel!" said Mathilde sharply. "You're being flat-out mean!"

"You won't think that when I tell you the worst of it," shrieked Izel. "Lybrarian Della Porta found out today that if the crux mission is reversed, someone here in Petrarch's Library will die."

There was a moment of stunned silence. Dorrie felt as though her heart was falling out of place. She raced out of the den, scarcely able to breathe. The door banged closed behind her. She wanted to be alone. She needed air and space.

She zigzagged her way through the library, pounding through corridors and down staircases, her sword rat-a-tatting against the spindles. Faces of those she'd come to love in Petrarch's Library flashed before her, eyes closed, still in death. At last, she tumbled out into the cool, stiff wind of the Bottom Shelf, gasping for breath.

The sea glittered with moon-brightened whitecaps.

Running down the stairway that led to the beach, Dorrie felt her foot go out from under her. She caught herself and watched something small and round bounce down the last of the steps and land silently in the sand. It was an orange, the kind the Archivist tended to read out by the dozens when he was upset and had drunk too much wine. She looked up and down the beach. Had the Archivist heard the terrible news as well? She walked along the edge of the cove faster and faster, passing a second orange and then a third.

A terrible thought took hold of her as she remembered the Archivist's strange mood that morning and how he'd stared at the symbols on the wall. What if, driven by the terrible news, the Archivist had decided to try to get the answers he wanted so badly from Mr. Biggs?

She scanned the water in the cove and saw nothing. About to chastise herself for jumping to such a crazy conclusion, a movement beyond the protective arms of the cove made her shift her gaze. She squinted. Unlike the other whitecaps, which melted away a few moments after appearing, one seemed to persist. Was it a sail? Her heart raced. She stared up and down the beach once more.

No light showed on Mistress Daraney's houseboat. Dorrie wondered if she was still at Ursula's. She looked back to where she'd seen the sail. The Archivist didn't need more trouble. If she could just overtake him, she could persuade him to return before he got into trouble.

Dorrie ran for one of the rowboats pulled up on the beach and turned it over. Throwing in a set of oars, she pushed it into the waves and clambered in. The tide was with her, and soon, she was passing through the rocky mouth of the cove and into the open sea.

The sail shone clearly now in the distance, Crackskull Island a distant dark hump behind it.

She pulled on the oars as hard and fast as she could, grateful for all the hours of practice she'd put in. Gaining quickly on the other boat, she saw that its prow was pointed toward the cove. It was heading in rather than out. Relieved that the Archivist had come to his senses, she stilled the oars. "Master Ishaq!" she yelled above the sound of the waves. "It's me, Dorrie!"

She strained to hear a reply, but none came. Putting her oars to work again, she soon closed the distance. The boat's sail, which had been full of wind, now billowed loose and untended.

Drawing alongside it, her heart juddered. Against the

mast slumped a figure. Dorrie shipped the oars with a clatter, hoping the Archivist hadn't been bashed into unconsciousness by the freely swinging boom. She had just tied the dinghy fast to the sailboat when the slumped figure sprang to its feet. It was Mr. Biggs.

With a startled cry, Dorrie stumbled backward. What had he done with the Archivist? Dorrie drew her sword, but before she could do anything useful with it, Mr. Biggs grabbed hold of the back of her coat and hauled her through the air to land painfully in the bottom of the sailboat. Her sword bounced free of her hand.

"Well, well, well…" he said, looming over her. "I'll have to thank the fates." He bent closer, his eyes hunting and cold. "I can smell it on you."

No idea what he was talking about, Dorrie tried to scramble away. Growling, he knocked her back down. Taking hold of the loop of yarn around Dorrie's neck, he tore the hidden vial free.

For a moment, he stared at it triumphantly. Then, his nails flashing white in the moonlight, he unscrewed the cap. Rushing the vial to his lips, he violently upended it, only to pull it away an instant later, livid.

"Empty," he hissed. Like a rattlesnake striking, he caught hold of Dorrie's hand, nearly crushing it in his own massive fist. Dorrie reared back, unable to break free. He stared at the blackened thumbnail. "Enjoyed my personal store of Whim's Gift, did you?"

"Whim's Gift?" Dorrie choked out, bewildered, as the sail flapped lazily in a burst of wind. "No, it's only Travelers' Tea."

Dorrie yelped as Mr. Biggs hauled her up to a sitting position by her shirtfront. "They're one and the same, girl, and both nicknames."

Dorrie's old images of Whim's Gift as some sort of machine melted away. Her thoughts turned desperately to escape. She glanced around wildly until her eye caught on the end of the sail's halyard, looped in a single loose figure eight once over and under the pegs. In her head, Mistress Daraney's voice warned again about how the sail and boom would fall if the knot slipped free.

Mr. Biggs jerked her closer. "I prefer its true name." He lifted the vial. "Vox Mortis."

The name sounded like fear and poison and the saddest ends. "W-what does that mean?" said Dorrie, desperate for time, her fingers feeling for her sword.

"Let me show you." The tones in Mr. Biggs's voice chilled Dorrie's blood and made it hard to think, hard to remember she had bones.

As Mr. Biggs drew slightly back, Dorrie's straining fingertips touched the cold metal of her sword.

If she could pick it up, she'd have one chance to hit the

knot in just the right place so the tip of her sword could push the halyard loop over the peg. One chance to drop the sail on Mr. Biggs and possibly get away. Her hand curled round the sword's hilt.

In a flash, she drew back her sword arm and drove the rapier toward the knot. Time seemed to slow, and the crash of the waves seemed to fade as she watched the blade hurtle forward. She sensed Mr. Biggs's arm swinging toward her. The rapier tip hit the knot, but too low. It glanced off with no effect.

"No!" she cried as Mr. Biggs's arm sent her sprawling to the bottom of the boat again. Holding her down, he pressed the vial against the center of her chest. Below its coldness, Dorrie could feel her heart bucking wildly.

"Now," Mr. Biggs said, his eyes boring into hers. "Tell me what you want to say, and I'll kill you. Tell me what I want to hear, and you'll live."

Dorrie stared back at him, adrenalin shooting through her, bewildered at the strangeness of his words. Then their meaning penetrated. Almost instantly, she felt a great tide of many things she knew to be true moving through her heart and demanding expression. She wanted to say that grass was green and that she loved her mother and that the thought of one of the lybrarians of Petrarch's Library dying because of her mistake terrified her.

But Mr. Biggs had said that these were the things he would kill her for saying. She choked on the words, holding them back. The things she wanted to say struggled to survive. Fear tried to smother them. Her chest felt like a battleground, her heart in danger of exploding to pieces. At last, she could bear it no longer. What would he want to hear?

"I-I-I give up," she gasped. The unbearable pain died instantly, but rather than relief, Dorrie felt a sensation deep in her chest, as though a small piece of her core had just crumbled to dust.

"Many thanks," said Mr. Biggs, peering into the vial. "Filled to the brim."

Dorrie fell back, too wretched and weak to do anything more.

Mr. Biggs brought the vial to his lips. As he drank, his fingernails blackened. He stood. "Powerful little things, aren't they? As it happens, a hundred of the Foundation's new allies are waiting patiently in the past for Vox Mortis vials to call their own. I haven't appreciated being delayed in sending them off."

"What allies?" whispered Dorrie.

Instead of answering, he tossed her back into the dinghy like a rag doll. She fell hard, bashing her knee and forehead. She gasped in pain, seeing stars.

"What are they going to do with the vials?" choked out Dorrie as Mr. Biggs rummaged in the bottom of the sailboat.

"Find plenty of ways to fill them, I hope."

Nausea rolled over Dorrie.

"We have a grand inquisitor to put back in power, and it

will take a good deal of Vox Mortis to open a way into the fifteenth century for the Foundation."

Mr. Biggs straightened. To Dorrie's horror, he held an ax.

"Since I'm the only one who knows where the vials are hidden at the moment, you'll have to forgive me for harboring a good deal of resentment toward the Lybrariad at the moment." With a splintering crash, he stove a hole in the bottom of Dorrie's boat. "I'm not in the most merciful mood."

A fountain of seawater bubbled up from the jagged opening. Without another word, Mr. Biggs took the oars, cut the boats apart, and set sail in the direction of Petrarch's Library.

Dorrie's brain sizzled. The hole was huge, and no amount of bailing was going to keep the dinghy from sinking. If she couldn't find a way to warn the lybrarians, Mr. Biggs was surely going to escape from Petrarch's Library. With him would go the chance to stop the Foundation from reversing the crux mission. Torquemada's power would grow again, and a lybrarian would die.

Dorrie paddled furiously with her hands, trying to force the half-submerged boat toward the lights of Petrarch's Library. She tried not to think about the sharks and poisonous jellyfish of Crackskull Island and what Mr. Biggs might have done to the Archivist there. She was getting nowhere. In fact, the current was taking her farther out to sea. She stared toward shore. It was a very long way away, but she felt she no choice. She had to try to stop Mr. Biggs. Kicking off her boots, Dorrie dove into the water and began to swim.

For a while, keeping her eyes on the rooftops of the library, Dorrie made steady progress, but soon, the water grew rougher. One wave slammed on top of her, pushing her far beneath the sea's surface. She came up sputtering, kicking hard, and wondered for the first time if she'd made a mistake in leaving the boat.

As Dorrie eyed the distance to the shore, an unfamiliar voice that seemed to come from deep inside herself spoke.

"You can't swim that far."

Dorrie kicked savagely and continued on, but her strokes felt clumsier.

"You'll never make it," said the voice, chewing at the connection between Dorrie's will and her body. Her arms and legs began to thrash without purpose or plan.

Dorrie had never understood how anyone could drown, thinking one only had to float when tired and then swim on. Now, as she sank beneath the water, she understood.

Chapter 20

Shore

DORRIE WOKE TO THE sound of low voices talking. Her eyelids felt terrifically heavy. There was a soft pillow under her head and something heavy and warm on top of her. She resented the voices that had pulled her out of the simple peace of her sleep.

Slowly, Dorrie opened her eyes. She was lying in a windowed alcove in a very large round room. Ebba and Marcus were sitting on chairs nearby.

"Where I am?" she murmured.

A relieved grin split Marcus's face. "In the human repair and preservation department." He poked at her. "How dare you stay unconscious that long? I almost got worried."

Ebba gathered Dorrie up in a bear hug. "Are you okay?"

"Yes, but what happened?" demanded Dorrie. "Where's Mr. Biggs?"

In whispers, so as not to disturb the injured lybrarians in other alcoves, Marcus and Ebba took turns telling Dorrie what had happened in Petrarch's Library while she had been out on the water.

"Mr. Biggs attacked Mistress Daraney in a corridor on her way back from Ursula's," said Marcus.

"Yeah," said Ebba. "He hit her over the head with an oar, stole her peg leg, and then disappeared through the Athens archway. It took her forever to find help obviously."

"She was furious," said Marcus. "Apparently, he was wearing her favorite bedsheet she'd left on a clothesline down in the cove."

"A bunch of lybrarians went after him. Mistress Daraney had others launch every boat in the cove toward Crackskull Island to see what had happened," said Ebba. "It was Mistress Daraney who spotted you with her eagle eyes. She said you were almost a goner."

Dorrie steeled herself. "Is the Archivist…"

"Dead?" answered Marcus. "Nah. The whole time you were out on the water, he was snoring in a rowboat on the beach."

Joy flooded Dorrie and then confusion. "But then how did Mr. Biggs get the sailboat?"

Ebba put her finger warningly to her lips. She pointed to an alcove with drawn curtains. Behind them, Dorrie could hear the murmur of adult voices.

"Master Francesco found Lybrarian Della Porta on Crackskull Island," whispered Ebba.

"What!" said Dorrie, sitting bolt upright.

"It turns out he hasn't really made any progress on deciphering Petrarch's journal," said Marcus. "His plan was to force Mr. Biggs to give him the information he needed to break the code. Instead, Mr. Biggs broke his arm and gave him two black eyes."

"And Mr. Biggs got away," said Dorrie miserably. Quickly, she told them what he had told her about his plans before leaving her to die in the ocean. She couldn't bring herself to tell them about how he'd used her to make Vox Mortis. That she had already shut up in a little box.

"So how exactly is he going to get the vials to the Foundation's new allies?" asked Ebba.

Dorrie frowned. "He didn't say." She pushed the covers back. "I have to tell the lybrarians what Whim's Gift actually is. They have to know."

Just then, Ursula bustled over. Despite Dorrie's protests that she was fine, Ursula wouldn't allow Dorrie to begin to speak until she'd demonstrated she could walk, see, hear, write her name, and do a cartwheel. Finally, she sent a message to Hypatia that Dorrie was ready to talk.

When Dorrie arrived in Hypatia's office, it was already crowded with most of the library staff.

Nervously, she began her story. When Dorrie had to explain

how Mr. Biggs had used her to make more Vox Mortis, she did so quickly with as little detail as possible, as though it had happened to someone else.

"Mr. Biggs treated you monstrously," said Hypatia when she'd finished. "You were in no position to resist him on your own. It was courageous of you to try to swim back to the cove to warn us. Thank you."

"Whim's Gift," Phillip said, sounding furious. "Nice polite name for such a foul substance. Though I hate to agree with him, Mr. Biggs is correct: Vox Mortis is its true name."

Hypatia steepled her fingers. "Well, now we know. To make use of Petrarch's Star, the Foundation needs a good deal of Vox Mortis, and to make Vox Mortis, the Foundation needs to get those vials of which Mr. Biggs spoke into the hands of their allies. We need to get to the vials first. At least we can now narrow the search to 399 BCE."

Francesco, who hadn't stopped pacing since the meeting began, stopped and rounded on Dorrie. "What were you thinking, going out there by yourself?"

Dorrie felt her face redden. "I-I…"

"You could have been killed!" said Francesco, his breathing ragged. "What would we have told your parents? Did you think about them?"

"She thought I was out on the water and in trouble," said the Archivist, "and she went to my aid."

Francesco ignored him, keeping his eyes on Dorrie. "Why must you always do things? If you just hadn't gone out there, then Mr. Biggs wouldn't have—"

"Francesco," Hypatia said sharply.

Snapping his mouth shut, Francesco stalked out of the room. The door slammed behind him, shaking the frame.

Dorrie stared after him, crushed, and finished the thought. "Then Mr. Biggs wouldn't have been able to collect the Vox Mortis from me and couldn't have escaped."

"Nonsense," said Phillip firmly. "He would have found another way."

"Please try to forgive Francesco," said Hypatia. "He is under great strain."

Dorrie summoned her courage. She had to know. "Lybrarian Della Porta said that if the crux mission on the *History of Histories* page is reversed, Torquemada's powers will grow, but also…someone here in the Library will die. Is that true?"

An electric silence filled the room.

"For a man who deals in secret codes, Lybrarian Della Porta has precious little ability to keep his mouth shut!" Phillip said at last.

"I think, for now," said Hypatia, "it's best that the staff keeps that piece of information to itself."

"It's true. Someone will die," Dorrie said later to Ebba and Marcus as she banged things around rather violently in her bedroom, supposedly to tidy up. She'd hurried through the empty den after her meeting with Hypatia, slammed the door, and hadn't ventured out since. Now she threw herself back down on her pillow. "But they wouldn't tell me who. How am I supposed to keep going to practicums and watching over those idiotic anti-suffragists while we all just wait to see who we've managed to push in front of a train?"

She had dreaded emerging from her room for dinner and had even briefly considered visiting the Inky Pot instead of the Sharpened Quill, but after she heard the den was empty, she at last consented to go with Ebba and Marcus. They stopped at the Celsus to check their mailboxes. Dorrie found a note from Savi telling her he was back and inviting her for a lesson in the Gymnasium courtyard during the dinner hour.

When she burst into the courtyard a few minutes later and saw him coming through another door, she threw her arms around him so hard, he nearly fell over.

"I'll have to bring a picnic more often," he said, setting down a basketful of cheese and apples. "Here," he said, handing over her lost sword. "Mistress Daraney found it in the sailboat wreck. Hypatia told me what happened." His tilted her chin to look in her eyes. "How do you fare?"

His simple question undid Dorrie. The tears she'd held back

since she'd faced Mr. Biggs came. She wept and told him everything. When she got to the part about Mr. Biggs forcing her to fill the Vox Mortis vial, wrathful fires appeared in his eyes.

Dorrie swallowed down one last shuddering sob. "When I was in the sailboat and aiming for the knot, I was sure I would hit the mark because I *needed* to, because I was in such trouble." Dorrie looked up at Savi. "But I did miss."

"Oh, Dorothea," said Savi, "only in storybooks does a perfectly exquisite crisis guarantee a perfectly executed victory over the circumstances."

Dorrie wiped her eyes, her shoulders sagging. "And then in the water, I just panicked. It was awful. I couldn't make any choices. I couldn't tell my arms and legs what to do. I just failed."

"We lybrarians play games with very high stakes," said Savi. "And Fear is…always in the mix."

"But how do you get rid of it?"

Savi raised an eyebrow at her. "Once there was a young warrior. Her teacher told her that she had to do battle with Fear. She didn't want to do that. Fear seemed too aggressive; it was scary; it seemed unfriendly. But the teacher said she had to do it and gave her the instructions for the battle. The day arrived. The student warrior stood on one side, and Fear stood on the other."

Dorrie found herself listening intently.

"The warrior was feeling very small," said Savi, "…and Fear was looking big and wrathful. They both had their weapons. The young warrior roused herself and went toward Fear, prostrated herself three times, and asked, 'May I have permission to go into battle with you?' Fear said, 'Thank you for showing me so much respect by asking permission.' Then the young warrior said, 'How can I defeat you?'"

"And what did Fear say?"

"I was getting to that," Savi said peevishly. He cleared his throat. "Fear replied, 'My weapons are that I talk fast, and I get very close to your face. Then you get completely unnerved, and you do whatever I say. If you don't do what I tell you, I have no power. You can listen to me, and you can have respect for me. You can even be convinced by me. But if you don't do what I say, I have no power.' In that way, the student warrior learned how to defeat Fear."

Dorrie stared at Savi, impressed. "You should write that down."

Savi hauled the sand-filled glove to its apex. "Pema Chodron already did. I memorized it out of *When Things Fall Apart: Heart Advice for Difficult Times*. A book from your wheren actually. Lybrarian Davis gave it to me." He cocked his head. "Where did she say she borrowed it from? Something absurd-sounding. Ah, yes, from the 'self-help section.' Anyway, I thought you might find the idea useful."

Dorrie stood and faced the glove. "Is all that what you do when you're afraid?"

"Me?" said Savi. "Oh, no. I like to imagine myself already dead before I go into a situation where I might die. Then I feel I have nothing to lose. It steadies my nerves."

He let the glove drop, and Dorrie lunged at it.

Dorrie spent the following week on edge, sure that at any moment, the news would come of Torquemada's rise to greater power and a death of one of the Library's own. But during announcements the day after Mr. Biggs's escape, Mistress Wu, her back ramrod straight and her eyes flashing, had insisted that even in the face of Mr. Biggs escape, practicums and apprenticeships were to go on as usual.

And as the lybrarians continued with their attempts to track Mr. Biggs, go on they did. Dorrie, who wanted only to be left alone to brood on how she might still help stop the Foundation, found that desire nearly impossible to fulfill.

For one thing, with Fatima's help, Marcus had finally earned the money he needed from the Inky Pot's patrons. Every time he saw Dorrie, he bugged her about needing her help to get back to Athens to pay Kalliope. Dorrie had put him off repeatedly, unable to even consider stealing the Archivist's skipkey again. Instead, one morning, after taking a deep breath, she explained to the Archivist about Marcus's attempt to assist Timotheus and then asked him if he'd take Marcus back to Athens. The Archivist had looked gobstopped but for some reason had found Dorrie's description of their adventure with Aristotle so funny that after he was done wheezing, he'd agreed, and then his face had turned serious. "I owe you at least a keyhand escort to Athens. I'm truly sorry my wandering down to the beach cost you so much."

Not wanting to talk about it again, Dorrie had shifted the conversation to her mission in England and the plans she and Ebba had made for another stakeout. The Archivist had been very sympathetic to Dorrie's fear that the newspaper thief might turn out to be Annie.

One lunchtime not long after, Dorrie and Ebba slipped into the Scooby-Doo Library to find that not only had Spinoza slopped all the painstakingly gathered seawater from his tub onto the floor, but he had also managed to flop himself out of it.

"He's getting too big to keep here," Ebba said, her face pinched with worry.

"We could release him down in the cove," said Dorrie carefully, not sure how Ebba would take it.

Ebba pulled the seal into her lap and scratched below his little ear holes. "I'd love that, but there aren't any other monk seals around here. He'd be all alone." She looked at Dorrie. "Do you think the Archivist would let Spinoza loose in the Athens harbor when he takes Marcus?"

The Archivist had agreed to Ebba's request as well, and the

next Saturday morning, Ebba and Dorrie saw them all off at the Tyre archway, Ebba giving Spinoza five separate final nuzzles and choking back tears. When Marcus slammed into Dorrie's bedroom many hours later, he looked anything but triumphant.

"What is it?" Dorrie demanded. "Didn't Kalliope write the oration?"

"Oh, she wrote it," said Marcus, yanking a piece of papyrus out of his satchel.

"Then what's the problem?"

"When I handed it to Timotheus, he went white as a chiton. He told me that unless he's playing music, he sometimes gets paralyzing stage fright. Just the thought of delivering the oration made him almost pass out."

"So what are you going to do?"

"Kalliope says you can have someone else speak on your behalf in the courts if you're too ill to stand up." He looked over the papyrus. "I told Timotheus I'd do it."

At her first Staying Afloat practicum after Mr. Biggs's escape, Mistress Daraney decided to make use of the brisk wind and give a sailing lesson. Dorrie and Millie were told to share a boat. Dorrie hadn't spoken to Millie since their eyes had met in the den when Izel had told the apprentices how Torquemada's power would grow if the crux mission was reversed.

Silently, they pushed their boat over the sand, into the surf, and over the first few low breakers. But when the first real wave bubbled around Dorrie's waist, she tensed and stopped moving forward.

"Keep pushing," came Millie's annoyed voice, "or we're going to get clobbered by the next one."

Dorrie looked up. It wasn't even a particularly big wave, but her mouth went dry. There was no time for figuring out where Fear was standing, let alone bowing to it respectfully. She did what it told her and stumbled out of the water, leaving Millie to manage the boat. Without Dorrie to help steady it, a wave hit it broadside, nearly capsizing it.

"What are you doing?" shouted Millie.

"I'm sorry, I'm not...I'm not feeling well," Dorrie said, retreating up the beach as the next wave brought the boat crashing back to shore.

At the next practicum, her legs again refused to take her any farther than the waist-high water. She'd had to tell Mistress Daraney that she was still feeling ill and spent the rest of the practicum sitting on the beach working on knots while the others sailed beneath a gloriously blue sky.

Reports from 399 BCE came in daily with the depressing news that Mr. Biggs was still at large. Disappointingly, Dorrie also learned that Critius's empty house had been thoroughly examined and that no vials had been found. Dorrie used the bad news to fuel the aiming practice, which she now forced herself to do every morning before breakfast. Kenzo was thrilled to work the lever for the price of a bout at the end of each session.

Thrusting her rapier toward the glove, Dorrie often imagined it was Mr. Biggs. Especially when she remembered what it had felt like to have the Vox Mortis vial pressed against her chest. She shuddered at random moments whenever she remembered that she had once drunk its awful contents voluntarily.

As she hatched and discarded absurd plans for going out into Athens, 399 BCE to track down Biggs herself, Dorrie watched the blackness of her thumbnail continue its retreat.

One day in the Scooby-Doo Library as Marcus paged madly through a book on how to give a Greek oration and Dorrie took another practice lunge with her sword at the jiggling skeleton's breastbone, Ebba emitted the kind of quiet *huh* that commanded instant attention.

Dorrie met her eyes as she looked up from *True Spine-Tingling Ghost Stories from around the World.*

"Remember how you said that all of Mr. Biggs's nails turned black when he drank the Vox Mortis?"

"Can't forget," said Dorrie.

"Well, look at this." She held up the open book.

Dorrie and Marcus peered at it. One page held words and the other an illustration. The illustration was of a dark cave mouth in a forbidding-looking wall of rock. It showed a skeleton inside the cave. The last bits of bone on each of the skeleton's fingers had been drawn black against the gray-green wall so that he looked to be sporting bear claws.

"The story's called 'The Cave of the Black-Fingered Skeleton,'" said Ebba. "It's all about this cave in Mali, so of course I was interested. It's in the desert near Timbuktu, and nobody will go near it." She flipped forward a page and began to read. "'Even today, local people avoid this cave. Many treasure-seekers have abandoned efforts to explore it, telling stories of being driven off by a skeleton with black finger bones. The local griots—the storytellers—say a dark light emanates from the cave.'"

Ebba looked from Marcus to Dorrie. "You think we should tell the lybrarians about this?"

Marcus grabbed the book and held it up for inspection. "The title of the book is *True Spine-Tingling Ghost Stories from around the World*. Why would anything in it correspond to reality?"

CHAPTER 21
A MODEST PROPOSAL

A T LAST, DORRIE AND Ebba again headed for London to begrudgingly conduct their second stakeout and— with a good deal more enthusiasm—to achieve a second objective.

They had checked out two of the warmest coats the circulation desk possessed, as well as burlap sacks in which to carry the painstakingly printed copies of the *Suffragette*.

The London keyhand had raised his eyebrows when Dorrie and Ebba showed up at the archway with the valise and the bulging sacks, but again, he ferried them through the archway with no questions asked.

Despite the danger Mr. Biggs and the Foundation posed— or maybe because of it—Dorrie felt a giddy pleasure at the thought of putting the newspapers in Annie's hands. Ebba seemed to share her mood. Straining beneath the weight of the sacks, they went straight to McAndrews Laundry.

"Annie's in at noon," Daisy said, stirring a steaming vat of bluish water.

They asked her if they could leave the sacks for her.

"What is this, a post office?" Daisy complained, but she allowed it.

The League's headquarters was bustling when they arrived. Lady Agnes and the Countess of Ilchester were getting ready to lead a delegation to a meeting at Parliament, where they'd been invited to argue against the idea of legalizing the vote for women. There were packets of information to assemble and rosettes to affix to the lapels of coats.

"Uncle Cromer has made it possible," Lady Agnes said proudly as she wafted around the room. She'd insisted that Ebba and Dorrie stay in her wake to assist her once she thought of something useful to do.

Ebba and Dorrie only escaped when one of the anti-suffrage sashes being ironed by a maid burst into flames, and they hurried away from Lady Agnes to help prop open doors and raise windows to get rid of the smoke.

At last, the leaders of the League were ready to sally forth.

Mrs. Richardson, who wasn't going, looked as relieved as Dorrie and Ebba to be getting rid of the lot of them. She shooed Dorrie and Ebba toward their coats. "Go have a lovely lunch."

Eager to make sure the newspapers had gotten into Annie's hands, Dorrie and Ebba hurriedly buttoned up.

"Wherever is Mr. Sacks-Sandbottom?" said Lady Agnes, her voice querulous.

"He hasn't returned from his speaking engagement at the Jameson Club," said Mrs. Richardson.

"But what about Lord Cromer's letter? It has to be delivered to the editor of the *Times*. I told Mr. Sacks-Sandbottom that quite clearly." Lady Agnes fussed with her hat. "The letter is a tour de force. Lord Cromer let me read it last night. He demonstrates quite inarguably that Mrs. Pankhurst and her brethren are not political prisoners as they claim but hysterical criminal maniacs that Mother England must care for as such."

She gave Dorrie, Ebba, and Mrs. Richardson a sly conspiratorial look, which made Dorrie want to step on her toes.

"Lord Cromer is great friends with the editor of the *Times*. He got the editor's word that the newspaper won't be printing a thing Mrs. Pankhurst has to say." She fluffed her fur collar. "And even if those outragers do manage to print another edition of the *Suffragette*, it will do them no good. Uncle has convinced the Home Office to make it illegal for newsagents to sell it. Isn't that brilliant?"

Dorrie and Ebba exchanged horrified looks as Mrs. Richardson put on her own coat.

"Lady Agnes!" called the countess from outside. "Our driver is blocking traffic. We really must go."

Lady Agnes turned her eyes on Dorrie and Ebba. "Be dears and drop off Uncle's letter for us, will you? The *Times* office is right across the park. The address is on the envelope. I put it in the cash box on Mr. Sacks-Sandbottom's desk. Thank you ever so much." Without waiting for an answer, she swept out onto the sidewalk. "Oh, Mrs. Richardson," she called from outside. "Perhaps you could—"

"Coming," said Mrs. Richardson. She gave Dorrie and Ebba a forbearing smile. "I think I'll go out for a nice, quiet lunch myself. I'll be back to let you in at two o'clock. Just close the door behind you when you leave."

"Oh, they're despicable!" Dorrie said as she and Ebba pushed open the door to Mr. Sacks-Sandbottom's office. It was frigid, nobody having closed the window since the ironing mishap.

"Get the letter and we'll run to tell Annie," said Ebba.

Dorrie ran to the desk and flipped open the lid of the cash box. Her timing couldn't have been worse. Just as she picked up Lord Cromer's letter, a forceful gust of wind from the window swirled through the room, its mischievous fingers sending a pile of bank notes swooping and tumbling through the air like a flock of escaped birds.

Dorrie found herself spinning around and snatching at the

bills. It was Ebba who thought to slam the window shut. The bills drifted to the floor.

"Oh, that's not good," said Dorrie.

Madly, she and Ebba swept around the room, raking paper money off the floor and the desk and from on top of a file cabinet and every other inconvenient place the bills had sought out as their final resting places.

Suddenly, Dorrie heard voices out in the main room. She and Ebba froze on their knees behind the big wooden desk, bills clutched against their chests. One of the voices belonged to Mr. Sacks-Sandbottom.

Remembering how he had accused Ebba of taking Lady Whitcomb's necklace, Dorrie had a very clear vision of the kind of thoughts that would cross his mind if he came into the room and saw them there.

Ebba must have experienced a similar vision, because after she slammed the cashbox lid closed, they made simultaneous dives for the space beneath the desk. They heard footsteps and the door to the office closing.

"You are my agent. My family has entrusted this business to you," said a woman's voice. "Now where are our bottles? You said the delivery would arrive weeks ago."

"That was the date we were given," said Mr. Sacks-Sandbottom, sounding harried.

"I want to see that document again myself."

To Dorrie's horror, Mr. Sacks-Sandbottom's legs came into view. Dorrie and Ebba clutched at each other as he jerked a drawer open. Dorrie heard what sounded like the twists and turns of a combination lock and then a flutter of paper.

"Here. It's just as I said," said Mr. Sacks-Sandbottom.

Now a skirt came into view as well as the upside-down head of a snarling fox, swinging back and forth like a fierce pendulum.

Dorrie and Ebba stared at one another. It was Lady Whitcomb!

"You see?" said Mr. Sacks-Sandbottom over the sound of paper being handled.

"Then something is either awry," said Lady Whitcomb, "or I'm being trifled with."

Dorrie heard a slosh of liquid.

"You're having more, Lady Whitcomb?" asked Mr. Sacks-Sandbottom in such a way that Dorrie could almost hear his eyebrows going up.

Lady Whitcomb laughed derisively. "Yes, I will have another nip if I please. Stop popping your eyes at me in that monkeyish manner or I'll send you to Timbuktu to check on the delivery yourself."

An envelope fell to the floor and landed perilously close to Ebba's foot.

Lady Whitcomb laughed again. "What? Did I frighten you?"

Dorrie stilled her breath as a long, gloved hand came into view, feeling for the envelope. It was addressed in loopy handwriting and stamped heavily. A picture in one corner gave Dorrie the impression of a brooding bat, its wings wrapped round itself.

Please don't see us. Please don't see us, Dorrie silently begged as the hand snatched the letter up.

"If you want to continue in my employ, you really must do something about those nerves," said Lady Whitcomb. "Telegram my agent at the manor every day. I want to know the hour the delivery arrives."

"Yes, milady." Mr. Sacks-Sandbottom left the room with Lady Whitcomb.

In a rush, Dorrie and Ebba crawled out from beneath the desk and thrust the money they'd collected back into the box. Opening the window back up, they hauled themselves over the sill and into an alley.

With trembling fingers, Dorrie stuffed Lord Cromer's letter in her pocket, and they ran all the way to McAndrews. Annie wasn't at the counter.

"She's out back," said Daisy. "And don't sit out there gabbing with her. She's got work to do. You've got two minutes."

They found Annie sending pillowcases through a mangle. As soon as she saw them, her face broke into a grin. "I don't know how you managed it, but your print job was brilliant. Really." She seemed to take in Dorrie and Ebba's distress, and her grin fled. "What's wrong?"

"The Home Office has made it illegal for newsagents to sell the *Suffragette*."

"Impossible," said Annie.

"It's true," cried Ebba and Dorrie.

Annie stared at them. "How did you…? Wait, don't tell me. Your mother's cousin has a friend." She brought her fist down on the top of the mangle. "The cheating monsters! Maybe my sister has it right with her rocks and matches. At this moment, I'm feeling a great urge to set fire to the Home Office!"

"Annie!" said Dorrie, alarmed. "You don't mean that. Not really. Right?"

"Two minutes is up," Daisy yelled from the back door.

"I'm not at all sure," said Annie.

"Out!" yelled Daisy as Annie gave the mangle's handle a hard turn.

When they emerged from McAndrews, Dorrie yanked out Lord Cromer's letter. "And now we're supposed to make sure this stupid letter gets safely to the *Times*? After all he's done?"

"It deserves a garbage heap," said Ebba.

Staring at the letter, Dorrie experienced a wild desire to tear it to pieces. Lord Cromer was a cheater and a manipulator. If she threw it down a sewer grate, nobody would be any the wiser in Petrarch's Library or in London. She could tell Lady Agnes she lost it. With great pleasure, she imagined Lord Cromer's words rotting below apple cores and fish heads, falling to pieces. A flicker of shame called her back. "Except there's that whole first principle thing."

They had reached the steps of the London Library.

"Do you think Annie would really, you know, try to burn something down?" asked Ebba.

Dorrie listlessly speared a piece of litter with the tip of her umbrella, and just like that, a possible plan elbowed itself forward. If Savi could use satire, why not Annie and the suffragists? Dorrie's felt a shiver of excitement. Why couldn't Annie write something that would *seem* like a letter from someone arguing against women's suffrage but would actually convince people that women should get the vote?

She imagined Annie slipping such a letter into the envelope along with Lord Cromer's and delivering them both to the newspaper office. She'd simply say that they were *both* from Lord Cromer. If no one was paying too much attention, maybe they'd both be printed!

"Ebba," she said, turning slowly to her friend. "We have to go back."

"The Lord Savior on a five-legged horse!" said Daisy when they presented themselves again fifteen minutes later. "What do you want now?"

"I promise, we just need to talk to Annie for one minute," said Dorrie.

Ebba took off her coat. "Here. We'll pay to have this ironed."

Daisy threw it back at her. "Five minutes."

Annie was now stirring a vat of soapy liquid with a paddle.

"So let me get this straight," she said four out of the five minutes later. "You are suggesting I deliver an envelope to the editor of the *Times*. It will contain a letter written by Lord Cromer telling the world that suffragists are a bunch of lunatics and giving reasons why they should be treated like criminals and why no woman should ever have the vote." She paused in her stirring. "Do I have that much right?"

"Exactly," said Dorrie and Ebba together.

She began to work the paddle up and down. "It will also contain a second letter: a work of satire I will produce in my copious free time this evening. It will appear to argue that suffragists are lunatics and should be treated like criminals and that no woman should ever have the vote but in actuality argue that suffragists are perfectly sane women who should indeed have the vote." She stilled the paddle again and raised her eyebrows at them.

"Exactly," Dorrie and Ebba said again in unison.

"Lots of writers make their points that way," Dorrie said. She quickly pulled out a bound collection of satiric essays that the Lybrariad's representative at the London Library had helped them find.

Annie took the book, amused, even in her dark mood. "You've thought of everything." She looked at the contents.

"'A Modest Proposal for Preventing the Children of Poor People from Being a Burthen to Their Parents or Country, and for Making Them Beneficial to the Publick' by Jonathan Swift—oh, yes, I remember that one." She looked up. "'Eat them' was the proposal as I remember it." She looked farther down the list. "'For Witches' by Hercule-Savinien de Cyrano de Bergerac."

Dorrie had crowed with pleased astonishment when she'd seen the essay listed in the contents.

Annie stared at his name. "I thought Hercule-Savinien de Cyrano de Bergerac was a fictional character in a play."

Dorrie cleared her throat and looked over her shoulder, as if Savi might be behind her with steam coming out of his ears. "Yeah, a lot of people do. Actually, he really lived. He wrote a lot of stuff."

"So what do you think?" Ebba asked.

Annie gave her bottom lip a short chew. "It's a sneaky thing to do, but given all the cheating and conniving coming from that lot, perhaps there's justice in it. She looked thoughtfully into the suds. How about…'Ten Reasons Why Suffrage for Women Would Destroy Civilization?'"

"That could work," said Ebba.

"I'm not the slouchiest of slouches with a pen," said Annie, "but I'm going to have to take tonight to do it. I won't be able to deliver the letter until tomorrow."

Dorrie felt a slither of uneasiness. She glanced quickly at Ebba. For all Dorrie knew, Lady Agnes was right and Annie had been stealing the stacks of the *Anti-Suffrage Review*. If she had, what would keep her from tossing Lord Cromer's letter in the garbage as Dorrie and Ebba had longed to do?

"But you'll definitely deliver it?" said Dorrie, thinking of Hypatia's insistence on the value of the Even Eye. "Because as much as I hate what Lord Cromer is saying…"

"I'll deliver it," said Annie.

Dorrie fished for the envelope in her bag and handed it over slowly to Annie.

She and Ebba reached the League's headquarters at the same time as a jubilant Lady Agnes. The printer's van had just pulled up outside. A man in an apron threw the new copies of the *Anti-Suffrage Review* on the doorstep.

"Oh, leave them there for now," said Lady Agnes to Mrs. Richardson. "I'm sure they'll be fine. No suffragist all day, the papers will lay." She gave a trilling little laugh. "And I have so much to tell you!"

Dorrie and Ebba exchanged pained glances.

Lady Agnes didn't notice. She spent the rest of the afternoon telling Dorrie, Ebba, and Mrs. Richardson about the wonderful effect she felt she'd had on the Lords. At last, it was time to leave. Dorrie and Ebba were in their coats and about to say their good-byes when a shriek from Lady Agnes rent the air.

"She's done it again!" she shouted, pointing frantically at the door, her hand on her chest. "She's just run away with some of the newspapers!"

Dorrie and Ebba tore for the door and wrenched it open. They ran outside, letting it slam behind them.

Far down the sidewalk, a figure in a hooded cloak was covering a lot of ground fast.

"Oh, please don't be Annie," whispered Dorrie.

"We have to go after her," said Ebba. "It is our real mission here, remember?"

They pelted down the sidewalk, passersby giving them room and looking surprised at their flying skirts. The figure was turning down a smaller road. When they got to the corner, they could see another wider road quite a distance away—and no running figure.

"She has to be in here somewhere," said Dorrie. "She couldn't have made it all the way down to that other road."

They hurried along, finally coming across a narrow, cobbled alley, dank and full of offal and piles of rotting garbage.

"Do we dare go down there?"

"Yes, we dare," Dorrie said, feeling for Ebba's hand.

Sticking close to the wall, they made their way toward a little door. A grime-encrusted window lay closer to them. Cautiously, Dorrie brought herself to it and peeped inside. It was a shabby room. A woman who looked tired and ill sat rocking with her eyes closed in a chair near a little iron stove, on top of which stood a pot. The door of the stove was open, and in its faint glow, Dorrie made out the face of a girl about her own age, kneeling beside it. She tore at the bundle until the papers fell apart and methodically began to feed them into the little stove, making the faint glow temporarily brighten.

"That's the thief?" whispered Dorrie.

"She doesn't care what the paper says," Ebba whispered. "She's just trying to keep her house warm."

"What are we supposed to do now?" asked Dorrie.

Ebba dug in her bag. "Knock on the door. I've got an idea."

Dorrie did. Through the window, she watched the girl freeze, looking alarmed. The woman slowly opened confused eyes but made no move to get out of the chair.

Slowly, the girl got to her feet, came to the door, and opened it a crack. She had sandy-blond hair, and her face and hands were sooty. Her eyes were full of fear.

"We don't care that you took the newspapers," said Ebba, holding out a handful of shillings. "But could we trade you this for them?"

The girl just stared at the coins.

"We won't tell anyone," said Dorrie. "You just have to promise not to take them anymore."

Nodding, the girl quickly took the money and, after disappearing for a moment, came back with what was left of the papers.

It was with great pleasure that Dorrie and Ebba laid the remaining copies of the *Anti-Suffrage Review* on one of the tables in the League's headquarters in front of Mrs. Richardson and a disappointed-looking Lady Agnes.

"It wasn't Ann—" Dorrie stopped herself. "It wasn't that suffragist from the soapbox at all."

As Dorrie and Ebba made their way back to the London Library, Dorrie giggled, remembering how unhappy Lady Agnes had looked at their explanation of who exactly had been stealing the newspapers and why.

"Hey," said Ebba as they climbed the stairs of the library. "You know what this means? We can stop slinking around the room in the principles practicum. We completed our mission!"

Dorrie paused for a moment. "Annie *is* going to deliver that letter, right?"

Chapter 22
A Name and a Face

THAT EVENING BACK IN Petrarch's Library, Dorrie felt flush with their success in discovering the identity of the newspaper thief. After dinner, Ebba hurried off to her camel-riding lessons, and Marcus, intent on earning more Filthy Lucre to cover his expenses on his next trip to Athens, begged Fatima to busk again at the Inky Pot. The Archivist hadn't been at the Sharpened Quill. The revelation of Della Porta's failure to decipher the journal had reinvigorated the old keyhand's belief that it was indeed written in a real, if lost, language. He had made trips out into several wherens, following up on new leads for a Rosetta stone that could jump-start the translation. He's also taken to working late into the night.

Excited to tell him about how her mission in England had finished, Dorrie hurried to his office.

He wasn't there, but it was clear when she pushed open the door that he'd recently been hard at work. The water in the teakettle was still gently steaming, and the room was strewn with papers. Several doors of the cabinet that held the *History of Histories* books were wide open, with a good number of the volumes spread across the floor and furniture. One had a feather sticking out from between its pages. Her heart beat a little faster. She immediately wondered if this was the same volume he'd marked with a feather the day she'd ended up out on the water. The day he'd been so upset.

The letters on the spine danced and then became legible: *History of Histories—Europa—309 PLE—January.* The book seemed to call to her. She couldn't help but wonder if it were the twin to the one out of which the missing page had come. The one that could tell her who among the lybrarians would die if the Foundation succeeded in reversing the crux mission. She edged closer, part of her longing to know and part of her wanting to run far away.

She let her gaze leap around the page, alighting on descriptions of missions that had saved people from drownings, hangings, beheadings, and a very nasty-sounding poisoning, but nowhere on the page did she see Ursula's name or Savi's or Hypatia's or Phillip's. Francesco was listed as the keyhand on several of the missions but never as the imperiled subject.

Her breathing slowed. Benedetta Diaz, Bjorn Olmstead,

Adelaide Stone, Gerhardt Blum…none of the imperiled subjects sounded even faintly familiar…except… She stared at the last entry on the page, unsure… "Sophia Ana de Reyes." *Where had she heard that name?*

There was a lightly penciled star beside the entry. She read the whole thing. "321 PLE January: On this seventh day of April 1481, in Castile, Spain. Foiled. A plot to burn at the stake for heresy, Sophia Ana de Reyes, author of poems, whose writing inspired Pope Sixtus to reject Tomas de Torquemada's request to extend his Inquisition into Aragon and other parts of Spain, France, and Italy. Lybrarian: Raul Enriquez. Keyhand: Francesco d'Avila."

She was looking at the crux mission! A word faintly penciled below the poet's name caught her attention: Dorrie sucked in her breath. She could make out an *M* and then an *I* and then… She stopped breathing for a moment. The word spelled out "Millie." A penciled line led from Millie's name to a scrawled note in the margin: "ancillary rescue." Dorrie's heart began to pound, a powerful dread rising in her. In a flash, she knew. Sophia Ana de Reyes was Millie's mother, and it was Millie who would die if the Foundation reversed the Torquemada crux mission.

"Is it true?" Dorrie asked a half hour later while sitting in front of Ursula's fire, a hot cup of strong tea in her hand.

With Savi away, she hadn't known where else to go, so she'd plunked down in front of the entry to Ursula's cottage and waited. At last, Phillip and Ursula had arrived hand in hand, Phillip humming a tune.

Now Ursula handed Phillip a mug as well. "I'm afraid so."

Dorrie felt her hands began to shake, and she sloshed tea onto the stone floor.

Phillip gently took the mug from her and set it on the table. "Twelve years ago, Francesco set out on a mission to save the life of Sophia Ana de Reyes by breaking her out of a dungeon. She had become the subject of a Lybrariad mission after the Spanish Inquisition arrested her for heresy because of some poems she'd written. When Francesco arrived at her prison, he found that Sophia had given birth to a child. One that only Torquemada knew existed. Millie."

Dorrie stared straight ahead into the crackling flames. No wonder Francesco had spoken to her so harshly during the meeting with Hypatia. She imagined the terror her own father would feel if Dorrie's life was in danger and how angry he would be at the person who had placed her there. Her shoulders sagged.

"What happened to Millie's mother?" asked Dorrie.

"She was killed in an ambush planned by Torquemada a

week after Francesco rescued her from the dungeon. A poem she had written while imprisoned would ultimately ruin Torquemada's chances of extending his Spanish Inquisition into other parts of the world, but Torquemada didn't know about that when he murdered her. He just wanted her dead so no one would find out he'd fathered a child."

"That's horrible," whispered Dorrie.

"He tried to kill Millie as well," said Phillip. "But Francesco was able to save her."

"Who else knows?" Dorrie asked finally.

"Now?" said Phillip. "The Library staff, the keyhands, and Hypatia of course, but Francesco only told us of the direct danger to Millie some weeks ago. The day before Mr. Biggs escaped."

"Why did he wait?"

Phillip frowned. "He knew the Lybrariad was working as hard as it could to stop the Foundation from reversing the Torquemada crux mission, even without knowing that Millie's life hung in the balance. He'd never told anyone about Torquemada being Millie's father. I think he wanted to protect her from that knowledge by keeping her danger a secret." He folded his hands over his generous belly. "And he had another reason to hold back. When Francesco returned from his mission in Castile with a baby in his arms, he didn't talk to the rest of us about what had happened. He went into a meeting with Hypatia to report on Sophia's death, and after he came out, he was no longer serving as a keyhand. Nobody knew why. I regret to say that a rumor that he'd been suspended went unchecked."

"I'd heard that rumor," said Dorrie. "So what really happened?"

"He gave up his keyhand status himself," said Phillip. "In the terrible moment when he'd been ambushed by Torquemada's soldiers and they'd killed Sophia, a woman he'd come to love, Francesco came to within a hairsbreadth of killing Torquemada. Lybrarians are prohibited from dealing a killing blow, even in self-defense and certainly not to exact vengeance."

"The twelfth principle," said Dorrie softly. They hadn't yet got to it in Hypatia's practicum, but Dorrie had seen it listed.

"Francesco didn't kill Torquemada," Phillip said, "and that was his heroism, but he didn't trust himself anymore. He had felt the desire to kill Torquemada so keenly that he was afraid of losing control again. Taking on the job of director of security, he was able to spend more time in the Library and take better care of Millie, and he didn't have to go out on missions so often. It felt…safer."

Dorrie's sympathy for Francesco grew. "So if Francesco hadn't rescued Millie and her mom from the dungeon, what would have happened to Sophia's poem?"

Ursula hung the kettle back on its hook. "It would never

have seen the light of day, and Torquemada would have extended his Inquisition."

"And Millie?"

"Torquemada would have killed her."

"And if the reversal of the crux mission happens…"

"Then that will be her history."

Dorrie didn't want to move. Didn't want to make a scene. But something was going to happen. She could feel her control crumbling. She slowly bent forward, her arms folding around her head. A moan escaped her.

She heard Ursula's footsteps and hated that she heard them. Hated that she had to continue to be aware. To know. She felt Ursula crouch down beside her. She put a hand on Dorrie's back.

"I know this has been terribly hard to hear," said Ursula, "but we have to ask you to keep this information to yourself. Millie does not know that her life is in danger, and Francesco wants to keep it that way."

"Shouldn't she know?" said Dorrie, straightening up.

"Francesco believes it would be too hard for her to live a normal life under such a black cloud."

"Well, it's hard to live a normal life when you're dead too!" cried Dorrie. "And she *is* living under a black cloud right now. She thinks Francesco is ashamed of her for being Torquemada's daughter."

Ursula looked troubled.

"And shouldn't she have the chance to fight for her life?" Dorrie asked. "I'd want to know if my life were in danger."

"Perhaps you're right," said Phillip. "But those are Francesco's wishes."

When Dorrie returned to the attics, the den was deserted. She went straight to her room, planning to wake up Ebba. Amazingly, she was still awake, sitting amid a sea of books, nothing left of the candle at the bottom of her bed but a flickering flame in a melted pool of wax.

"There you are!" she said before Dorrie could speak. "I went to the Scooby-Doo Library three times, the Inky Pot twice. The Celsus—"

"There's something I have to tell—"

"No! There's something I have to show you first," interrupted Ebba. "Remember when we were under Mr. Sacks-Sandbottom's desk and that envelope fell on the floor?"

"Yeah," said Dorrie uncertainly.

"Do you remember the little picture in one corner? You know, where a return address usually goes? At least in some wherens."

Dorrie thought back. "Yeah. The thing that kind of looked like a folded-up bat?"

"That's funny," said Ebba, tilting her head. "I thought it looked like a lady in a hat. Anyway," she said, opening *True Spine-Tingling Ghost Stories from around the World*. "I didn't say anything at the time, but it was as if I'd seen the picture before." She tapped her finger on the illustration of the black-fingered skeleton. "And I had!"

At first Dorrie saw nothing. She tilted the book so that more of the candlelight reached it. Above the skeleton head, fine lines made a perfect copy of the picture on the envelope. The hairs on the back of her neck rose. "It's the same!"

"Exactly!" said Ebba. "And that's not all." She dug out her copy of *The Foundation: Essential Dictums* and thrust it into Dorrie's hands.

"What?"

"Remember the three stacked diamonds?"

Dorrie, exhausted and still burdened with the news about Millie, grew impatient. "What about them?"

"Well, doesn't the folded bat picture look like it's hiding three stacked diamonds?"

Dorrie stared at the picture above the skeleton's head and then at the white book's. At first, the images seemed to have nothing to do with each other, but then, as if tilting one of those magic picture prizes from a box of Cracker Jack, she could suddenly see the three diamonds embedded in the folded bat.

She sucked in her breath. "One is inside the other! Maybe Lady Whitcomb is connected to the Foundation!"

"That's how it seemed to me," whispered Ebba.

Dorrie cast her mind back over all she remembered of her encounters with Lady Whitcomb. She grabbed Ebba's arm, her eyes widening. "Didn't she mention Timbuktu when we were under the desk?"

"And bottles," said Ebba. "Yes, Lady Agnes said Lady Whitcomb's family owns ginger beer factories, but what if she was talking about waiting for Vox Mortis vials?"

Dorrie's heart began to thunder. "Ebba, Mr. Biggs said that only he knew where the Vox Mortis vials were stashed and that he had to send them off to all the Foundation's new associates in the past. I've been assuming, since he used the Athens, 399 BCE archway, that the vials were hidden in the city. But it's been weeks since Mr. Biggs escaped, and none of the missions have been reversed yet."

Ebba wrinkled her nose. "That might just be because the Foundation's new friends haven't finished making enough of that foul Vox Mortis."

"Or maybe he had to travel a great distance to get to them," said Dorrie. She began to pace the tiny bedroom. "Just because we saw Mr. Biggs in Athens that one time last quarter doesn't mean that's where the Stronghold actually connects with 399 BCE or where the vials were being stored."

"They could be any place in 399 BCE," Ebba whispered.

"Like in that cave," Dorrie said grimly. "And if Mr. Biggs is trying to get to Timbuktu from Athens and he has to travel the regular way—walking and by boat and all that—of course it would take him weeks."

Ebba threw aside *The Foundation: Essential Dictums.* "But if we use the Timbuktu, 1567 archway, we could be there in a few hours."

"And maybe we could get to the vials first," cried Dorrie.

"If his ship sinks or an adder gets him anyway," said Ebba.

Dorrie frowned. "What do you mean?"

"Well, if Mr. Biggs stowed the vials in the cave there around 399 BCE, they'll only still be there in 1567 if he never got to retrieve them."

"A lot might happen to a person between Athens and Timbuktu," said Dorrie, hoping. "Ebba, we have to talk to Millie."

CHAPTER 23
VALIANCE AND VERITY

M ILLIE HAD BEEN SHOCKED when Dorrie asked her to wait for her after their Staying Afloat practicum, and Izel positively boggled when Millie had shrugged her shoulders and agreed. In near silence, Dorrie led Millie to the Scooby-Doo Library. To her credit, Millie made no complaint about the rat-infested tunnel or even the fact that Darling, who had finished destroying her enclosure, was lying on the back of the couch, cracking a chicken bone to pieces. Ebba was sitting beside her, idly playing with Dorrie's practice sword. She hastily stuck it in the elephant leg with the other weapons when Dorrie and Millie arrived.

"So what's this all about?" asked Millie, standing stiffly just inside the door.

Dorrie glanced at Ebba to draw strength and hoped she was

doing the right thing. "I'm not supposed to tell you, but your life is in danger."

"Oh yeah?" Millie barked, sounding very much like Francesco. "How?"

Dorrie drew another breath. "You're the person Lybrarian Della Porta was talking about when he told Izel that reversing the crux mission would cost someone in Petrarch's Library their life."

Dorrie told her all she'd learned from the *History of Histories* book and how Millie's survival was entwined with Francesco's mission to save her mother twelve years ago and how Francesco had kept the identity of Millie's mother and father a secret to protect Millie from the burden of knowing that her life was in jeopardy.

Millie's eyes had glittered throughout Dorrie's explanation— but with what emotion, Dorrie wasn't sure.

"I'm sorry if you wish I hadn't told you," said Dorrie, bracing for anger, "but I just kept thinking that I'd want to know if my life were in danger."

A look of deep joy slowly bloomed in Millie's face. "So he wasn't ashamed of me," she murmured.

"Definitely not," Dorrie said. "Just terrified of...well... you...uh...disappearing."

Millie's eyes shone. "And my mother's poem made all the difference in keeping Torquemada in check?"

Dorrie nodded.

"You understand, right?" said Ebba carefully. "You know that if the mission Francesco ran gets reversed—"

"That I'll die? Or never live? Or whatever?" Millie snorted in her old scornful way. "That just makes me really mad! That's something I can fight. It's nothing compared to thinking Francesco thought there was something wrong with me. That I was someone who was too evil-spawned to be a lybrarian."

Dorrie felt a mixed pang of empathy and resentment, Millie had often said in one way or another that Dorrie wasn't good enough to become a lybrarian simply because she hadn't grown up in Petrarch's Library. "I know what that feels like," she said with a bit more sharpness than she meant to.

Millie met her eyes. "I guess you do." She seemed to squirm a little. "Sorry about that."

Dorrie shrugged. "Yeah, well, I feel kind of stupid even thinking about it right now, but thanks."

Millie got to her feet. "Now what?"

"Well," said Dorrie, exchanging glances with Ebba, who began to dig in her satchel for the books to show Millie, "we have a lead to follow."

"Our evidence is kind of flimsy, not enough to bring to the Lybrariad, but Ebba and I think there's a small chance the Vox Mortis vials might be out in this cave in the desert not too far from the Timbuktu, 1567 archway."

319

Dorrie and Ebba explained why as Darling, who had finished her bone, slid off the couch to gnaw on the fireplace poker.

"I'm in," said Millie when she'd heard their idea.

That night, as quietly as they could, Dorrie and Ebba crept out of their room with the burlap bags they'd stuffed with their supplies, and met Millie in the den. Together, they picked their way with utmost care through the chambers of Petrarch's Library, having to dodge and hide from several research runners despite the late hour.

In the Chinese library, by the dim light of the glowing calendar to the right of the Timbuktu archway, they changed into the desert clothing that Ebba had checked out with the excuse that her family wanted to get prepared early for their trip to Mali at the end of the quarter.

Done dressing first, Ebba pulled a fat *Encyclopedia of Mammals* out of her pack. "It has a very vivid description of a camel in it," she whispered. "I hope the saddle comes too."

While Dorrie pushed the plug more firmly into one of the sloshing water skins, she watched Millie strap on a curved sword, then a dagger. Millie was in the process of strapping on a second dagger when she caught Dorrie's stare.

"What?" she said.

"Do you really need to bring so many?"

Millie shot home the last buckle. "Francesco says you should never go out into a wheren with fewer than three weapons." She peered into her pack. "I brought eleven. All made in Petrarch's Library." She tossed a small sword to Dorrie.

Busy opening to the right page of the encyclopedia, Ebba declined Millie's offer of a scimitar. "I've got my slingshot."

Millie rummaged further. "I also brought a tinderbox, two pounds of jerky, a fishing line and hook, a tent, a needle and thread for stitches, bandages and salve, and a snakebite kit."

Dorrie stared at it all. "Nothing like planning for success."

Millie gave her an unyielding look. "Nothing like planning for survival."

Feeling exposed but preferring to attempt the camel read-out inside Petrarch's Library rather than out in the unfamiliar Spoke Library, Dorrie kept anxious watch on the corridor while Millie kept her eyes trained on the archway to warn of any late-arriving lybrarians.

Rigid with concentration, Ebba knelt by the book and placed her fingertips on the drawing. She began to whisper the passage aloud. Dorrie saw her begin to sweat, and in another moment, a little hump of something velvety appeared beneath her fingers.

"I feel her!" gasped Ebba.

Slowly, the little mound became a pair of immense lips pulled back from a set of yellowed, Halloween pumpkin teeth. The book bent and flexed as more of the nose emerged and then a rolling brown eye surrounded by lashes thicker even than Saul's. With a sudden plunge, the camel shook itself free of the page, its neck festooned with lengths of woven red strapping hung with tassels. It towered over them.

Dorrie marveled at it.

"Oh, you great, big, darling, beautiful creature," Ebba crooned as it tried to stick its head in what looked like a Ming vase.

"I sure hope it's well-trained," said Millie.

Ebba patted the camel. "You know, the book didn't say anything about that." She got busy reading out a second one.

A few minutes later, the apprentices and two camels stood in the empty Spoke Library in Timbuktu. Dorrie had been surprised at how willing the camels had been to go through the archway.

Getting the camels out into the faintly moonlit street through the low doorway proved not nearly as easy. The apprentices had nearly despaired of being able to get any further with their plan when the camels, for reasons known only to themselves, changed their minds with such suddenness that they nearly crushed the three girls as they clambered through.

After a bit of a struggle, Ebba got both camels to kneel. She explained to Millie and Dorrie how to get on and how to stay on when the camel stood so many times that Millie finally shut her up with, "I know, I know"—but then did topple off when the camel stood and had to start all over again.

At last, with Dorrie and Ebba perched on the second camel, they were on their way.

Dorrie felt for the compass she'd tied onto her sword belt. Before she could consult it, her camel broke into a gallumphing run. Dorrie screamed and threw her arms around Ebba. They flew past low doorways flanked by water cisterns and assortments of jars, and when the camel took a sharp turn, Dorrie almost had her head knocked off by a beam sticking out of a stucco wall. She ducked just in time. When she dared lift her head again, they were bursting out of the end of a street and into what looked like an endless sea of sand. The camel slowed down and came to a splay-legged stop.

The second camel joined them, Millie hanging off to one side.

"These are *not* well-trained camels," Millie said as she fell again.

After Millie remounted, and the other camel turned around and bit Dorrie's foot, Dorrie finally had a chance to get their bearings. Their hurried research on caves in the desert surrounding Timbuktu had turned up a few results, but one had excited them. A book had described a cave at the base of a rock formation called the Crocodile Cliffs as being unpleasant and infrequently visited, and five miles northwest of Timbuktu.

"We can't just keep calling them 'first camel' and 'second

camel,'" said Ebba as they plodded across the sand in the deep dark.

Millie snorted. "They don't deserve names."

"They're letting us ride them," said Ebba. "And they might be helping us find the vials." She took off one of the two scarves she had wrapped around her head and tied it around her camel's neck. "I dub thee Verity." She looked back at Millie. "Would you mind dubbing yours Valiant?"

Millie only snorted again.

They rode for what felt like an impossibly long time, and despite Dorrie's constant checking on their direction, no crocodile-shaped cliff had yet come into view. Dazzled by the electric brightness of the stars and the sea of moon-brightened sand, Dorrie had never felt so thoroughly away from everything she knew. Soon though, the temperature began to drop, and Dorrie felt her fingers going numb. A cramping stiffness in her muscles made her feel like she was simply going to topple off the next time the camel swerved left or right.

At last, something changed on the horizon. Excitement and nervousness pricked Dorrie. Soon, the solid dark silhouette of a crocodile head could be seen against the star-spangled sky behind it.

They stopped in a hollow among the dunes to stretch their legs and drink water. Dorrie and Millie slid clumsily to the ground and landed in heaps. Rubbing her legs and saying

"Ow, ow, ow, ow," Dorrie struggled to her feet and took hold of Verity's reins as Ebba slid down as well, managing to keep her feet.

"I sure hope the attack skeleton isn't real," Ebba said a few minutes later as she folded away an empty water skin. She fished some dates out of a pack and fed a few to Verity, which the camel seemed to relish. The wind, which had picked up, ruffled her scarf.

"C'mon, we'd better go," said Dorrie. "We've got to leave just as much time to get back as it takes us to get the cave, and we want as much time as possible to look for those vials." As they gathered their things, the wind began to gust more strongly, driving stinging sand before it.

Verity and Valiant didn't seem to like the change. They simply refused to kneel. In desperation, Ebba poured the rest of the dates onto the ground in front of them. Just when it looked like they were going to fold their legs, a great cloud of fast-moving sand pricked them all over, and both camels bolted, reins streaming behind them.

"No!" shouted Ebba, trying to run after them, her feet churning inefficiently in the deep sand, Dorrie and Millie at her heels.

Within seconds, the two camels had disappeared over a dune into a cloud of swirling, airborne sand as neatly as if they had used a skipkey, taking all the girls' supplies with them except for Dorrie's compass and the weapons hanging from Millie's belt.

Ebba stumbled to a stop. "Are they going to be okay?"

"They're camels!" shouted Millie. "We're the ones in trouble!"

Ebba raised her voice over the sound of the wind. "Do we have to head back?"

Dorrie glanced nervously in the direction of the cliffs, which were lost for the moment in the swirling sand. They hadn't seemed too far off, but now…with no water… She glanced at Millie. Her lips were stubbornly set. Dorrie imagined Millie disappearing before their eyes. "I say we keep going."

"Me too," said Millie.

They trudged in silence, tucking their chins against the wild flying sand. At times, the clouds of sand obscured the cliffs completely, and Dorrie was afraid they'd miss them.

At last, the jutting spine of rock that now loomed above them. Dorrie's hands touched rough rock.

With no clue to guide her but desperate to get out of the driving, pitiless sand, Dorrie blindly chose to go right, the others hanging on to her. Wearily, her fingers sought a refuge in the cliff face. They had gone on like this for some time when without warning, the face of the cliff seemed to give way, and Dorrie found herself falling—Ebba and Millie with her. They landed in a tangle. Beneath them, a vast nest of bones and skulls clattered and slid.

Shrieking, Dorrie and Ebba scrambled out of it in different directions.

"They're not going to hurt you," said Millie, tossing her bangs and kicking at a bone that looked like a rib.

Dorrie tried to slow down her breathing. "Yeah, well, I'd rather not sit on them." She looked around.

They stood in a small cave with rough walls. At the height of their heads, the small opening through which they had fallen showed flying sand bright like snow seen outside the window of a lit room.

"How are we seeing each other?" asked Millie. "It should be pitch-black in here. Where's the light coming from?"

"The bones," whispered Ebba.

Slowly, Dorrie looked down. They did seem to be exuding a ponderous, dark sort of light.

Millie put a hand on one of her daggers. "It feels like…like bad things have happened in here."

Dorrie tried not to let Millie's words unnerve her. "Better start looking for the vials."

"If they're here, I bet they're near that folded-up bat picture," said Ebba.

Each taking a section of the cave, the apprentices set to work searching for it on the chamber's walls.

Just when Dorrie felt she had nowhere left to search, Millie called out. "Look at this."

Dorrie and Ebba hurried to her. In a fold in the cave's wall, Millie pointed out a narrow opening in the shape of a peapod. Peering into the space beyond it, Dorrie made out a narrow passage. Its walls were the same rough stone as those of the cave. It was filled with an even heavier version of the unsettling light.

Millie stepped through the opening and turned back to them. "Are you coming?"

Dorrie said a silent good-bye to her hopes that if the vials were there, the vials would be easy to find, possibly already packed in a convenient carrying case. She forced herself to follow, Ebba close behind. The passage narrowed further, its walls converging at what looked like a mere crooked crack.

"Look!" shouted Ebba.

High above the crack, the figure of the folded bat lady had been scratched into the rock.

"Just like on the envelope," whispered Ebba. "And in the book."

Beyond the crack, the light dimly showed another rock wall less than a foot away. Hope burning in her eyes, Millie thrust her arm through and reached in all directions.

"Nothing," said Millie angrily.

Dorrie squeezed by her and maneuvered her head through the widest part of the crack. Her palms broke out in a sweat. She was looking down a cleft in the rock so narrow that Dorrie could barely fit her whole head into it. Far, far away, the cleft seemed to widen. The thought of squeezing her whole body into that crevice and then traveling its length was terrifically unpleasant. She forced herself to speak. "I think we have to go farther."

Dorrie led the way. Twisting and turning like a corkscrew, she managed to claw her way into the cleft.

She began to shuffle sideways, trying not to think about getting stuck, scraping a new bit of skin off with every step. Behind her, she could hear Ebba struggling her way through the crack and then, with many curses, Millie.

After far too many steps taken, the cleft finally widened. With great relief, Dorrie tumbled into a chamber, Ebba close behind.

"Are they there?" Millie called, a note of raw desperation in her voice as she struggled to reach them. For all her brave talk, she sounded deeply afraid.

Dorrie's eyes swept the chamber, trying to make sense of its contents.

The floor was littered here and there with scraps of papyrus, parchment, and paper. In the cavern's center stood a great flat-topped block of stone, covered in black stains and what looked like dried pools of red and yellow wax. Someone had affixed five enormous metal plates to the wall. The figure of the bat had been etched into the top of each one. They were covered with lines of writing in dozens of languages.

Millie appeared beside Dorrie, her cheek freely bleeding.

"What's all this?" said Ebba dropping onto the floor to sift through the scraps.

Dorrie and Millie examined the plates.

"They're covered with names and addresses," said Dorrie as the lines of writing shifted into readability.

"And dates," said Millie. "Each name has a date next to it."

Dorrie gave a cry and pointed. "There's Lady Whitcomb's name!"

"And look at this," said Ebba, standing with a rough-edged piece of parchment.

Dorrie and Millie leaned close, and Dorrie's breath caught. Though most of the page was blank, someone had begun to write a letter upon it. A letter dated the fifth of March 1077 began:

"Dear Count Sieciech,

Long have you patiently waited, outnumbered by the ignorant, for the glorious return of the Foundation. Long have you kept—"

It ended in a blot of ink, as though an accident had made the writer give up, perhaps to start the letter over fresh on another sheet of parchment. The apprentices stared at one another.

"The Foundation *is* using this place," said Dorrie.

With great energy and hope, they darted around the room, searching it for the vials as they had the first chamber with increasing franticness, but again with no luck. Millie finally turned and slapped the wall hard, breathing roughly, her head bowed. "They're not here."

Dorrie glanced at Ebba, feeling helpless, as Millie's breaths echoed in the silence.

When Millie at last turned back, her face was stiff. "We'd better get back and tell the Lybrariad what we found."

Dorrie took a last look at the metal plates. For the first time, she noticed one of them was different from the others. Rather than being arranged in a list of names and addresses, the words on it were laid out in the shape of a letter, complete with a salutation, a close, and a signature. She peered more closely at it. "I don't believe it," she shot out. She touched a line of the writing. "Those are symbols from Petrarch's alphabet!"

"Are you sure?" Millie asked.

Dorrie nodded vigorously. "The Archivist has them painted on his wall. I stare at them every morning!"

"We really have to go," said Ebba. "We're on foot, and once the sun hits the desert..."

A thought struck Dorrie as Ebba and Millie began to ease themselves back through the crevice. A thought she didn't dare explain now in case she were wrong. Heart racing, she snatched up the letter to the count from the stone block where Ebba had laid it and tucked it inside her clothes.

The second struggle through the cleft reopened old scrapes and created new ones. They had just stumbled out of the middle passage and into the cavern of bones when a monstrous shape thrust itself through the cave mouth above their heads, making them all shriek.

Millie pulled out a sword and a dagger. Dorrie, unable to afford the luxury of squeamishness, dove for a leg bone.

"Verity!" shrieked Ebba.

The shape pulled back her rubbery lips to display an impressive set of yellow-brown teeth, set off nicely against a blue scarf.

Chapter 24
An Unexpected Meeting

DURING THE JOURNEY BACK across the desert, the implications of their failure to find the vials worked their way more deeply into Dorrie's heart. Millie hardly spoke at all, and Dorrie couldn't bring herself to talk with Ebba about anything else while the specter of losing Millie rode along with them. A glance at her thumbnail added to Dorrie's anxiety. There was hardly anything left of the black stain. She wondered for a very uncomfortable moment if she'd be able to get them back into Petrarch's Library.

On the edge of Timbuktu, which they almost missed entirely, Ebba pushed the camels' reins into the surprised hands of a man at the head of a long caravan of camels loaded down with slabs of salt, and they hurried on by foot.

Two hours before breakfast would be served at the Sharpened Quill, Dorrie, Ebba, and Millie sprinted into the Celsus, hoping Hypatia was up and at work. When they reached her office, they could hear the low murmur of a conversation on the other side of the door.

Dorrie knocked firmly. There was a pause in the talk, and then the door was thrown open by Mistress Wu, who blinked at them in great surprise.

"We need to talk to Hypatia," Dorrie said.

"Yes, well, now's not really a—" she broke off, seemingly just having eyed the gash on Millie's cheek and the general worn and worse-for-wear look of all of them. She stood aside.

A few feet into the room, Dorrie stopped short, causing Millie and Ebba to plow into her from behind. "Savi!" she said, shocked somehow to see him standing beside Francesco.

"What the devil happened to you?" asked Francesco, striding toward Millie to get a better view of the gash.

She batted his hand away. "It doesn't matter."

"We've found something," Dorrie said breathlessly. "It has to do with the Foundation." Hoping the lybrarians wouldn't react too badly to the news that she and Millie and Ebba had been in Timbuktu, Dorrie told them how the apprentices had come to suspect that Lady Whitcomb might be in touch with the Foundation and how they'd come to believe that the Vox Mortis vials might be in the Cave of the Black-Fingered Skeleton and how they'd gone there hoping to find them before Mr. Biggs got to them.

Francesco's eyes had grown wild with hope at this but then dimmed when Millie explained that the Vox Mortis vials hadn't been in the cave. He strode away to the window, his hands knotted behind his back.

Hypatia watched him solemnly, Savi looked down, and Mistress Wu's eyes dampened. Millie went to stand beside him, her shoulder barely brushing his arm, and after a moment, they turned back to face the room together, Francesco's hand on her shoulder.

Dorrie told the lybrarians about the room with the ink- and wax-covered stone block and the strange metal plate that showed Lady Whitcomb's name, along with those of hundreds of other people. She laid the letter addressed to the count on Hypatia's desk. "And Ebba found this."

Hypatia looked the bit of letter over. "Now that is interesting." She passed it to Savi. "Savi has been looking for signs of Foundation activity in 1647 all quarter. He's become aware of one Baron Flageletti in Italy who not only has a black nail but has been awaiting the appearance of a set of bottles for some weeks now. A delivery that is very late and very important to him."

"Just like Lady Whitcomb," said Ebba.

"The bottles are to appear beneath the seventh flagstone from the foot of the stairs in his wine cellar," said Savi.

"How does he know?" asked Dorrie.

Savi and Hypatia exchanged glances.

"He received a letter," said Savi.

"So did Lady Whitcomb!" said Dorrie. "With a little bat thing on it."

"Addressed in that room beneath the Crocodile Cliffs, it would seem," said Savi. "And then sent on their way."

"But four hundred years apart," said Francesco.

Hypatia turned to Dorrie. "You're certain Mr. Biggs said he was the *only* one who knew where the Vox Mortis vials were hidden?"

Dorrie nodded.

"And he intended to send them to the Foundation's new allies?"

Dorrie nodded again. "He was angry the Lybrariad had delayed him."

"We'd been assuming the allies were all in 399 BCE," said Savi. "But it would seem that they're all over time. In centuries to which the Stronghold doesn't even connect. Lady Whitcomb in twentieth century London, Baron Flageletti's in seventeenth-century Italy, not to mention this Count Sieciech, wherever he resides," said Savi.

Hypatia took back the count's letter. "Perhaps for Mr. Biggs, 'sending' the Vox Mortis vials means simply leaving them in one or more safe, out-of-the-way places where they can lie undisturbed until unearthed by one of the Foundation's allies in a later century."

"But what about that Baron," asked Dorrie. "His wine cellar didn't exist thousands of years ago, did it? It's not like Mr. Biggs could slip it under the seventh flagstone in 399 BCE."

"No," said Savi, "but Mr. Biggs could hide the vials in a place that does still exist in later centuries. Perhaps some Foundation agent is poised to find them and distribute them, and so make it look to the Lady Whitcomb's of the world as if some impressive 'magic' has happened indeed."

Hypatia turned to Mistress Wu. "Dispatch a few lybrarians to the wherens of the three new Foundation allies," said Hypatia. "See if they'll let anything slip. Also, please ask Keyhand Obaji to lead a party out to the Crocodile Cliffs as soon as the circulation desk can have one outfitted."

"I'll go too," Francesco and Savi said at the same time.

"There's one more thing," said Dorrie. "There was a fifth plate we couldn't read. It was written with symbols from Petrarch's alphabet."

Hypatia's eyebrows rose.

"It was laid out like a letter," said Dorrie. "Is there any chance the bit of letter to the count says the same thing as the beginning of the letter engraved on the metal plate?"

All eyes in the room turned to the scrap of parchment in Hypatia's hands.

"And if it does, would it give the Archivist a kind of Rosetta stone?"

Hypatia's eyebrows rose further. "Mistress Wu, please fetch the Archivist and ask him to join the Timbuktu team."

Many other orders were given. Lybrarians came and went. There was much conferring and squashing against one another in the crowded room. When Francesco took Millie aside to talk privately, Ebba elbowed Dorrie.

"Let's get out of here," she whispered, "before they remember to punish us for going out to Timbuktu by ourselves."

In the empty attics, Dorrie and Ebba changed out of their desert robes. Outside the den windows, Roger bellowed mournfully. Dorrie agreed to hurry to the Sharpened Quill before breakfast ended to get them food while Ebba took care of Roger's dining needs.

However, halfway there, as Dorrie passed the Pyonyang archway, its calendar caught Dorrie's eye, and she jammed on the brakes. This was the day of Timotheus's trial, but the Archivist was likely long gone to Timbuktu by now. Marcus was probably waiting for him at the Tyre archway.

Doubting she could get in any more trouble than she was already going to be in once the lybrarians could focus, Dorrie sprinted down to the Archivist's office. Fifteen minutes later, she arrived at the Tyre archway, panting, the chitons the Archivist had checked out for the occasion in her arms and the skipkey in her hand.

Marcus was there, pacing. "Where have you been?"

"Long story, but the Archivist can't come."

"What!"

Dorrie threw him one of the chitons. "I'll take you."

"But I haven't even begged yet. I demand to know what's going on!"

"I can't explain right now!" cried Dorrie, ducking into a musty closet full of dictionaries to change.

"Hurry up," said Marcus. "Jalileh must be above deck. If we go now, we won't have to fight off another tray of hors d'oeuvres."

On the other side of the archway, the boat was bobbing more briskly than it was during their last visit. Marcus lost his balance and overturned an urn full of scrolls. It rolled across the hold noisily, crashing into the boat's hull. Dorrie glanced nervously at the closed hatch. Rain beat on it loudly. She hoped it had masked the sound of the urn smashing to pieces. Dorrie lifted the skipkey's pin.

The *Hura* had slid away and the Lyceum's library had materialized around them. Luck was with them as they crept from the room; the Lyceum was virtually deserted.

"Maybe Aristotle gave his students the day off to see the trial or something," said Marcus as they scuttled out into the street. It was just as rainy in Athens as in Tyre. As they walked along the muddy road, Dorrie told Marcus all about what they'd discovered in Timbuktu.

By the time they got to the Courts District, the rain had diminished to faint, misty moisture in the air.

"Wish me luck," said Marcus, digging in his leather pouch.

Dorrie showed him her crossed fingers. "I wish I could watch. I still can't believe women aren't allowed in there."

"The oration," cried Marcus as he dug more frantically. "I forgot it!"

A bell began to ring, signaling the start of the trial.

Marcus stared at Dorrie, his eyes wide.

Dorrie gave him what she hoped was a loving shove toward the entrance. "Meet me at Kalliope's when you're done."

Marcus nodded, looking blank. Giving his hair a shake, he ducked inside.

Though less crowded than the first time she'd visited, the agora was still busy. Her mouth watered as she passed a stall where meat sizzled. A customer turned, and Dorrie found herself face to face with the Tyre Spoke Lybrarian.

Jalileh, her mouth full, looked as shocked as Dorrie felt.

"What are you doing here?" Dorrie asked, her confusion overriding her caution.

Jalileh hastily swallowed, looking shifty. "I am…well… I was…" She drew herself up defiantly. "Things got unbearably quiet on the *Hura*, and I just thought…why not nip over to Athens for a day or two."

"You moved the Tyre Spoke Library to Athens!" Dorrie said.

Jalileh looked hurt. "Well, it's nothing to get judgmental about. It's still fully attached to Petrarch's Library, and really, nothing of note is going on in Tyre." She leaned in confidentially. "What happened is that when I sailed down to Athens a few weeks ago, I won tickets to a critically acclaimed production of Aristophanes's *The Wasps*."

"You've moved the *Hura* to Athens before?" said Dorrie, goggling at her.

"Well, just that one other quick time," said Jalileh. "For the mental health. I had no idea I'd win the tickets." She looked nervously around. "Which keyhand brought you?"

Now it was Dorrie's turn to look shifty. "The...uh... Archivist."

A look of profound relief crossed Jalileh's face. "Oh, I'm sure he'll understand. Not that there's any need to bother him with details about running into me," she added quickly. "As soon as the play is over, I'm going to simply fly down to the harbor and sail right back to Tyre."

Dorrie saw her chance and began to back away. "I actually have to go meet the Archivist now, but...I-I won't say anything."

Jalileh beamed at her.

Dorrie turned, cursing her luck.

She found Kalliope bent over behind her table, picking up pieces of broken pottery.

"Well, hello!" she said, standing up when she caught sight of

Dorrie. She brushed off her hands. "Oh, that's right. Today's the big day. Timotheus walked by earlier, looking pale as milk."

"Yeah, I just left Marcus at the Courts. I'm waiting to… to…see how it all turns out."

"Keep me company if you'd like," said Kalliope. She looked darkly at the broken crockery. "Though I have some more cleaning up to do."

Dorrie slipped behind the table and bent down to help. "What happened?"

Kalliope swept up some smaller bits. "Dissatisfied lunatic vagrant. Showed up in town a couple weeks ago. Spends his days and nights in the ruins of Critius's house, trying to move great blocks of stone around with his bare hands and a few ropes and boards, cursing and sweating and muttering to himself. People are afraid of him." She jerked her chin toward a table. "He took one look at that little perfume bottle and went apoplectic."

Dorrie let go of the pieces of pottery she'd gathered, and they fell in a noisy shower back onto the ground. Sitting in a bowl with a wooden spoon and some very ugly rings was the twin of Mr. Biggs's vial.

Kalliope looked from Dorrie to the vial. "You look about like he did when he saw it. He called me a thief and demanded to know where I'd gotten it, which did not endear him to me. I told him I bought it fair and square from a garbage picker ages ago."

Dorrie lifted the vial out of the bowl.

To prove his claim, the lunatic opened up that old sack he carries around with him, and it was full of the little bottles.

Dorrie felt the blood rush out of her face. She whirled to face Kalliope. "How many?"

"Hundreds. He demanded mine. I didn't like his manner, so I refused."

An outrageous possibility clutched at Dorrie. Jalileh had said she'd taken the *Hura* to Athens once before. "What did he do then?"

"He cursed me, knocked one of my best vases off the table, and left."

Fear slithered through Dorrie. "What does he look like?"

"Big. And cruel if you ask me. And he wears a very strange chiton. I'd never seen anything like it. Flowers painted all over it, it looks like."

"Mr. Biggs," Dorrie murmured, remembering how he'd stolen Mistress Daraney's sheet.

"Excuse me?" said Kalliope.

"Nothing," said Dorrie, her thoughts whirring. The night Mr. Biggs had escaped, it had been Mistress Daraney who had reported that he'd disappeared through the Athens archway. Mistress Daraney, who could get lost going from the Celsus to the Sharpened Quill.

"You said the man had been spending a lot of time in the ruins of Critius's house. Did he find the little bottles there?"

"It's possible," said Kalliope, looking puzzled at Dorrie's interest. "But I don't think so. He's been carrying that sack around with him ever since he showed up in Athens. He never seems to put it down."

"Oh!" Dorrie cried, unable to stay silent as the explanation for Mr. Biggs's presence here fell into place.

"Is everything all right?" Kalliope asked.

"No!" Dorrie longed to scream. Mr. Biggs hadn't escaped through the Athens, 399 BCE archway as Mistress Daraney had reported. Not at all. Mistress Daraney only thought he had. Dorrie's mind spun dizzily. Mr. Biggs had escaped through the Tyre, 327 BCE archway while Jalileh was in Athens winning tickets to the play. Only he probably hadn't realized his mistake!

Jalileh herself had explained why he wouldn't. When the apprentices were setting off for their field trip to Tyre, she'd told them the *Hura*'s anchor had once come loose and that this had caused confusion in Petrarch's Library because as the boat had drifted past various towns, the word "Tyre" over the archway had been replaced by each of their names in succession.

When Mr. Biggs had escaped, the letters above the archway would have spelled out "Athens." After getting bonked on the head, Mistress Daraney could be forgiven for not noticing the year after "Athens" was 327 BCE, not 399 BCE.

Dorrie felt feverish. Mr. Biggs had made the best of the

situation. He'd managed to recover the empty Vox Mortis vials from wherever he'd hidden them seventy-two years earlier. But if Mr. Biggs already had the vials, why hadn't he already "sent them" by placing them where they could be found by Lady Whitcomb and the Foundation's other new allies? A new thought bucked through Dorrie.

What if Critius's house was important for a different reason than Dorrie had first thought? What if it was the place where Mr. Biggs was supposed to leave the vials so that hundreds of years later, the Foundation's allies could find them? That would explain why Mr. Biggs had been working so hard to get down to whatever deep, dark, unsavory corner of Critius's house was supposed to serve as the Foundation's giant mail slot to the future.

Dorrie caught hold of Kalliope's hand. "Do you know where Mr.... Where the man went?"

"Banged off down the road toward the harbor," said Kalliope, looking concerned. "Been doing that three times a day since he showed up in Athens. Marches down close enough to get a view, then turns around and goes back to his ruins."

Of course! Dorrie thought. He'd been checking to see if the *Hura* had returned. And if he saw it was anchored again in the harbor, he would try to get back on board—she was certain. He'd want to get back inside Petrarch's Library and find the archway back into the earlier Athens he'd meant to get to, where he'd have easy access to Critius's house before it had collapsed and where he could get back into the Stronghold.

Dorrie breathed raggedly, Millie's face flashing before her eyes, then Torquemada's. She couldn't let Mr. Biggs succeed. She couldn't!

For a moment, she considered running back to the Lyceum in the hopes of getting to Petrarch's Library that way before Mr. Biggs had a chance to reenter it through the *Hura*, but she didn't dare take the risk. He already had a head start, and from the maps she, Marcus, and Ebba had looked at, the Lyceum was just as far from the agora as the harbor.

"Which way to the harbor?" she asked Kalliope.

CHAPTER 25
THE ORGAN PLAYER

A FEW MINUTES LATER, DORRIE was racing down the street Kalliope had pointed out, having left a cryptic message with her for Marcus, telling him to look for Jalileh and the *Hura* down at the harbor.

Running as hard as she could for as long as she could and then walking until she could run again, Dorrie wondered how far ahead Mr. Biggs was and whether Marcus was going to be able to get to the harbor before the *Hura* sailed.

At last, the rocky hillside full of cottages and grape vineyards and goats gave way to a narrow bare beach, its edge tufted with grass. Panting, Dorrie surveyed the harbor. Far off to the right, smaller boats were moored to bustling docks that jutted out over the water. The larger boats, riding at anchor, were actually closer as the crow flew to where Dorrie stood.

She gulped for breath in the mist, eyes flitting from boat to boat, realizing she had never seen the *Hura* from the outside. The prow of one of the boats had been carved to look like a great beaked bird. Had Jalileh mentioned that detail?

Dorrie's ears picked up the regular splashing sound of oars. She squinted. A small boat was being rowed across the water from the direction of the docks toward the bird-headed boat by someone large and powerful with hair as silver as the mist. It was Mr. Biggs.

"Oh no," whispered Dorrie, cold fear catching her in its talons. There was no time to run down to the docks and try to find another boat. She'd never overtake him that way. Her only chance of getting to the *Hura* first was to swim there.

Not giving herself time to think, she forced herself to sprint across the beach and into the first little hissing gray-green waves, then on through the waist-high breakers. Staring at the next oncoming wave, she knew if she didn't dive below it, it would break on top of her. Clumsily, she ducked, her toes clawing at the shifting rocks beneath her feet.

Heart banging high in her chest, she ducked another wave, feeling a spurt of panic as her toes lost contact with the pebbles.

A glance at Mr. Biggs told her he was making good time, skimming over the waves with stiff, efficient strokes of the oars.

Past the breakers now, Dorrie began to swim, trying to remember what it had felt like to be in the water before the night

Mr. Biggs had left her adrift, back when she felt strong and fear-less. But after only a few strokes, Fear began to speak again.

"You'll never make it," it said, each word it uttered further separating Dorrie's will from her strength.

"Look how far away the *Hura* is," said the voice.

Dorrie raised her eyes to where the *Hura*'s hull rose dark out of the sea.

"You'll sink like a stone before you get halfway there."

Dorrie began to flounder, arms and legs thrashing.

Savi's face wavered before her, and she fought to remember what he'd read to her about Fear. About how to defeat it. Only it was hard to think with the voice as loud as a banshee, telling her to give up, to let the waves carry her back to shore before she died. She tried to shut her ears to the Fear, to fight against it, but she felt herself dropping down. Her head went under.

She felt herself bumped. She imagined Mr. Biggs's boat running her over, holding her under. Flailing, she fought for the surface and for a moment found air. Mr. Biggs's boat was still distant, but a few feet ahead, a sleek, dark-whiskered head had also broken the surface of the water.

"Spinoza!" gasped Dorrie. In the refuge of her pure delight at seeing the seal, Dorrie remembered how the young warrior had defeated Fear.

Trying to banish it or slay it or shut it up wouldn't work. The way to defeat Fear was to let it speak, but choose not to do as it bid. Dorrie felt a surge of energy. She had to decide to swim despite Fear's talk. Slowly, she began to kick and stroke, her arms and legs taking up their old recalled rhythms. Kick. Stroke. Kick. Stroke.

With Spinoza shooting in and out of the water ahead of her, Dorrie focused on the ladder dangling against the hull of the *Hura*. She risked another glance back. Mr. Biggs was now only fifty yards from the boat. Dorrie almost sank again as his face registered furious recognition. Asking every tired muscle to work harder, she swam on until with one last tremendous reach, her hand caught hold of the ladder's bottommost slimy rung.

Arms trembling, she hauled herself up to the next rung and the one after that until she was halfway up the side of the boat. Below, she heard the sound of Mr. Biggs's boat crashing into the *Hura*. A glance down showed Mr. Biggs making his way quickly upward, a sack tied to his waist.

Dorrie tried to climb faster, her breath ragged. Below her, she could hear Mr. Biggs closing the distance between them. At the top of the ladder, she toppled over the gunwale and staggered forward, scanning for something to use to fight him off, but it was too late. Mr. Biggs landed on the deck like a great heavy panther. He knocked her backward, and she fell hard on the deck. Before she could get up again, he was standing over her, pressing the point of a flat sword against her chest.

He glared at her, his teeth bared. "How considerate of you to volunteer your services as guide and safe passage ticket."

The painful prick of the sword point infuriated as much as frightened Dorrie. She longed to send him reeling back with a kick, to hurl the vials into the sea, but he had all the power.

"I wouldn't think heroic thoughts if I were you," said Mr. Biggs. "Or I shall find it necessary to swear a solemn oath to use someone you love to make my next bottle or ten of Vox Mortis. Maybe that brother of yours? Or that charming little sister?"

Dorrie felt the surge of the outright terror she'd felt when he'd collected Vox Mortis from her in the sailboat. The feeling of a bit of her soul crumbling.

"Get up," said Mr. Biggs, drawing back the sword just enough to let her roll out from under it.

Knees shaking, Dorrie pushed herself to her feet. Mr. Biggs forced her to walk to the hatch and open it. She hesitated for a flicker of a second, and he instantly prodded her in the back in a way that Dorrie knew had drawn blood. Taking hold of her arm, he dragged her down the ladder.

He stopped for a moment at the archway. "You are now going to take me to the Athens, 399 BCE archway. You will choose a low-traffic route, and should we see anyone, you will remain quiet as a tongueless corpse. Do you understand?"

The thought of doing his bidding revolted Dorrie, but when he shook her roughly, she nodded her assent.

He dragged her into Petrarch's Library, and they set off. Dorrie pointed out turn after turn, standing obediently silent when a passing pair of lybrarians made it necessary to hide behind a wardrobe.

As they drew ever closer to his desired destination, ideas flashed and fizzled in Dorrie's head. If she could only find a way to break away from him and grab the sack of vials. If she could only alert someone without Mr. Biggs knowing. She'd never wanted to see Master Francesco more in her life. As they approached the Biblioteca Marciana, a marvelous, desperate possibility occurred to her. If there was any place where she might have a fighting chance to lose Mr. Biggs, it was in the Scooby-Doo Library. She just needed to get Mr. Biggs there.

She stopped.

"Keep moving," he growled.

"It gets crowded ahead," said Dorrie.

He pressed the point of the blade meaningfully into her back again. "Choose an alternative route, please."

She called on the spirit of Marcus for a felicitous lie. "I know a way," she whimpered, "but you have to walk along a cliff, and I'm afraid of heights."

"I'm not, and I'll hold on to you very tightly. Now, move."

She led him through the Biblioteca Marciana, onto the Middle Shelf, and into the flooded corridor. As they splashed through the ankle-deep water, Dorrie tried to sort out her plan, her heart thunking madly. They climbed the little flight of steps and gained the whitewashed corridor. At the black door, Dorrie reached for the knob but Mr. Biggs held her back, his eyes narrowed.

Dorrie swallowed nervously. Had she betrayed too much eagerness? Had she seemed too willing? Mr. Biggs pressed his ear against the door, listening for a moment, and then kicked it open, his gaze sweeping the room.

Dorrie pointed at the skeleton's closet across the room. "The Athens archway is through there."

Roughly, Mr. Biggs hurried her toward it. Dorrie tried not to tense, tried not to reveal she planned on doing anything other than exactly what Mr. Biggs told her to do.

Again, he listened at the door, and again satisfied no one was on the other side, he flung it open. With its customary clatter of bones, the skeleton hurtled forward on its track, chains dragging. Snarling, Mr. Biggs slashed at the skeleton with his sword. As ribs showered to the ground, Dorrie wrenched herself free from Mr. Biggs's grasp and, darting beneath his arm, tore the heavy sack from his hand. He lunged after her, his fingers catching in her hair. Thinking only of the shortest path to the spinning wall, Dorrie launched herself onto and over the couch, kicking over the candelabra on the way.

Turning back, Dorrie saw Mr. Biggs duck as the chandelier plummeted toward him, but he didn't stop, and she had to swerve out of her intended path or risk being grabbed. Leaping off the table, he landed in front of the portrait himself, cutting her off.

"Oh, you'll pay for that," he said, his eyes gleaming slits.

One menacing footstep at a time, he began to approach her. Dorrie stumbled backward, clutching the sack and upsetting a clock, a chair, and finally the elephant leg, sending its collection of weapons crashing to the ground. Her back hit the unyielding edge of the table behind the sofa.

A terrible, humorless smile spread across Mr. Biggs's face. His sword raised, he took a step toward her. Only a great booming cacophony of notes wheezing from the organ made Mr. Biggs pause. He spun to face the unseen player. It was Darling, her long scaly body draped over the keys. Her tail thrashed.

For a moment, Mr. Biggs seemed to lose his focus staring at his old pet. Dorrie, eying her own sword among the spilled weapons, dove for it.

Furious, Mr. Biggs snapped his head back around and crouched. Before he could spring at Dorrie, another mournful blast sounded from the organ, and the vast trapdoor between Dorrie and Mr. Biggs dropped out of sight. The bottomless pit yawned. Dorrie was left windmilling on its edge, her toes hanging over its edge, the sack of Vox Mortis vials in her hand swinging wildly. She regained her balance.

For the first time since she'd met him, Dorrie saw alarm

in Mr. Biggs's eyes. Breathing hard, she regained her balance. "Stay where you are," she cried, her breath coming in snatches as Mr. Biggs edged to the left. "Or I'll drop them in."

Darling growled as if egging Dorrie on.

Mr. Biggs looked of two minds on the matter.

"I'll drop every one!" Dorrie shouted.

After staring at her for another moment, Mr. Biggs lifted his hands as if to signal defeat. "Well, well, well. Look who's clawed her way into the catbird seat! What do you plan to do with your upper hand? Leverage a Vox Mortis vial for yourself out of the deal? So you can make some for yourself, perhaps?"

Dorrie stared at him, horrified and shocked at the thought. "I never want it anywhere near me again."

"Words, words," said Mr. Biggs, his cold, piercing eyes pinning Dorrie's. "No one who has tasted Vox Mortis, and enjoyed the power it bestows, can walk away from it. And you only know the half of what it can do."

Dorrie hesitated, feeling darkly enchanted, the enormous weight of the sack dangling over the pit making her arm shake. She glanced at her thumbnail. The black stain was entirely gone.

"Oh, I can assure you," said Mr. Biggs, his nostrils dilating. "I can sense the presence of Vox Mortis, and you have now been deserted, my friend."

Dorrie fought off a disturbing rush of panic and sorrow.

Her old fears about her power being the source of her value to the lybrarians thickened in her. She stared at the sack. Her hand wobbled, setting it swinging.

"You don't have to fling them into the abyss," Mr. Biggs said quickly. "You can bring them back to your people, with me as your prisoner and one in your pocket for you to have always. How would that sound?"

Slowly, Dorrie raised her head. She relived the agonizing moment on the sailboat when Mr. Biggs had used fear to twist her truth and had distilled her silence into Vox Mortis. "Terrible," whispered Dorrie. She opened her hand.

"No!" Mr. Biggs howled, lunging for the sack as it plummeted downward and nearly falling into the pit himself. Another blast sounded from the organ, and with the same speed as it had appeared, the pit vanished.

Mr. Biggs smashed the floor with his fist and then straightened up, his eyes glittering. Behind him, the toads on the shelf grinned from left and right. "You poisonous little dwarf," he spat out.

Dorrie quaked as he gave the blade in his massive hand a spin. "The question now is: How will I kill you?"

Dorrie, every limb trembling, saw a chance. One chance. One absurdly small chance. She raised her rapier, trying to breathe, trying to choose not to do fear's bidding and throw Mr. Biggs the sack of vials.

Mr. Biggs shifted his weight to his back foot with ominous deliberation.

Dorrie did the same.

His gaze shifted from her eyes to her heart as he lifted his blade. "You should have chosen a real sword."

Dorrie doubted she could manage one parry. As he drew back his arm, she didn't wait to find out but sent the tip of the rapier hurtling forward, not toward Mr. Biggs as he expected but at the ugly brass toad to his right. This time, she expected nothing, waiting only as time slowed again to see if the hours she'd practiced would be enough. The tip struck the toad's eye true. As Mr. Biggs thrust his sword toward Dorrie's chest, the wall jerked around, and he lost his footing. His blade hissed harmlessly past Dorrie's shoulder, and Mr. Biggs fell to the ground. He gave out a cry of fury and pain as the turning wall wedged him in the gap, imprisoning the top half of him on Francesco's landing and the bottom in the Scooby-Doo Library.

Hearing running footsteps outside the black door, Dorrie turned, rapier still aloft, just in time to see it fly open. Ebba, Millie, and Marcus pounded into the room.

"Are you all right?" Marcus asked as he sprinted toward her, his soaked chiton dripping.

Ebba's eyes bulged. "Is that Mr. Biggs?"

"What happened?" cried Millie.

Dorrie grinned faintly at them, relieved and exhausted. She lowered her sword. Her knees buckled. "I found the Vox Mortis vials."

Chapter 26
Something to Sing About

THE NEXT FEW DAYS passed in a dreamy sort of daze for
Dorrie. Every meal, tedious chore, and loll in front of the
Apprentice Attics fire was shot through with the sublime pleasure of knowing that Mr. Biggs and the Vox Mortis vials were
now safe in Petrarch's Library.

At first, the Lybrariad hadn't been at all sure where the vials
had gone. Then a report had come in. While sleeping in her
little bedroom off the Bodleian Library's main reading room, the
elderly lybrarian-in-training from Dorrie's principles practicum
had nearly lost consciousness when the sack of vials had shot out
of an air vent in the wall over her bed and hit her in the head.

Dorrie had been happy to hear that her teeth, which had
only just been repaired after the aurochs incident, had sur-
vived intact.

When Dorrie, Marcus, Millie, and Ebba had sat down in Hypatia's office with the staff lybrarians to tell them what had happened in Athens and on the *Hura* and finally in the Scooby-Doo Library, they had listened raptly, the Archivist beaming and Savi looking quietly proud.

Dorrie got to hear again about how when she hadn't shown up to meet Ebba as planned, Ebba had grown increasingly worried and about how she'd finally remembered Timotheuss' trial. Thinking Dorrie might have gone to the Tyre Archway, Ebba arrived there just as Jalileh and Marcus were returning to the *Hura*. He had scrawled a note explaining that Mr. Biggs and Dorrie could be in Petrarch's Library and slapped it up against the invisible barrier. Ebba had sounded the alarm, and a massive search had begun. A Tyre keyhand eventually arrived to pull Marcus back into Petrarch's Library. Marcus, Ebba, and Millie had decided to search the tunnel and the Scooby-Doo Library for Dorrie, sure that no one else would think to do it.

"It appears," said Hypatia, "the Cave of the Black-Fingered Skeleton has been in active use by the Foundation for close to five thousand years, and the plates on those walls have been used as an address book of sorts. Lady Whitcomb, Baron Flageletti, and Count Sieciech all received letters, hundreds of years apart, inviting them to become allies of the Foundation. The Foundation must have installed agents in the cave early on from its foothold in ancient Egypt—agents who passed on the secret of the cave and instructions for continuing the mailings to new younger agents and so on through the years."

"But why would they do it?" asked Dorrie. "What would be in it for them?"

Hypatia shook her head. "Gold? Threats? Promises of glory in an afterlife or a future Foundation empire?"

"A lifetime supply of chocolate?" suggested Marcus.

Hypatia smiled. "We don't yet know."

"So who was going to pick up the Vox Mortis vials from Critius's house?" asked Ebba. "And in what century?"

"That point has occupied us greatly," said Hypatia, glancing at Master Francesco. "We do not yet have an answer, but it's possible the Foundation may have seeded another chain of hereditary operatives charged with receiving and distributing the vials in particular times and places."

"And what about the scrap of a letter Ebba found?" Dorrie asked, her eyes turning to the Archivist, hardly daring to hope.

The Archivist's eyes glowed.

"I believe the words addressed to Count Sieciech do indeed say the same thing as the first bit of the letter etched into that plate in the cave." His voice shook a little with what Dorrie took to be barely suppressed excitement. "Not every letter is represented, but it's enough to begin working on a true translation."

Dorrie grinned at him.

"We are grateful for the Archivist's persistence," said Hypatia.

"And to you for the great courage and presence of mind you showed in Athens and while Mr. Biggs held you prisoner."

Dorrie felt her face grow pleasantly warm.

Hypatia folded her hands. "So the effect of the Vox Mortis has at last worn off?"

Uneasiness filled Dorrie. "That's what Mr. Biggs said." She showed Hypatia her whitened thumbnail and waiting for someone to suggest that the offer of her apprenticeship needed to be reviewed or rethought or just outright rescinded.

"Well, that's a relief!" said Francesco, startling Dorrie. "Perhaps now you can settle down to your training, and I won't have to worry about the next archway you'll find a reason to leap through."

Dorrie released her breath and shared a surprising, if brief, smile with him.

In the days following the staff meeting, Dorrie, Marcus, Ebba, and Millie had to repeat the story of what had happened in Timbuktu and Athens and the Scooby-Doo Library many times, first to the library's Board of Directors, then to a gathering of keyhands, and finally to every single apprentice in the place. Dorrie hadn't minded, but she didn't share everything. Only Ebba and Savi heard about her moment of temptation as she dangled the sack of vials over the pit.

Ebba had hugged her and said she could understand being sad about letting go of such a tremendous ability.

When she'd met Savi for a lesson in the courtyard, he'd squeezed her shoulder and told her to stop being so hard on herself and then insisted on her explaining to him again, in rhyming couplets, how wonderfully the practice sword he had picked out for Dorrie had served her.

"Now," said Savi. "I think you've earned that duel you've been aching for all quarter."

"Really?" Dorrie asked, grabbing up her rapier. A thought crossed her mind. "This isn't a bribe because you already know that next quarter, I'm going to be apprenticed to Lybrarian Della Porta while you're away in China or Ethiopia, is it?"

"Ah." Savi lowered his own blade. "Well, that was the plan, but I'm afraid Lybrarian Della Porta has been suspended for taking actions unbecoming to a lybrarian. Unfortunately, you'll have to make do with me instead."

Grinning, Dorrie tried her first thrust, which Savi parried. "Miserable. Simply miserable," he said, the corners of his mouth upturned. "*Allez!*"

The day after Mr. Biggs's capture, Mistress Wu had announced with great pleasure at breakfast that the annual Autumn Sing would be held on the last day of the quarter up in the Old Field, which lay near the top of Petrarch's Library. "Bring blankets and chairs if you'd like, but anything you take up to the Old Field must be brought back down at the end of the night. Last year, some enterprising apprentices managed to bring up an eight-foot-long sofa, which is still there, providing shelter and nourishment for countless field mice and possibly some larger creatures. No field needs more than one couch."

There was stifled laughter around the apprentices' table and some finger-pointing.

The Autumn Sing was held on a beautiful starry night. Dorrie was crushed with about half the other apprentices on the couch Mistress Wu had complained about. From there, she had a beautiful view of the snapping fire and, in the far distance, the glinting sea that no longer filled her with dread. One after another, various lybrarians had risen to sing. Mistress Lovelace surprised them by singing a bawdy tavern song, and Fatima and Marcus performed one of the songs that had made them all their money in the Inky Pot, to great applause from the apprentices and Fedya.

Fedya had sent up great plates of baklava to be enjoyed with the cocoa and hot spiced cider, but Dorrie passed the plate along, still uncertain. One of the Sumerian lybrarians had just finished a haunting wordless tune full of aches and aspirations when Marcus returned to the couch after getting his third cup of cocoa.

Dorrie made room for him. He sat and promptly snatched more than his share of the blanket. "Hey!" Mathilde protested from farther down the couch.

"Sorry, not sorry," said Marcus. "Hero coming through."

Mathilde yanked the blanket back in her direction.

"Yeah," said Kenzo. "If Marcus hadn't made Dorrie go to Athens, she would never have found Mr. Biggs or the vials there, and he would have kept digging through old Critius's ruins till he got to where he wanted to put the vials, and then they would have been spread all over time and all over the world, and—"

Millie interrupted his praise song. "I can't believe you actually managed to get Timotheus off the hook," she said to Marcus.

"Uh. Thank you?" he replied, looking around his feet for the box of marshmallows.

"No, really," said Dorrie, who realized suddenly that Marcus had said very little about his success since their day in Athens, other than that Timotheus had been found innocent.

"What can I say?" said Marcus. "I went extemporaneous."

"Extempa-what?" said Kenzo.

"He made it up as he went along," explained Fatima.

"Did Aristotle give you the evil eye after the trial?" Dorrie asked.

Ebba sniffed. "Or did he have to hurry off to murder a baby dolphin?"

"Actually, he came over and talked to me."

"Really?" said Ebba.

"So what'd he say?" Dorrie asked.

Dorrie was surprised to see Marcus look embarrassed. "Oh, just stuff."

"Like what?" she pressed.

"That I made some good points. Like I'd changed his mind about whether it was just of him to bring charges against Timotheus."

"Wow," Dorrie said. "That's a big deal!" She looked across the fire to where she had seen Egeria and Bang sitting with friends earlier. She lowered her voice. "So did you tell Egeria yet?"

"Uh, not really." Marcus craned his neck to look farther down the couch. "There better be some marshmallows left!" he bellowed.

Dorrie and Ebba exchanged looks, eyebrows raised, as Marcus caught the box that Amo threw.

Dorrie nudged Marcus again. "You're not going to tell her, are you?" she said, not able to help looking smug at her realization. "Because you *did* end up caring what happened to Timotheus. You really did do all that fundraising and research and oration-practicing for him, not to impress Egeria."

"Well, not at first," Marcus said, horrified. "And quit knocking my cocoa arm. And quit talking about it!"

"Hey," Ebba said, pulling out *True Spine-Tingling Ghost Stories from around the World*. "Anybody want to hear me read 'The Cave of the Black-Fingered Skeleton' out loud?"

There was a chorus of groans. Only Millie raised her hand.

"Oh, that reminds me!" said Fatima, burrowing in her satchel. "I can't believe I forgot to give you this." She pulled out a newspaper. "Something else you should read."

Ebba took it. "The *Times*."

Quickly, getting in each other's way, Dorrie and Ebba began to turn the thin pages, looking, hoping, dreading…and suddenly, there it was. On page eight. To the left was a letter signed with Lord Cromer's name. To the right, another letter took up several columns. "'Ten Reasons Why Women Should Not Get the Vote' by Annie Knox," Dorrie read breathlessly.

"She did it!" Ebba crowed.

Dorrie read the first couple "reasons" out loud to the others.

"Those are pretty good," Saul said. "The title's kind of boring though. I wish she'd made it something more colorful like 'Ten Reasons Why Suffrage for Women Would Be the Worst Thing Ever to Happen to Civilization.'"

"I knew you felt that way underneath," said Mathilde.

Saul threw his hands up. "It was just constructive criticism!"

"Well, I sure hope the article helps the suffragists," said Dorrie. "I will *not* miss spending time with Lady Agnes."

"Mrs. Richardson was pretty nice though," Ebba said.

"She was," Dorrie said thoughtfully, wondering why exactly Mrs. Richardson hadn't wanted women to get the vote. She'd never bothered to ask her.

Walking back to the attics with Ebba and Marcus, Dorrie felt tired but content, thinking about how good it would be to see her parents and Miranda again in just a couple days. As Marcus and Ebba drew ahead, deep in discussion about the potential hazards and pleasures of fizzy lifting drink, Dorrie heard footsteps behind her. It was Millie. She fell in step with Dorrie.

"Hey, I just wanted to say, you know, thank you. I'm really kind of excited I'm going to keep on living."

Wanting to laugh, Dorrie gave Millie a sidelong glance, not sure, having no experience of joking with the other apprentices, if she had meant that to be funny. Millie's mouth looked a little crooked, and there was extra light in her eyes. Dorrie took a chance and grinned.

Millie grinned back. She took a deep breath. "If you want to practice rapier some time together next quarter…"

"I'd love that," said Dorrie.

Next quarter. The words sounded delicious to Dorrie. The Foundation still had Petrarch's Star, but without a source of Vox Mortis, they weren't going to be able to make it serve them for at least some time to come. The Lybrariad could breathe. Petrarch's Library—and Millie—was safe for the moment.

Dorrie and Millie caught up with the others at the Xianyang, 220 BCE archway, where Marcus had stopped to shake a pebble out of his boot.

Beyond the archway, a patron in a flat-topped black hat hovered over a piece of silk painted with characters.

It occurred to Dorrie that unlike everyone else in Petrarch's Library, she had no idea what the invisible barriers felt like when one wasn't passing through them. Did they feel smooth like glass? Warm? Cold? She reached her hand out to touch it and, with all the grace of a one-legged table, found herself falling through the archway and knocking off the patron's hat in the process.

She scrambled backward quickly, regaining the corridor just as the man, looking indignant, turned to see who had assaulted him.

Marcus, Ebba, and Millie were staring at her dumbfounded.

"I don't believe it!" Dorrie cried, examining her thumbnail. It was the same pinky-white it had been since she'd returned from Athens, so it couldn't be the Vox Mortis. Then how had she done it?

"Yes!" cried Marcus.

Dorrie stared from the other apprentices to the archway and back again. "Anyone want to go visit Kalliope and get some really bad fish sandwiches?"

MASTER PHILLIPUS AURELOS THEOPHRASTUS BOMBASTUS VON HOHENHEIM'S
SECOND GUIDE TO PETRARCH'S LIBRARY

PEOPLE

Rachel Davis: Mission lybrarian serving the Lybrariad and assistant to the director of the Western Colored Branch of the Louisville Free Public Library out in 1913, Louisville, Kentucky. The library in that segregated wheren was the first established to serve African Americans. While it's considered rude in Petrarch's Library to talk about the adventures, triumphs, or misfortunes a lybrarian has yet to live out, there's nothing to stop *you* from finding out more about her on your own.

Giambattista Della Porta: Former branch lybrarian based at the Academia Secretorum Naturae out in sixteenth-century Naples, Italy. Since he's no longer serving as a lybrarian, I can tell you that though he found it difficult to conduct himself according to Lybrariad principles, he was in fact, a brilliant cryptographer. Had Petrarch's journal been written in code, he certainly could have cracked it. Apparently, later in life, he continues to practice the "new" science and invents things like the camera obsura. He has his own brushes with the Roman Inquisition. The Lybrariad will help him as it can—observing our principles while doing so, of course.

Benjamin Franklin: Though he was asked to serve as a mission librarian, Benjamin Franklin (citing an overloaded schedule) opted instead to take a part-time position at Petrarch's Library, managing its printing and reproduction department. He also agreed to publish an in-house newspaper: *Gouty Ben's Weekly Digest.* He commutes from 1742 Philadelphia, where he's busy publishing another newspaper called *Poor Richard's Almanack*, working on his new invention, tentatively called "the Franklin stove" and trying to put together a club for talking about philosophy.

Kalliope: Since Kalliope is not a lybrarian, it would perfectly appropriate for me to tell you all about the rest of her life. Unfortunately, I can't. Because no one bothered to write any of the details down in any sort of history book. It's possible that people in later centuries are reading her orations, but if they did survive, they of course bear a man's name. Perhaps

"Dinarchus" or "Isaeus." What a shame. You could refer to Guy Carleton Lee's *Orators of Ancient Greece* written in 2004 to see if you feel Kalliope's presence there.

Master Hunayn ibn Ishaq: Currently serving as keyhand and Archivist for the Lybrariad. The Archivist's interest in translation runs deep. When he was young, his skills were so respected out in his home wheren of ninth-century Baghdad that a powerful Caliph hired him to serve at the Bayt al Hikmah or House of Wisdom, a library and center for scholarly studies. He squeezed in work there while he could while serving also with the Lybrariad. When he was asked to become a keyhand, he requested to serve out in 327 BCE, rather than in his home wheren of ninth-century Baghdad, at least in part for the opportunity to research less well-known early written languages.

Ida B. Wells: Journalist, courageous critic of the lynching of African Americans in the south of the United States, suffragist, speaks out about all forms of racial injustice. What is lynching you ask? It's violence dealt out by a mob on an individual, where there has been no trial. Usually deadly violence. Ida B. Wells is as courageous as they come. Some years ago, after buying a first class train ticket, she was outraged when the crew tried to make her move to a "colored" car. She refused and fought them tooth and nail, as they dragged her physically out of her seat. Out in 1913, she's living and working in Chicago, trying to address racial injustice there.

Aristotle: Philosopher who founded the Lyceum, a school of philosophy, where he teaches biology and history among other things. After hearing about Dorrie, Marcus, and Ebba's adventures in Athens, my interest in Aristotle was piqued. I went down to the main reference room to find a biography, and Callamachus suggested a modern one from the Passaic Public Library called *Introducing Aristotle* by Rupert Woodfin and Judy Groves. Loved the cartoons. The authors say, "All that we know of Aristotle indicates that he was a good man, both kindly and generous." Ebba contests the assertion. He writes. A lot. And well. Cicero, a fellow writer out in first century Rome, recently spoke of "the suave style of Aristotle...a river of gold."

Sophie Scholl: Young German Nazi resistor. At this time, the history books say that in the summer of 1942, while her father was imprisoned for making a critical remark about Hitler, news of war crimes committed by Germany horrified Sophie. After reading an anti-Nazi sermon by Clemens August Gra von Galen, her brother and some of his friends established a non-violent resistance group called the White Rose, which Sophie insisted on joining. The group wrote pamphlets encouraging

Germans to resist the Nazis. She was arrested in 1943 for distributing the pamphlets. In court, she said, "Somebody, after all, had to make a start. What we wrote and said is also believed by many others. They just don't dare express themselves as we did." She was executed by the Nazis soon after. The Lybrariad is currently looking for a way to change that.

Dr. James Risien Russell: Doctor living and working in London of Scottish-Carribean descent. Born in British Guiana in 1863, Dr. Russell earned a ridiculous number of degrees, professorships, and fellowships, and now has a very busy medical practice out in London 1913's West End. He specializes in diseases of the nervous system. We hope he's too busy to follow up on any references made by his patients to a visiting niece by the name of Ebba.

Critius: A writer and political figure out in fifth-century Athens. We know Kalliope didn't care for him. Interestingly, before he became one of the Thirty Tyrants, he enjoyed spending time with Socrates. Have you heard of Plato—another philosopher? Critius was related to Plato's mother. When someone is so callous as to be willing to condemn hordes of fellow citizens to death as Critius did, I resent having to acknowledge that said person had a reputation for being a good writer. He did.

Tomas de Torquemada: Inquisitor. It's difficult to imagine him as a child, innocently toddling about picking daisies, and yet he wasn't born a man. As Mr. Sabatini told us, he was the architect of the Spanish Inquisition and oversaw it until his death in 1498. "His history," says a commenter named Prescott, "may be thought to prove that of all human infirmities there is none predictive of more extensive mischief to society than fanaticism."

Lord Cromer: His full name (including titles and honors bestowed) is Evelyn Baring, First Earl of Cromer, Order of the Bath, Order of Merit, Order of St. Michael and St. George, Order of the Star of India, Order of the Indian Empire, Her Majesty's Most Honourable Privy Council, Fellow of the Royal Society. My name suddenly seems rather pithy. I mention all of this to give you a sense of the connections he enjoys in his society and his comfort with wielding power. He doesn't know it, but he's enjoying one of the last years of his life at the moment and will never embrace the idea of women's suffrage.

Count Sieciech: Count Palatine at the court of Duke Wladyslaw I Herman of Poland out in the eleventh century. Though only a count, he has managed to weasel and intimidate his way to the center of power—and more or less rules Poland at the moment. His ways are not delicate, and he's busy trying to kill off the duke's sons in order to gain the throne. It's no wonder the Foundation reached out to him.

ORGANIZATIONS

Alpha Suffrage Club: Ida B. Wells spearheaded the creation of this club out in 1913, Chicago, with white suffrage colleague Belle Squire. Black women who wanted the vote faced opposition by white men and women, as well as black. By 1919, thousands of black women will have joined, seeking out a way to act to end lynchings of African Americans and to create a means for black women to participate in political life. Twenty-first century reference sources tell us that the Alpha Suffrage Club will play a powerful role in the election of the first African American alderman in Chicago.

National League Opposed to Woman Suffrage: Well, you've seen what the members of the League are up to out in 1913 London. They like things as they are and don't want them to change. They've been opposing women's suffrage since 1910. Twenty-first century sources tell us they'll be at it until 1918, when the Representation of the People Act will pass (absurdly only extending the right to vote to women over thirty years of age) and take the wind out of their sails.

Women's Social and Political Union: The WPSU was begun in 1903 by people dissatisfied with the lack of progress in gaining voting rights for women, by the National Union of Women's Suffrage Societies (NUWSS). Annie is a member of both organizations, but prefers soapboxing to breaking windows. The WSPU didn't start out advocating destructive acts as a means of pushing Parliament to grant voting rights. They concentrated on holding demonstrations, including a series in the Parliament building. When Prime Minister Sir Henry Campbell-Bannerman refused to act with legislation even after an envoy of three hundred women representing over 125,000 suffragettes made their case, members of the WSPU began to interpret its slogan "Deeds Not Words" in new ways. Out in 1913, the WPSU at the moment is led, some say run dictatorially, by the Pankhurst family: Mother Emmeline Pankhurst and her two daughters Cristabel and Sylvia.

PLACES

The Lyceum: The school founded by Aristotle out in fourth-century BCE Athens. Aristotle has a sometime habit of strolling beneath the covered walkways of the school and through the gardens as he lectures. For that reason some call it the Peripatetic School. I leave it to you to figure out why. Students don't only spend their time at the Lyceum, trailing Aristotle. The

Lyceum boasts baths, a gymnasium, and a palaaestrae where students can box and wrestle. It later centuries, the Lyceum's location was lost, its walkways buried, but I hear from Mr. Kornberger that a few years ago out in the twenty-first century, the Lyceum was excavated, and the site now is now open to the public. I wouldn't mind a visit myself.

The Agora: In an agora, as Dorrie, Ebba, and Marcus found, one can buy or sell just about anything. But it literally means "gathering place." In the agoras out in ancient Greece, people assemble to talk politics and business, debate, visit temples, and conduct other business. They also go to hear philosophers hold forth. Some who didn't go for that reason might find themselves doing that anyway. Before Socrates was arrested, he would install himself in the Athenian agora and question shoppers about the meaning of life. Some years later, Diogenes, a philosopher who has made a virtue out of poverty, has installed himself there in a ceramic jar and given himself a similar mission.

Timbuktu: City. Don't be alarmed if you see it spelled as Tinbuktu, Timbuctoo, or Timbuktoo. Any of these will do. It's being established as a permanent settlement out in the twelfth century on the southern edge of the Sahara desert in Africa. Its residents will live in large part on the trade in salt, gold, ivory and slaves for a while to come. Out in the fourteenth century it becomes part of the Mali Empire and develops as a center of learning and scholarship, and enjoys a thriving book trade. Later, the Songhai Empire, and then after them, the Moroccans will claim it. I haven't yet had time to research what's going on there in the twenty-first century. Feel free.

Books, Newspapers, and Assorted Other Expressive Works

The *Anti-Suffragist Review*: The newspaper first of the Women's National Anti-Suffrage League and then of the National League Opposing Woman Suffrage. It's been produced now (in 1913) since 1908 and will go on being printed until 1918. It expresses beliefs such as "They call it [votes for women] equality and justice. It is nothing of the kind. It is the subjugation of men to women."

The *Suffragette*: Newspaper of the WPSU between 1912 and 1915. Before that, the WPSU's newspaper had been *Votes for Women*. In-fighting resulted in the Pankhursts expelling its editors, Emmeline and Frederick Pethick-Lawrence, from the WPSU leadership when they didn't want to go along with the new plans for the WPSU to engage in arson.

The *Times*: London newspaper that has been going since 1785. It's sold out in that wheren as a two and a half penny broadsheet called the *Daily Universal Register*. Out in the 1800s, it is fondly called *The Thunderer* as it publishes quite a lot of strong opinion. Callamachus tells me it's still being sold out in the twenty-first century.

"Against Witches": An essay written by Savienen Cyrano de Bergerac. Or Savi, as you know him. In it, as you probably remember, he lays out every argument he can think of to persuade readers that witches do not exist. If you're from Dorrie's century, or one of the later ones, which you'd have to be to be reading this, you probably think that the argument would be an easy sell. Not so out in Savi's time, where he tells me nine out of ten people believe they exist, souring milk when they please, and making darker mischief. He's not quite ready to publish it and has put it away for now.

"For Witches": An essay written by Savienen Cyrano de Bergerac. Or Savi, as you know him. In this one, as you probably remember, he tries to persuade readers that witches *do* exist—but not really. As he informed Dorrie, it's a satiric essay. If you're from Dorrie's century, or one of the later ones, which you'd have to be to be reading this, you probably think that it would have been *obvious* to his readers that he wasn't being sincere. Savi expects that if and when he publishes "For Witches," nine out of ten people will believe that he's being one hundred percent sincere and read the satire with breathless pleasurable dread.

"A Modest Proposal for Preventing the Children of Poor People from Being a Burthen to Their Parents or Country, and for Making Them Beneficial to the Publick": A satiric essay written by Jonathan Swift in which he suggests that eating poor children is the answer. Though Savi has barely finished penning the first draft of his own piece of satire, it already irritates him that young European and American people in the nineteenth and twentieth centuries are frequently given "A Modest Proposal" to read, as the best modern example of the satiric essay. It may be. If you want to write a satiric essay pointing up the unfairness or absurdity of some parental practice or another, "A Modest Proposal" will serve well as a guide.

Torquemada and the Spanish Inquisition: A History: A book by Rafael Sabatini published in London in 1913. Millie, in her quest for more information about Tomas de Torquemada, requested this book just weeks after it became available. Though as a denizen of a later century, you have at your fingertips many newer books on Torquemada's terrible exploits, Sabatini's account is told with a certain dramatic flair. After all, Callamachus tells me, he'll soon be writing high-seas adventure stories like Captain Blood, and the Sea Hawk, which end up getting made into something new to me called "movies."

Discourses Concerning Government: This alas, was the book that got Algernon Sidney into so much trouble and put his head at such a sad distance from his neck. He strongly opposed the prevailing belief in the "Divine Right of Kings" to do as they pleased to citizens. He wrote that "God leaves to man the choice of forms in government... He who institutes, may also abrogate." He believed governments should serve the populace, not dictate to it. "General consent...is the ground of all just governments." Out in the eighteenth century, this book is currently being read by Thomas Jefferson and others involved in inventing the United States of America.

African American Women in the Struggle for the Vote, 1850–1920: Book by Rosalyn Terborg-Penn, written out in the twenty-first century. As you now know, out in 1913, all American women are not in the same place. Some women besides being women, are black and are struggling against racism as well as sexism. Lybrarian Davis tells me this book tells the stories of women who are finding the strength and strategies to battle both destructive stupidities at once. I've asked Mathilde to pass it on to me when she's finished with it.

The *Cherokee Phoenix*: First printed out in 1828 Georgia in the United States, the *Cherokee Phoenix* is the first newspaper printed in a syllabary of the Cherokee language. For many years, its editor Elias Boudinot and Principal Chief John Ross have editorialized against the Indian Removal Act of 1830.

***Against Women's Suffrage: Some Reasons*:** A pamphlet by Grace Saxon Mills. The National League for Opposing Woman Suffrage passes it out at many of their events out in 1913 London. I'm afraid Dorrie, Ebba, and Mathilde are so indignant about the idea of women being denied the right to vote, they can only scoff at the reasons laid out by Mrs. Mills and haven't really studied them. But if you do decide take a closer look at the pamphlet, it's interesting to trace in *Some Reasons* a record of what people who oppose suffrage for women *fear*. Always worth understanding what people fear.

***Fourteen Reasons for Supporting Women's Suffrage*:** This is a manifesto created by the National Union of Women's Suffrage Societies. Millicent Fawcett leads this organization. The National Union favors peaceful debate and logical argument as their means of choice, rather than window-breaking. They fear that such direct actions will alienate potential supporters.

The Wasps: This is a play written in the fifth-century BCE Greece by Aristophanes. It's *funny*! A comic gem! A total pantaloons-wetter! It's about this son whose father is a "trialaphile." He can't stop volunteering for jury duty. He's addicted to it. The plot revolves around his son trying to keep his father away from the Athenian law courts by any and all means. No really. It's uproarious. I understand completely why Jalileh was so excited to win a ticket to see it. It's probably playing right now somewhere in at least a dozen twenty-first-century wherens. Ask your parents to take you.

When Things Fall Apart: Heart Advice for Difficult Times: Book by Pema Chodron. Pema Chodron lives and writes out in the twenty-first century and has written more than a dozen books on the challenges presented by the whole "being alive" thing. She draws many of her practices and insights from Buddhism. Her books have titles like *The Wisdom of No Escape* and *Start Where You Are*. In them, among other offerings, she shares methods for working with chaotic situations. They've become terrifically popular in Petrarch's Library. Callamachus can't keep them on the shelves.

ORGANISMS, INVENTIONS, AND OTHER UNCATEGORIZED MARVELS

Angelus Marshmallows: Though out in ancient Egypt, the Pharaohs are enjoying a heavenly confection made from the sap of a mallow root mixed with nuts and honey, many centuries are doing completely without anything like a marshmallow. Out in the nineteenth century, French candymakers are whipping up mallow root into difficult to make foamy sort of confection, but only the rich can afford it. But it's out in the twentieth century that marshmallows are taking the world by storm. Inventors theren have substituted gelatin for sap. Frederick Rueckheim, the inventor of Cracker Jack, has been producing Angelus Marshmallows for six years now and they are his second most popular product.

Baklava: Heavenly dessert. The Turks and the Greeks are arguing loudly in the later centuries over which culture invented it. Setting that aside, it's made of flaky thin layers of pastry, and chopped nuts held in glorious sticky togetherness by honey or syrup. Eat it whenever you have the opportunity. Even if it's Fedya offering you a piece.

Gyromitra esculenta: I can't disagree with Marcus's comment that this mushroom looks like a purple brain. It grows in many parts of Europe and North America. Though ingesting the fungus raw can cause headaches, lethargy, vomiting, diarrhea, delirium, dizziness, coma, and death, people in many centuries continue to try to eat it, claiming cooking it thoroughly makes it safe. Let it be a feast for your eyes and not your stomach.

Mediterranean Monk Seal: Spinoza's species. Though plentiful in ancient Athens and in many centuries following, it has fallen on hard times in the twentieth and twenty-first centuries. Where once their habitat extended throughout the Mediterranean, where they would give birth and socialize on a magnificent range of beaches, the shy creatures have retreated exclusively to underwater caves inaccessible to humans. Amanda used the google machine to do some research for me out in Passaic and says that only about seven hundred of Spinoza's relatives are thought to still be alive in that century.

ACKNOWLEDGMENTS

So many things to acknowledge.

Writing a second book is not easier than writing a first one.

It *is* possible to sprain one's sitting muscle.

I was not, every time I told the children not to bother me because I was working, in fact, working.

Most importantly, I want to acknowledge that I depended heavily on friends, family, colleagues, and partners in creative crime to help me get these words into even this attempt at best order. Whatever distance the result has fallen short of the possible given the good advice, support, insights, wisdom, and talents on offer is, of course, the apprentice's responsibility alone.

Thank you to friends, family members, and fellow writers Johanna Lindholm, Kate Bennis, Patty Culbertson, Rebecca Downey, Christina Downey, Matthew Rohdie, and Carolyn Fay who kindly used some of their precious time on earth to read the manuscript in its ancient, medieval, renaissance, revolutionary, restoration, second empire, and/or early modern forms. Each gave me invaluable feedback.

Thank you to my daughters, Lil and Georgia, who took their continuity and character consistency policing duties very seriously. Thank you to my son Finn, who didn't read a word but whose ways in the world fuel my imagination.

Thank you to Aubrey Poole, Katherine Prosswimmer, Elizabeth Boyer, and Diane Dannenfeldt at Sourcebooks for bringing passionate, skillful attention to the editing process.

Thank you also to the Sourcebooks design team for working so hard to produce such a wonderful look for the book.

Thank you to Susan Hawk, my funny, engaged, stalwart gem of an agent, for keeping a steady hand on the tiller.

And most of all, I want to thank Stephen Brannan, who, when he came upon me quite lost in the story jungle, suspended his own quests and devoted his prodigious skills as teacher, guide, and editor to helping me find a path.

ABOUT THE AUTHOR

Jen Swann Downey lives and works in Virginia where she revels in moments with her family, friends, and the occasional tree. This is her second novel for young people. She tries to walk away from Omelas.